P9-CTP-543

09/2020

PALM BEACH COUNTY
LIBRARY SYSTEM
3650 Summit Boulevard
West Palm Beach, FL 33406-4198

PARADISE PEAK

Don't miss any of Janet Dailey's bestsellers

The New Americana Series
Sunrise Canyon
Refuge Cove
Letters from Peaceful Lane
Hart's Hollow Farm

The Tylers of Texas
Texas Forever
Texas Free
Texas Fierce
Texas Tall
Texas Tough
Texas True

Bannon Brothers: Triumph
Bannon Brothers: Honor
Bannon Brothers: Trust
Calder Storm
Green Calder Grass
Lone Calder Star
Calder Promise
Shifting Calder Wind
American Destiny
American Dreams
Masquerade
Tangled Vines
Heiress
Rivals

JANET DAILEY

PARADISE PEAK

KENSINGTON BOOKS
www.kensingtonbooks.com

To the extent that the image or images on the cover of this book depict a person or persons, such person or persons are merely models, and are not intended to portray any character or characters featured in the book.

This book is a work of fiction. Names, characters, places, events, and incidents either are the products of the author's imagination or are used fictitiously. Any resemblance to actual persons, living or dead, events, or locales is entirely coincidental.

KENSINGTON BOOKS are published by

Kensington Publishing Corp.
119 West 40th Street
New York, NY 10018

Copyright © 2020 by Revocable Trust Created by Jimmy Dean Dailey and Mary Sue Dailey Dated December 22, 2016

All rights reserved. No part of this book may be reproduced in any form or by any means without the prior written consent of the Publisher, excepting brief quotes used in reviews.

All Kensington titles, imprints, and distributed lines are available at special quantity discounts for bulk purchases for sales promotion, premiums, fund-raising, educational, or institutional use.

Special book excerpts or customized printings can also be created to fit specific needs. For details, write or phone the office of the Kensington Special Sales Manager: Attn. Special Sales Department. Kensington Publishing Corp, 119 West 40th Street, New York, NY 10018. Phone: 1-800-221-2647.

Kensington and the K logo Reg. U.S. Pat. & TM Off.

Library of Congress Card Catalogue Number: 2020937093

ISBN-13: 978-1-4967-2171-6
ISBN-10: 1-4967-2171-3
First Kensington Hardcover Edition: October 2020

10 9 8 7 6 5 4 3 2 1

Printed in the United States of America

PARADISE PEAK

CHAPTER 1

Travis Alden could easily recognize the sights and sounds of hell: the bared teeth of predatory inmates, the sharp clicks of metal handcuffs, and the profanity-laden screams that echoed against the concrete walls of a six-by-eight cell.

But this place—whatever it was—held none of those things.

Cautiously, Travis stepped closer to the edge of the mountain overlook, his worn tennis shoes crunching on loose gravel, and looked down at the peaceful landscape. Evergreen trees and pines stood proud above the thick brown foliage that hugged their massive trunks. Distinctive outlines of leaves, trees, and bushes melded as his gaze roved further out, scanning the rugged mountain range that sprawled for miles in every direction.

The Great Smoky Mountains slumbered beneath a blue morning mist. The high peaks in the distance gradually grew clearer as the sun's orange glow lit up the eastern Tennessee sky, its slow ascent above the mountaintops burning off the misty shroud one sleepy inch at a time.

Despite the bright warmth of the approaching sun, a thin plume continued to thrive on one distant peak. The gray plume billowed upward, obscuring the streaks of orange, pink, and purple coloring the sky, and cast a thin shadow over the mountain from which it rose.

A swift mid-February breeze pushed across the landscape, swept past Travis's ears on a high-pitched whistle, bringing with it the pungent scent of smoke. The skin on the back of his neck prickled. The uneven terrain before Travis—a slumbering giant—seemed to breathe and stir. Almost as if it sensed his presence, that darkness within him, knowing he didn't belong.

Travis jerked back onto the graveled path and raised his head, squinting up at the sun's glow instead of studying the steep drop below.

"You in God's country, son."

A grizzled man, wearing a brown jacket and jeans, stood ten feet away by the entrance of a hiking trail. He carried a fishing rod in one hand and a large cooler in the other. The old man's blue eyes surveyed Travis. Then he raised one arm and pointed the fishing rod in the direction of the mountain range Travis had studied. Orange sunlight glinted off the metal tip of the pole.

"That there's the park." The man's gray mustache lifted with his slow smile. "But Paradise"—he swept his raised arm toward a large mountain jutting up high behind him— "is that way." His smile widened. "Paradise Peak, that is. That what you're looking for?"

Travis gripped the frayed straps of the backpack on his shoulders and swept his gaze over the other man's form, searching for the bulge of a weapon in his jacket, along his waistband, or tucked beneath the hem of his jeans. The action was automatic—a distasteful, but necessary, habit Travis had formed during his twenty-year stint in prison. He'd been forced to defend himself on more than one occasion over the years.

Finding nothing suspicious on the man, Travis relaxed his hold on the bag's straps and nodded. "Can you tell me how many miles it is into town?"

"Only seven or eight, but it'll feel like thirty on account of the climb." The man glanced at Travis's shoes and frowned. "You been hitching?"

"I tried." Travis looked down, cringing as he recalled the suspicious stares he'd glimpsed through windows of cars and trucks as drivers had sped past his raised thumb. He didn't blame people for not trusting a nomadic stranger, and after three days with no success, he'd stopped asking for rides. "I started in Franklin 'bout three weeks ago." He studied his mud-caked shoelaces and the loose stitching along the seams of the soles. "Mostly on foot."

The wind picked up, gusting between them, and the man asked, "You walked two hundred miles across these mountains during the tail-end of winter?"

It sounded like a perplexed statement instead of a question.

"Two hundred and thirty-three," Travis said.

He'd counted every one. Each night, as he'd huddled beneath canopies of trees for warmth or stretched his aching frame out on a bed of dead underbrush and stared up at the stars, he'd calculated every step, added the estimated mileage that lay ahead, and subtracted the hours of sleep and periods of rest he'd need when the climb became too painful.

The man whistled low. "What you come all that way for?"

Margaret Owens. Absolution. To save his—justifiably—damned soul. Travis hesitated as he met the man's narrowed gaze, not wanting to lie, but unsure of how much to share with this stranger. In his experience, most people weren't all that understanding. Or forgiving.

"To start over."

Travis's throat tightened and he looked away. He raised his eyes above the blur of moisture coating his lower lashes and studied the burst of color brightening the sky as the sun rose higher above the distant peaks.

The sight conjured a small measure of peace within him, stirred a soothing sensation through his veins, and made him wonder how it might feel to be a good man. Not a great one (he doubted he'd ever be one of those), but at least an honest, trustworthy one. A man who always tried to do the right thing and had no blight on his name. The kind of person he wished, with every breath he drew, he could become.

"It must've been hell."

Travis shook his head and returned his attention to the man, whose scrutiny had intensified. "Not at all."

Travis had entered hell at eighteen and had emerged from it three weeks ago when he'd been released from prison at thirty-eight. By contrast, the mountain trek he'd undertaken over the last few weeks had been full of fresh air, bright skies, and majestic heights that had lifted his head and at times, his weary spirit.

"Weather's been clear most of the way," Travis added, gesturing toward the sunrise. "No snow, and only one thunderstorm that dropped lightning instead of rain."

"We've had a drought for a while now. Bad for us, but good for your trip it seems."

Gravel crunched underfoot as the man stepped closer. Travis faced him again, tensing as the man lowered the large cooler to the ground, wiped his hand on his jeans, then extended it.

"Red Bartlett." Smiling, he nudged his hand closer.

Travis stared at Red's palm, the deep creases stained with dirt, and considered the open invitation his upturned fingers offered. Releasing the straps of his bag, he slowly placed his hand in Red's. "Travis."

Red squeezed, his callused fingers gripping the back of Travis's hand as he shook it firmly. He searched Travis's expression, perhaps waiting for more, but when Travis didn't speak, he said, "Welcome to Paradise Peak."

Travis smiled, his chest swelling. It was the first time in twenty years that he'd been welcomed anywhere . . . or touched without animosity.

"I expect you're exhausted," Red said. He released Travis's hand and retrieved the cooler from the ground. "How's a decent meal and good night's rest sound to you?"

"Good, but . . ." Travis shoved his hand in his back pocket and fumbled through the bills lining it. Fifty, sixty dollars at best, remained. "How mu—?"

"Don't know if you've noticed," Red said, rolling his shoulders, "but I got a few years on me. There's fifteen rock bass in this cooler, and there's another cooler stocked with more bass and trout by the river at the bottom of that trail." He raised an eyebrow. "I been out here three hours—since five in the a.m. My arms hurt, my back's screaming, and I don't relish the idea of stomping back down there and hauling that heavy sucker up here. I'm interested in a trade, and your muscle would be a big help."

Travis frowned. "That's a kind offer, but not a fair trade."

Red threw his head back and laughed. "Don't bow your back up, son. I didn't mean to offend you, and this ain't no charity, if that's what you're worried about. That ain't all there is to the trading, and there ain't no five-star hotels my way. I'm offering you a plain ol' fried fish dinner and one night's stay in a rickety cabin with a lumpy cot." He grinned. "When the temperature dips back down tonight, you'll feel like you're sleeping on a slab of ice, and that's after you spend the majority of today cleaning, filleting, and cooking those fish before you eat 'em." Red's tone was firm, but his lips twitched. "Damned shame I didn't stumble upon you earlier, otherwise I'd have made you catch them, too. Save me the trouble."

Travis smiled. Maybe it was Red's friendly demeanor, or it could've been the way being called "son" sat well within his soul, but either way, Travis liked the idea of helping Red. He hadn't been able to help anyone in a long time.

"In that case, I'd say it's a fair trade, and I thank you for it." Travis headed for the trail, asking over his shoulder, "Cooler's at the bottom of the trail, you said?"

"Yep." Red pointed toward a small clearing beyond the gravel path, where a blue truck was parked. "That's me over there. I'll load this up, and when you get back we'll head out."

Travis paused, a sense of dread seeping into his gut as he stared at the truck. He nodded, turned away, and walked down the path, his steps heavy and sluggish.

Gravel gave way to dirt and small rocks as the narrow hiking path curved along the steep incline of the mountain. Travis ducked beneath low-hanging limbs, stepped carefully around roots that protruded from the ground, and found the cooler sitting on a smooth rock by a wide river.

He drew to a stop near the river's edge and inhaled the cool mist rising from the rippling water, savoring its refreshing caress on his sweat-slicked face and neck. The surrounding woods were thick, and though the path had led to a lower elevation, the sky was still visible and the same sense of peace he'd experienced higher up the mountain was palpable below as well.

"Paradise," he whispered, weighing the word on his tongue.

The name was appropriate—this place sure looked like heaven. But somewhere on the next mountain, somewhere even higher in the town of Paradise Peak, Margaret Owens still grieved the loss of someone she'd loved. Someone he had taken from her.

Shame searing his skin, Travis grabbed the cooler, hoisted it into a firm grip, then hiked back up the path to the clearing.

Red stood by the lowered tailgate of the truck and smiled as Travis approached with the cooler. "Thanks, son." He walked around to the driver's side, motioning over his shoulder. "Toss it in the bed with the other and we'll head out. You can dump your bag back there, too."

Travis deposited the cooler, raised the truck's tailgate, then climbed into the passenger seat. He removed his backpack and placed it in his lap, eyeing the loose seat belts strewn across the wide seat.

"You still holding tight to that bag of yours," Red said. He smoothed his mustache and grinned. "What you got in there? Gold?"

"No." Though the notebook paper, pens, thermos, and three changes of clothes were as valuable as gold to him. "All I own is in it." Travis grabbed one seat belt strap and searched the bench seat for the other. "I prefer to keep it close."

Red remained silent for a moment, then pointed to the slim crack between the back rest and leg rest of the bench seat. "Other half of that belt is probably stuck between the seats. Dig around a bit and you'll find it."

Thanking him, Travis did as Red suggested and found the matching strap. He shifted his backpack to the side, fastened the seat belt across his lap, and glanced at Red. "Thanks for the ride."

"No worries," Red said. "So long as you don't mind riding in a throwback. This jalopy's got some age on it, like me." He patted the dash. "But I can't bring myself to give her up."

Travis looked at the cab's old-fashioned interior. There was a wide dash trimmed with wood grain and blue paint and, from what he could tell, the old-school radio, glove compartment, and padding on the doors were all original.

"It's a nice truck," Travis said. "I've never seen a classic in as good shape as this."

Red cranked the engine, an expression of pride crossing his face. "She's a 1969 three-on-the-tree shifter. Two hundred and sixty thousand miles to her credit, and she still climbs these mountains like a dream. My niece has been hounding me to get rid of it for years, but I'd have to be dead for someone to pry it away. Even when I do get a new one, I won't give her up." He cocked his head to the side. "You're welcome to drive us up the mountain if you'd like to test her out."

Travis gripped the edge of his seat. "I don't drive."

Red's brows rose. "Never?"

"Not anymore."

Travis stared straight ahead as an unwelcome mantra whispered through his mind. He recalled Judge Manning's voice as clearly as if he'd spoken the words yesterday rather than twenty years ago: "Neil Travis Alden possesses a reckless disregard for life, and as a result . . ."

Face burning, Travis swallowed hard. "Thank you for the offer though."

Red studied him closer but didn't comment further. A few moments later, he eased back in his seat and drove the truck onto the highway.

The climb was steep, and the engine's rumble grew louder as the truck ascended the mountain. At first the thick tree line on both sides of the road loomed over the truck and obscured the view. Bare branches bowed low with the heavy push of wind, and brown underbrush rustled in the wake of the truck. But when the road curved upward on a sharp angle, a wooden sign, etched with PARADISE PEAK, emerged into sight. The passing trees dropped away, leaving the view to Travis's right clear.

And, man, what a view it was.

Mountains sprawled across the open landscape, their high peaks touching the blue, misty sky, and with each mile the truck climbed, the sun grew stronger. Its powerful rays brushed the fog aside and poured golden warmth onto the paved highway, over the hood of the truck, and into the cab.

Paradise Peak had awakened.

Travis sat up straighter and craned his neck to take it all in.

"Thing of beauty, ain't it?" Red asked.

Travis pulled in a small breath. "Like nothing I've ever seen."

"We're 'bout to hit the top and that sun's gonna strike you right in the eyes." Red pointed. "Flip that visor down and you'll get a better look."

Travis lowered the visor, his fingertips lingering on the shiny surface of a photograph attached to it. A woman smiled back at him from the picture, her auburn hair shining beneath the sun above her, her stance relaxed against the green pasture and horses grazing in the background.

But her eyes—deep blue, and wary despite her smile—held his attention. Her gaze was direct and full of distrust. It was a look he'd seen before. One that made him cringe with shame.

"Not getting any ideas, are you?"

Travis snatched his hand back and pressed it against his thigh. "No. Not at al—"

"Relax." Red laughed. "I'm just giving you a hard time." He glanced at Travis. "Not much of a kidder, are you?"

"Guess not." He couldn't afford to be.

"That's my niece, Hannah Newsome." Red slowed the truck as he maneuvered a curve. "She came to live with me five years ago. Best stable manager I've ever come across—family or not."

"Stable?" Travis studied the horses' lithe muscles and shiny manes in the picture.

"Yep. I own Paradise Peak Ranch—the place we're going to on the other side of the mountain." Red grinned. "Well, I co-own it."

Travis leaned closer and eyed the picture again. He took in the wide-open fields that led to high misty peaks. "How many horses do you have?"

Red's smile fell. "Only a couple. But we're hoping for more soon." He gestured toward Travis's right. "Downtown's that way, but I don't have time to show you around now. Gotta get these fish cleaned and stored before they spoil. That all right with you?"

Travis nodded. "Fair trade or not, thanks again for offering me a place for the night. Not many people would do that."

Red shot him another glance as he slowed the truck down a steep incline. "Why? They got reason not to?"

Travis shifted in his seat. Clutched his bag closer. "I'm a stranger. Nowadays, it's hard for anyone to trust a stranger."

Red grunted. "Ain't that the truth." He took a left and the truck rocked over a deep rut as it traveled up a graveled track. "But this is my home, and I was raised to be good to people so . . ." He looked at Travis and shrugged. "Guess I'll just have to trust you till you give me a reason not to. You're welcome to do the same with me."

Travis tried to smile, tried to reassure him, but he couldn't. He'd learned years ago that the bad in him could sometimes override the good.

Instead, he faced the view before him and watched the

gravel track widen as they reached an open field. A wooden sign, this time bearing the words PARADISE PEAK RANCH, appeared. He looked out the window as the truck passed the sign, watched as one weather-beaten cabin passed, a second cabin, then a third. He squinted past the glint of sunlight hitting the windshield and studied the three-story rustic lodge ahead on the left side of the road. It was large and might have been impressive back in the day, but now, the structure looked as outdated as the neglected cabins they'd passed.

"This is the main lodge," Red said, turning into a small dirt parking lot and stopping the truck in front of the lodge. "That's where I stay. I'd offer you a room here, but my co-owner is renovating the place, so I don't have any decent ones available." He pointed past the lodge to a large—if run-down-looking—stable. "You'll spend the night in the cabin up that trail past the stable and on the other side of the stream. Not much to it, but there's a good view."

Travis's gaze followed the narrow dirt trail winding between the stable and a wide paddock with wooden fencing. "That'll be fine, thanks."

Red opened his door and hopped out. "Help me unload the coolers and I'll get you set up to clean the fish."

Travis exited the truck, put on his backpack, and joined Red at the lowered tailgate of the truck. He unloaded both coolers and all of Red's tackle, propping the fishing pole against the truck.

"Here." After retrieving a large knife from a bag tucked in the corner of the truck bed, Red held it out. "This needs a good cleaning before you start. I got sloppy on my last filleting and didn't have time to clean up after myself. There's a fish-cleaning table across the field near the stable. Take one cooler up there and clean the knife before you get started. There's a water hose outside the stable you can use, and some soap's inside the cabinet next to the hose. While you're doing that, I'll let my niece know I'm back, then grab some ice and plastic bags and bring the other cooler to you."

Travis stared at the knife for a moment. Its blade, though dull and caked with grime in places, glinted beneath the bright morning sunlight. His fingers trembled at the thought of handling it, however benign the intent. He took it though and held it carefully at his side, the solid weight of it unwelcome in his grip.

Red headed for the lodge, saying over his shoulder, "I'll join you in a minute."

Travis watched as Red walked up a short path, climbed the front steps, and entered the lodge. Sighing, Travis adjusted his grip on the knife in his hand, picked up the cooler with the other, and started walking across the open field toward the stable.

Dormant grass, brown and brittle, crunched beneath his shoes, but the air at Paradise Peak Ranch was cool and clean save for the faint scent of smoke still hovering on the breeze. Gentle slopes and hills spread across the open landscape and, from this vantage point, there was an unimpeded view of the Smoky Mountain range. The plume of smoke he'd seen on the trail earlier still rose from a distant mountaintop, looking thicker from Paradise Peak Ranch.

On the other side of a narrow dirt path, to Travis's right, lay a spacious fenced-in field that looked serene against the tree line behind it.

His footsteps slowed as he reached the bottom of a small slope. Situated above him was a small structure comprised of thin wood planks and a shoddy roof. Seemed the worn cabins and lodge weren't the only blemishes on the property—the stable could be added to the list as well.

There were two entrances, the doors of each open and hanging at crooked angles, and what he assumed to be a loft was situated above the entrances, tufts of hay sticking out of its opening. A hose and small wooden cabinet were on the ground beside the right entrance of the stable, and, as Red had said, a small fish-cleaning table made of wood—looking as rickety as the stable—sat several feet to Travis's left.

Travis walked to the table, set his bag and the cooler beside it, and started up the slope. Eyeing the hose on the ground, he rotated the knife between his fingertips and quickened his steps.

"Stay where you are!"

He jerked to a halt and looked up. A woman, around the same age as he—probably a few years younger, stood on the threshold of the right entrance of the stable, glaring at him, her fists balled at her sides. Her long, auburn hair was pulled back tight in a ponytail, and angry panic flashed in her blue eyes. Her features were familiar, as was the distrust in her direct gaze.

Hannah. Red's niece.

She stared at the knife clutched in his hand; then her gaze drifted up his arm, over his chest, and fixed on his face. Her scrutiny pierced the blank expression he struggled to maintain and struck deep for dark secrets he wasn't ready to share.

Her voice, when she spoke, was quiet but full of steel. "Who are you?"

Hannah tightened her fists, tore her eyes from the long blade clenched in the stranger's hand, and met his stare head-on. Her legs shook, but she held her ground. Looking away would peg her as weak—something she refused to be again.

"I said, who are you?"

He didn't answer. Just returned her stare with a dark look of his own. Everything about him seemed dark—the fathomless depths of his brown eyes, the thick stubble lining his hard jaw, and the rich black strands of hair that fell over his tanned brow. His T-shirt—the same midnight shade as his hair—stretched tight across the wall of his chest, and dirt-stained jeans clung to his thick thighs. His bulky frame rose easily above six feet and would tower over her by at least five inches if she approached.

A tendon tightened in the sinewy forearm that held the knife.

Breath stalling, she reached back, her right hand feeling the way around the door frame of the stable's entrance, fumbling blindly across the wall for Red's rifle.

"I'm sorry. I didn't mean to scare you."

She froze at the deep sound of his voice, her palm curled tight around the rifle on its wall mount. "You don't. I just want to know what you're doing on private property."

"I'm with Red." He studied her right arm and the portion of the stable wall hiding her hand from view, then slowly lowered the knife to the ground by his feet. "This is his knife." His voice softened. "Red asked me to clean it for filleting the fish he caught. I met him on the mountain this morning, a few miles back. He drove me up here. You're Hannah, right?"

Mouth twisting, Hannah nodded and relaxed her grip on the rifle but kept her fingertips on the barrel. Red. Of course. He was forever picking up strays. This made the second stranger he'd hauled home this month. The last guy he'd dragged here had mooched off them for a week and left without repayment.

"Where is Red?" she asked.

He moved to answer, but an engine growled over his

words as Red's truck sped up the dirt path and drew to a jerky halt beside the stranger.

Red hopped out, his gaze darting from the stranger to Hannah, and he held up a hand. "It's okay, Hannah. He's with me." He smiled up at her. "I swung by the lodge to give you a heads-up, but I see you've already met."

"Not really. I still haven't gotten a name." Hannah straightened to her full height and eyed the stranger again. He looked away, gaze downcast and posture stiffening.

"His name's Travis." Red glanced at the knife on the ground, then moved to the other man's side.

"Travis what?" she prompted.

"That's all I got right now," Red said.

She glared at Red. "And you let him get away with that?"

Red's jaw hardened. "We just met. I conducted a friendly ten-minute chat with the man, not an inquisition. If you're that keen on a last name, try asking him nicely." He narrowed his gaze on her raised arm. "And maybe get your hand off my gun while you're at it?"

Face heating, Hannah slid her fingers off the rifle and lowered her arm to her side.

"Look," Travis said, "I don't want to cause any troub—"

"No trouble." Red clamped a hand on Travis's shoulder. "You've had a long hike and I promised you a night's stay. I don't go back on my word, and you're more than welcome here." He smiled tightly at Hannah. "We're glad he's joined us, aren't we?"

The censure in Red's stern gaze made Hannah step back. Red might be too trusting and naive in his interactions with people, but this was his land . . . and his say. Five years ago, when she'd needed him most, he'd welcomed her to Paradise Peak Ranch with open arms despite the situation she'd been in and the fallout he'd be forced to face with her abusive ex-husband. She owed Red more than she could possibly repay, and this newcomer—whoever he was—had done nothing to merit her continued suspicion.

She nodded stiffly and forced a smile. "Welcome to Paradise."

Emotion flickered across Travis's expression before he dipped his head. Disappointment and . . . vulnerability, maybe? Which, Hannah ruefully admitted, she must have misinterpreted. There was nothing vulnerable about the rock of a man standing below her. He didn't have a soft spot on him.

Travis retrieved the knife and straightened, casting her a sidelong glance. "May I come up? I need to use the hose."

Hannah swept her arm in that direction. "Sure."

He walked up the hill, each long stride bringing his massive bulk into sharper focus until he reached her side, his impressive height looming over her. Despite the chill in the air, heat radiated from him and blocked the February breeze that swept across the grounds. An earthy mix of pine, lumber, and smoke drifted past her as he knelt by her side, turned on the hose, and scrubbed the hem of his shirt along the wet blade in his hand.

She looked down and studied his hair as it ruffled in the wind. She'd been wrong in at least one respect—he did have one soft spot. That wealth of shaggy hair looked soft and welcoming. He was so close, if she reached out her hand, she could touch the dark strands. Could follow the muscular line of his neck and shoulders, which seemed more impressive than intimidating from this vantage point. Could trace the curve of his mouth and gain a clear view of features she'd yet to fully examine.

He stiffened and shifted away, obscuring his face from view.

"Hannah," Red called. "Come down here and take a look at this mess of fish I caught."

She shoved her hands in her pockets and headed down the open hill. The breeze kicked up, slunk beneath the cuffs of her long sleeves, and sent a chill through her. She shivered and caught herself glancing back, missing—for a brief but disconcerting moment—the warm shield of the stable . . . and the heat from Travis's massive frame.

"Had I known you'd be up and about before dawn," Red called as she approached, "I'd have invited you to go with me." Standing by the cleaning table, he took the top off a large cooler and tilted it. Ice slid forward, revealing a pile of fresh fish. "That old river was good to us today."

"You've always had better luck than me." Hannah leaned closer for a better view and smiled. "Looks like trout's back on the menu for a while."

Red grinned. "Knew that'd make you happy. When I stopped by the lodge, Margaret offered to bring—"

"Your delivery is here," a feminine voice chimed over the hum of a motor.

A utility vehicle arrived with Margaret behind the wheel. She parked the UTV beside Red's truck, slid out, and smoothed a hand over her long skirt.

"Those bags of ice are heavy." Margaret, smiling, tucked her long, gray curls behind her shoulders with French-manicured nails and gestured toward the plastic bags stacked on the back of the UTV. "I could use a bit of manly muscle to help move them. Is our new guest available to lend a hand?"

Hannah stifled a groan. Only Margaret would curl her hair, don a skirt, and paint her nails for a day of ranch work. And Margaret dropping everything to rush outside and meet someone new was no surprise. Ever since Margaret had taken over her late husband's 50 percent share of Paradise Peak Ranch and moved into the lodge a year ago, she'd been desperate to find and sweet-talk a new hand into renovating the place from the ground up—much to Red's amusement. Red would indulge any of Margaret's impractical notions; he'd been secretly sweet on her for decades and still was, despite the fact that Margaret's daily praises of her late husband, Phillip, made it clear that no man would ever equal his perfect memory in her mind.

But, in Hannah's opinion, there was nothing funny about Margaret turning Red's ranch into another run-of-the-mill Tennessee tourist attraction. Whether she owned half of it or not.

"I'll get those." Hannah walked to the UTV, hefted a bag of ice from the back and hoisted it onto her shoulder, then whispered to Margaret, "I thought you were gonna help me work on the stable roof."

She spread her hands, surprise in her eyes. "Well, of course I am," she declared loudly. "What makes you think I'm not?"

Hannah raised an eyebrow as she walked past Margaret. "You're an hour late, and you're wearing a skirt."

Margaret waved away the concern. "Pioneer women did everything in a skirt, and there's no reason I can't look my best while handing you tools."

"A skirt isn't practical for that kind of work." Hannah gripped the bag tighter. The ice numbed her fingertips. "I don't want you tripping and falling face first on a nail."

Margaret's mouth tightened into a pink lip-glossed line. "I appreciate your concern, but I'm perfectly capable of looking after myself." She blew out a breath. "Really. You're too intense, Hannah. You worry far too much about everything."

"What's this about working on a roof?"

Hannah ducked her head at the hard tone in Red's voice

and dropped the bag of ice on the cleaning table. "No big deal. I planned to patch a few spots on the stable is all."

"And what? You thought you'd climb up there and piddle around by yourself while I was out?" Red grunted. "I don't want you moving around on that rickety roof alone."

"You're busy," Hannah said. "I was saving you the trouble."

Red scowled. "Hogwash. You just wanted to keep my old butt on the ground so I wouldn't get hurt. Just 'cuz I got thirty years on you doesn't mean I can't keep up. I'm sixty-five, girl. Not dead."

"Must the two of you argue every day?" Margaret crossed her arms over her chest and tapped her toe in— *dear, Lord*—high-heeled shoes.

Hannah bit her tongue and looked away. And there stood Travis, now at the bottom of the hill, clean knife in hand, gaping at the lot of them.

"Well"—Hannah gestured toward Margaret—"you might as well meet all three of us. Travis, this is Margaret Owens, a friend of Red's and co-owner of the ranch. Margaret, meet Red's newest guest, Travis."

Instead of moving forward to offer a greeting in that low, polite tone of his, Travis stood motionless, his cheeks turning pale as he faced Margaret.

Hannah narrowed her eyes. "Is something wrong?"

"There certainly is," Margaret admonished, walking to Travis's side. "You two have just about run him off with your bickering." She smiled up at Travis. "I assure you, they're not always like this. Hannah's a bit grumpy in the morning, but it wears off by noon, and Red usually breaks in the day with one good argument. After that"—she shrugged— "they're fine." She held out her hand. "As Hannah said, I'm Margaret, and it's a pleasure to have you visit us."

Travis's stare moved from Margaret's face to her hand. Shaking himself slightly, he placed the knife on the cleaning table, then wiped his hand on his jeans several times before placing it in Margaret's grip. "Thank you, ma'am."

Margaret's smile widened. "Polite *and* strong. What a gentleman." She winked over her shoulder as she shook his hand. "You've made quite a find, Red." She faced Travis again and lowered her voice. "I'll just put a bug in your ear, shall I? Red told me you're staying the night, but if the idea crosses your mind to extend your stay, you're more than welcome. And as you probably saw on your way in, there's a ton of work to be done on this property. The stable roof needs to be repaired and several cabins need to be rebuilt. The main walkway needs to be restoned and—"

"Ease up, Margaret." Hannah shook her head.

The man was a total stranger who hadn't even given his last name yet, and already Red had promised him a bed, put a knife in his hand, and announced to all and sundry where they kept a gun. And Margaret was gearing up to offer him a job. Good grief, was she the only one of them who used a modicum of good common sense and caution?

"He just arrived," Hannah continued. "He's here to clean fish and spend one night in a cabin. He hasn't said anything about looking for work. Not to mention, listing all the problems this place poses is the surest way to run an interested party off rather than attract them."

Cheeks flushing, Margaret released his hand and stepped back. "I'm sorry, Travis. I didn't mean to bombard you. And, of course, Red would be the one to do the hiring, if there's hiring to be done. I'm only a silent partner in this business."

The tremble in Margaret's voice and lower lip made Hannah's shoulders slump. And the disapproving frown Red flashed her lowered them even further.

Hannah looked at her shoes and rubbed her forehead. "I—I need to get back to work. I'll stay off the roof and chop firewood instead."

She turned away and strode up the hill, then around to the back of the stable, stopping when she reached a small fenced paddock. Leaning on the paddock's wooden fence, she lifted her flaming face into the crisp breeze and inhaled.

The faint scent of smoke filled her senses and her gaze honed in on the thin plume rising from a nearby mountaintop. The sight made her blood pound quicker through her veins.

"Keep your eyes off that smoke." Red approached, his heavy tread crunching across the brittle grass behind her. "It's making you jumpy."

Hannah watched as the plume bent and widened on a gust of wind, the smoke spreading into a gray, misshapen stain against the skyline. "That fire's been burning for three days now."

"It's contained."

"Tomorrow'll be four."

"It's natural and contained like all the others." Red's calm voice drew closer. "And that man on the other side of the stable, cleaning fish, is not some bloodthirsty heathen. From what I can tell, he seems to be a decent guy who happens to be down on his luck."

She tensed. "So you say."

"You got cause for fear and concern," Red said quietly. "God knows, you do. But this constant sizing up and judging of everyone who crosses your path isn't doing anyone any good—least of all you. You're safe here. Stop looking for trouble where there is none."

"And be like you, instead?" Her hands shook. She wrapped them around the top fence rung, wincing as a splinter pierced her palm. "You want me to blindly trust every stranger that wanders up this mountain? Keep trying to save men who can't—or don't—want to be saved?"

Red sighed. "No. Not at all. But you know I'd never let anything happen to you, don't you?"

Yes. That much she knew. Hannah nodded. "I'd do the same for you and Margaret."

"Speaking of," Red said, "it'd be a nice change of pace if you could cut Margaret some slack. She loves this place as much as you do, and she's desperate for a new start. She's lost more than anyone should in life. And it wouldn't hurt to at least be civil to Travis. For all we know, the path he's traveled may have been as painful as yours and Margaret's."

Her eyes burned. She looked up at the sky and tried to ignore the hot tear rolling down her cheek. "I'm sorry. I'll try."

After a few moments, Red seemed to accept her apology, and the feel of his presence faded as he walked away. His steps slowed when he reached the stable, and his quiet voice, hesitant and heavy with pain, traveled back to the paddock.

"Hannah, not all men aim to hurt."

She waited until she was sure he'd rounded the stable and joined the others, then scrubbed the back of her hand over her cheek. "Maybe not." She refocused on the plume rising from the mountain. Stared as the curl of smoke rose higher. "But some do."

CHAPTER 2

Travis scrubbed harder at the blood on his shaky hand. The red stains were deep. They caked every crevice in his palm, discolored his cuticles, and lodged beneath his blunt fingernails. Scales and fish guts had dried on the bare skin of his forearms and the acrid smell of fish flesh still lingered in his clothes, his hair, and even his lungs.

A bit of soap and water were no match for five hours of scaling, gutting, and filleting the pile of trout and bass Red had caught. Travis tossed the hose aside, cut the water off, sat back on his haunches against the stable wall, and admired the grounds.

The midafternoon sun was high. A fine blue mist still hovered over the mountain peaks in the distance, but the view at the ranch was clear. Well, except for the thin smoke still trickling up from that nearby mountain.

Travis turned his head and watched as Hannah walked across a nearby field and dumped another armload of firewood onto a high stack of logs. She rubbed the small of her back, tilted her head and shielded her eyes, her attention focused on the rise of smoke in the distance.

"Thinking of giving her a hand?"

Travis faced forward at the sound of Red's voice and

watched as Red walked up the hill. Hours earlier, after he'd shown Travis his preferred method of filleting, Red had excused himself to return to the lodge and finish up some renovations on a room. But he'd returned to the stable once every hour to check on Travis as he cleaned fish and to speak to Hannah as she chopped and stacked firewood. He brought snacks and soda for the two of them twice, then returned to the main lodge.

Travis appreciated the company and the snacks, and knew Red meant well. But he also knew Red was keeping an eye on him as he worked near Hannah, which he understood and accepted.

"Wouldn't waste my time if I was you," Red continued. "Most occasions Hannah won't accept anyone's help no matter how politely it's offered." He stopped by Travis and studied Hannah as she stood in the field. "She's stubborn."

"She's afraid."

Travis stiffened as Red's attention shifted back to him. He hadn't meant to say that. Not out loud. He broke eye contact and watched Hannah again. She had turned away from the smoke rising from the mountain peak and stretched over the stack of firewood, tugging a large blue tarp across the logs. Even from this distance, he could make out her guarded demeanor, the tight set of her shoulders and rigid posture.

The sight of her, strong but haunted, and the memory of her panicked warning hours earlier stirred a strange urge within him. An unfamiliar longing to fold his limbs around her slender frame. To shield. To protect.

"Has someone hurt her?" Travis cringed as the quiet words left him, afraid they'd reveal too much.

Red's blue eyes didn't flicker; they continued studying him with unwavering intensity. "That's her story to tell," he said. "But, yeah. She's got reason to be skittish."

Probably as much reason as Margaret . . . if she knew who I really was.

Travis slumped, lowered his head, and picked at his filthy nails. "Is Margaret still working in the lodge?"

He hated to ask. Was ashamed that after hiking all this way, instead of having to search for days on end to locate her, he'd stumbled across her almost the moment he'd arrived without even looking, but still couldn't bring himself to walk the field separating them and reveal his full name.

How could he? From what he surmised, after the passage of twenty long years, Margaret no longer recognized him. She had no idea who he was; otherwise she wouldn't have greeted him the way she had. And if he were to tell her now, there was a very high likelihood Red would throw him off this beautiful property, shout him down the serene mountain, and ostracize him from the only person who'd given him a reason to keep breathing.

"She spiffed up a cabin and is straightening up the back deck now." Red grinned and glanced over his shoulder. "She's polishing furniture, washing her nice dishes, cleaning the outdoor fireplace, and tossing orders at me left and right. Having a guest for dinner. A night's stay is a rare occasion around here so she's eager to impress."

Frowning, Travis glanced around at the cabins dotting the picturesque landscape. "But this is a guest ranch, right? With this view, I'd imagine you'd be booked on a permanent basis."

A dismayed sound left Red's lips. "We used to be, but things have slowed over the last few years. With fewer guests, fewer cabins were used and kept up. The horses we boarded came few and far between." He rubbed the back of his neck. "Guess things on the outskirts of the ranch slowly died away and now it's started to creep into the main grounds."

The happy light dimmed in Red's eyes, and Travis scanned

his surroundings once more, wondering how a place that felt so welcoming, bright, and alive to him could be seen as dying by anyone.

"Here." Red dug in his pocket and withdrew half a lemon. "No amount of scrubbing with soap and water will clean those hands of yours. Come with me. I'll give you a quick tour and show you a little trick I learned."

Travis stood, threw his bag over his shoulders, and followed Red as he ambled down the hill and onto the dirt path between the stable and paddock. They walked up the incline silently for a few minutes and had just reached the top of the hill behind the stable when something pounded the ground rapidly to their right.

Travis froze as two horses shot past them, galloping away from the fence and seeking refuge across an open field.

"Easy." Red, two feet ahead of Travis, paused and waited for Travis to rejoin him. "It's not you—they spook easily." He pointed toward the two horses now slowing across the field. "Hannah named the gray mare Ruby and the black one Juno. They were neglected by their original owners. A good Samaritan rescued both horses and boarded them here last year. Hannah rehabilitated 'em, then bought 'em."

Travis eyed the horses as he kept pace with Red, noting they were different from the ones in the photo he'd seen in Red's truck. "Are there any others?"

Red shook his head. "Not for a while now, and we need more horses. And guests. We're bleeding money."

Travis looked around, taking in the sprawling pastures, tall trees, and majestic views. It'd be a shame for this place to wither up. "I'm sorry."

Red shrugged. "Ain't your fault, but thanks just the same." He led Travis down the other side of the hill and off the dirt path. "Though you could help do something about it. Margaret wasn't too far off base with that laundry list of needs. There's plenty of work to be had here if you happen to be interested."

Travis's steps slowed as they arrived at a deep, peaceful stream. A thin line of pine and cypress trees bordered the far side of the water, but the bank they stood on was clear.

"See that cabin to your left?" Red asked.

Travis glanced to his left, further up the dirt path, and noticed a two-story log cabin. A large deck extended from one side and a series of connected winding stairways led down to the bank of the river. Unlike the other cabins, this one was in pristine condition and well-loved if the decorative wind chimes and attractive landscaping were any indication.

"That's Hannah's place," Red said. Turning back to the stream, he pointed across the river, at a higher elevation. "See that cabin up there? The one just inside the tree line?"

Travis glimpsed a small log structure between the trees' thick branches. "Yeah."

"That's where you're staying. It ain't spiffy, but it'll keep the elements off you." Red walked to the edge of the stream and held up the lemon. "Use this and scrub up over here. This lemon will have you smelling good as new."

Travis took the lemon half from Red, squatted by the water's edge, plunged his hands in the icy stream, and scrubbed. As he worked, he watched the water ripple and swirl around his hands, roll over smooth rocks, and flow gently around a bend in the distance. A few minutes later, his hands were numb with cold but completely clean. He held his palms up and smiled as the sunlight glinted off the drops of water lingering on his fingers and the clean scent of fresh lemon drifted from his skin.

"See?" Red clapped him on the back. "Good as new. Thanks again for cleaning that mess of fish. You freed me up for a lot of other chores, and even though she'd never admit it, I know Hannah's looking forward to a big trout dinner." Red headed toward the dirt path and motioned for Travis to follow. "I'll show you the way to your cabin. We're not eating till five so you'll have about three hours to shower and rest up before you come down to the main lodge."

Five minutes later, after walking to the end of the dirt path, crossing the stream on a small wooden bridge, and hiking up a stone walkway through a tangle of underbrush and trees, they arrived at a shabby cabin.

"Like I said"—Red stomped the dirt off his boots on the narrow porch steps—"it ain't fancy, but it'll get you through the night."

Travis eyed the aged structure and surrounding trees. Tipped his head back and looked at the blue sky. Listened to the breeze rustle through the leaves and savored the peaceful freedom that coursed through him at the thought of a cabin—a space—that would be all his own. For one night, at least.

He smiled. "Oh, it's fine."

Red opened the front door and led the way in, pausing to gesture around the small interior. "The bed's a single and the bathroom's through that door. This plumbing's old but you'll get a good, strong stream of running water in that shower. Margaret came up here a couple hours ago, put fresh sheets and a thick blanket on the mattress and clean towels, soap, and a few other toiletries in the bathroom cabinet. That fireplace will need cleaning before you light it. The Wi-Fi ain't strong enough to reach up here, and there's no phone. Sorry about that."

Travis shook his head. "I don't have a laptop or anything. I've been living off the grid for a while and prefer it that way. As for a phone . . ."

Well, he had no one to call.

Travis removed his bag from his shoulders and set it on a small desk by the door. He ran his hand through the thick dust covering the surface of the desk, eyed the chair beside it and the wide window above.

Red stepped toward the desk. "A guest requested that years ago. Now, I can get that out of your way to give you more room if—"

"No," Travis whispered. "This is perfect. Just perfect."

A satisfied expression moved over Red's features and he eased past Travis. "Dinner's at five on the back deck of the main lodge." As he left, Red said over his shoulder, "Maybe by then, you'll feel up to sharing a last name."

Travis moved to the window and watched as Red walked down the porch steps, maneuvered his way along the stone path, then disappeared below the thick shade of the trees. Reaching out, Travis palmed the edges of the window and, after discovering there was no lock, he tugged hard and pried it open.

A cool breeze swept in, dislodging a small cloud of dust, and rippled around the musty room. The smell of bark, pine sap, and smoke settled on the air. He could see the wide stream from here, caught the sunlit glimmer of fresh, mountain water, and Hannah's deck and stairway were just visible between the trees lining his side of the stream.

Travis stared down at his clean hands, then walked into the tiny bathroom, stripped, and turned on the shower. There were clean towels, soap, and toiletries just as Red had said. After scrubbing every inch of his skin with soap and water, shampooing his hair and shaving, Travis felt a bit more whole. His hair, when he ran his hand through it, felt shaggy, but smelled a million times better.

He returned to the main living area, leaving the bathroom door ajar to air out the steam from his hot shower, and retrieved a clean pair of jeans and a long-sleeved flannel shirt from his bag. After dressing, he ran his palm over the plaid blanket Margaret had draped over the small bed. It was thick and warm, the comforting feel of it against his fingertips evoking a heavy tightness in his chest. He didn't deserve her kindness; he wasn't worthy of Red's either.

Travis moved to the small desk, used a towel to remove the dust, then sat in the chair. He grabbed his bag and withdrew a stack of letters, stuffed in unmarked envelopes and bound with string, and placed them on the upper right corner of the desk. Then, he retrieved a pile of blank notebook paper and pens, arranged them on the desk's surface to his liking, and picked up a pen.

Propping his elbows on the desk, Travis pressed the pen to paper and wrote as neatly as the tremor in his hand would allow.

Dear Margaret,

I found you today. Twenty years, seven months, and three days after we last saw each other. You looked me in the eyes, shook my hand, and smiled. You didn't recognize the reckless boy I was in the man I've become. But I recognized you.

Your hair is gray now instead of blond. It's still long. You were dressed as elegantly today as you always were in court. But even though you smiled, that same look you had in your eyes twenty years ago—the only time during the trial that you faced me—was still there. The look that said the world is cruel, and God is more cruel.

That same look was in Hannah's eyes, too.

Travis raised his head, his gaze seeking out the large deck and wooden stairways on the other side of the stream. He spun the pen between his fingers slowly, then drew a line across the paper.

~~*That same look was in Hannah's eyes, too.*~~

I came to Paradise Peak for you, Margaret. To see you. To beg your forgiveness. To help you in any way I can. And yes, I'd fix that stable roof for you. I'd rebuild every crumbling cabin, restone the walkways, and revive this ranch.

I'd restructure my face and change the sound of my voice if it'd leave no trace of the killer you knew in this body. I'd burn my bones and these letters to ash if the act would erase my sins, every trace of my existence from your world. I'd do all these things if they'd bring you comfort. If doing so would set you free from the pain I've caused.

I'll see you again in a couple of hours. Instead of hiding these words with the others, I should tell you all of this. I should tell you that my life—however miniscule its worth—is yours in whatever way you choose to use it. But if you knew who I really am . . . If you knew I was Neil Travis Alden—the man who killed your daughter—would you even want it?

"If you're seeking perfection," Hannah said, "you're never going to find it."

She stopped mopping the kitchen floor and stared across the island at Margaret, who, bifocals perched on her nose, leaned down and pinched dough around the rim of a ceramic pie plate.

Dinner was supposed to be on the table in half an hour, but Margaret was just now cooking dessert because she'd insisted they sweep and mop the lodge's foyer and kitchen floor prior to Travis's arrival. As they planned to dine on the back deck, Hannah had maintained that there was a high probability the man wouldn't even set foot inside the kitchen, and an even greater chance that if he did, he wouldn't give a fig as to whether or not the porcelain tile gleamed.

Hannah glanced at the countertop, which housed a new glass-top stove Margaret had purchased and had installed in the lodge's kitchen two months ago. She had to admit it was an improvement over the old-fashioned—and unde-pendable—model they used to have. But she'd also noticed that the changes Margaret was making to the lodge and the grounds were more frequent and noticeable. It was as if she sought to transform every square inch of the prop-erty into a pristine cookie-cutter tourist attraction.

"Perfection is impossible to attain," Hannah added, leaning on the mop handle. "You're going to wear your-self out working on that."

Margaret's fingers stilled and she glanced at Hannah over the rim of her glasses. "And that is where you and I differ. I believe that if a task is done correctly at each and every step, the result will be either perfect or nearly per-fect."

"I see." Hannah bit back a grin. "So that apple pie is going to taste different depending on how evenly balanced the edges of the crust are?"

Margaret straightened and plucked her glasses off her nose. "Of course not, but I'll feel like a better hostess if all parts of the meal look appetizing to our guest. Delectable food should please the eye as well as the taste buds, and the atmosphere should be equally elegant—which is why I set out the formal dinnerware. Phillip and I always ate off nice china."

"Hmm." Hannah smiled and resumed mopping. "Then I guess you should tell Red to take the paper plates off the china, toss out the beer bottles, and turn down the honky-tonk tunes."

Margaret's mouth dropped open. "What?"

Hannah rubbed the mop head hard over a stubborn dirt smudge on the tile. "Just sayin'."

Margaret spun around and, long skirt swooshing, stomped out of the kitchen, down the foyer, and to the sunroom leading to the lodge's outdoor deck. When the door to the deck squeaked open and the loud beat of country music drifted into the kitchen, Hannah sighed, propped the mop against the kitchen counter, and followed Margaret out onto the deck.

"Turn that down!" Margaret stood by Red with her hands cupped around her mouth, shouting above the music that blared from a set of speakers on the wooden railing. Her attention darted from Red to the speakers and the two empty beer bottles surrounding one of the formal place settings.

Red, standing in front of a large fryer with a bowl of hush puppy batter in one hand and a large spoon in the other, dropped a spoonful of batter in the fryer, then asked in a raised voice, "What'd you say?"

"I said"—Margaret reached around Red and punched a button on the speakers—"turn that down!" Her shout echoed in the ensuing silence. She looked up at the clear, late-afternoon sky, smoothed a shaky hand over her hair, then, cheeks reddening, faced Red. "I meant to ask if you could please turn down the music."

Red glanced at the speakers and grinned. "Turn it down? Or off?"

Margaret reached around Red again, fiddled with the speakers, and the music resumed—at a much lower volume. "Down, of course. I apologize for overreacting." She walked to the table in the middle of the deck and straightened one edge of the lace tablecloth, her gaze shifting quickly when it landed on the beer bottles. "I was hoping we could use the good dishes for dinner tonight instead of paper plates. Phillip and I always ate our evening meal off formal dinnerware. Is it okay if I put the paper ones back in the kitchen?"

Red dropped another spoonful of batter in the fryer. "Sure. Only reason I brought 'em out was to save us the trouble of washing dishes later."

"I don't mind washing them." Margaret removed the paper plates from each formal plate, stacked them together, and headed toward the lodge. She stopped and turned back. "Thank you for cleaning the kitchen, Hannah. I'll finish mopping the floor after I put the pie in the oven. That way, you'll have time to freshen up before dinner."

Hannah glanced down at her long-sleeved shirt and jeans. There were no stains or rips in the clothing, so as far as she was concerned, she was in good shape. "No need. After we eat, I'll have to traipse across the pasture, round Ruby and Juno up, and get them back in the stable for the night. I'll get dirtied up all over again."

"Yes, but wouldn't you feel more comfortable during dinner if you showered and put on a nice blouse and skirt, maybe?" Margaret asked.

"Would I feel more comfortable wearing a skirt while I eat?" Hannah smirked. "Nope."

Red laughed. The fryer hissed as he plopped in another spoonful of batter. "If you want Hannah to wear a skirt, you'll have to hog-tie her and adhere that joker to her skin with duct tape."

Margaret's lips twitched. "It doesn't have to be a skirt. Just something a bit nicer than jeans to make a good first impression. And I'd be happy to fix your hair if you'd like me to. I could curl the ends or—"

"No, thank you." Hannah tightened her ponytail. "I've already made my first impression on Travis." Which . . .

she should've handled better—she could admit that now—
but it was too late to change their unfriendly introduction.
"And I promise I'll wash my hands before I eat. Beyond
that, I'm sorry to say, my lackluster appearance will just
have to disappoint."

Margaret studied the paper plates stacked in her hands,
then said quietly, "You couldn't be a disappointment if
you tried, Hannah. You're a beautiful girl, no matter what
you have on." She looked up and her eyes, sheened with
tears, met Hannah's. "I can't help it. Sometimes you remind me so much of—" She waved a hand and turned on
her heels. "You rest. I'll finish in the kitchen so you can
keep Red company."

Hannah watched, hands hanging by her sides, as Margaret went inside the lodge and shut the door behind her.
The fryer hissed again.

Groaning, she walked to the table, pulled out a chair,
and sat. "Why is it, every time I argue with her, whether
I'm right or not, I always end up feeling like a total loser?"

"Because you like having her around."

Hannah crossed her arms and frowned at Red's back.
"Sometimes, maybe. Margaret's a good person—I'll give
her that—but I've adjusted to her for your sake. I miss
things the way they were before she moved in."

Red grunted. "And how was that?"

"Peaceful." Hannah slumped back in her chair. "Pre-
dictable. B—"

"Boring?" Red glanced over his shoulder and raised an
eyebrow.

"No. Better." She picked up a cloth napkin Margaret
had painstakingly folded into a swan. "Practical." Her lips
twisted. "Without a swan napkin in sight."

Red set the bowl of batter and spoon aside, grabbed a
slotted utensil and plate, and scooped the cooked hush

puppies out of the hot oil one at a time. "She's making improvements to bring in more business. Something we need real bad."

"She's erasing every recognizable corner of this ranch in an attempt to attract a crowd." Hannah dropped the napkin onto the table. The beak drooped. "Paradise Peak Ranch has always been a secluded, no-frills retreat—and crowds, we could do without. A few loyal guests who return regularly would do fine. Do you know she's thrown out all of the original bedding in the first-floor guest rooms and put up seashell wallpaper in one room?"

He shrugged. "Margaret said she's using different themes for every room."

"But seashells, Red. This is a mountain ranch. You see any beaches around here?"

"What do you want me to say?" Finished removing the hush puppies, Red set them aside and faced her. "She's trying to help in the best way she knows how."

"She's re-creating her old life." Hannah thumped the fancy plate in front of her. "Surrounding herself with expensive things. Plastering seashells all over the walls to remind her of the beach house she and her husband used to visit every summer. There are more pictures of Phillip on display in the lodge now than there are of you."

Red's mouth tightened. "He's only been gone a year. She's still grieving."

"I understand that, but this is still your home, and you should be comfortable in it. You should be able to use paper plates whenever you want. Play music as loud as you want. This place should be full of your memories, too."

"You're a walking memory," he said. "Not just for me, but for Margaret. You remind her of Niki, and you help Margaret remember what it feels like to be a mother again—that is, when you're not shoving her away. Being a mother is one of Margaret's best memories. You begrudge her that, too?"

Hannah's throat tightened. Oh, she hadn't meant to go off on a tangent. And when she did, she always said the most awful things. If Red had no qualms about Margaret bulldozing into his daily life, it was no business of hers. When would she learn to keep her mouth shut and leave well enough alone?

"No," she whispered. "I don't mean to push her away. I know she misses Phillip and Niki, and that she's an equal partner in this business. And I do want her to feel at home with us. I just . . ." She rubbed her hands over her jeans. "The more changes she makes, the more it unsettles me. I liked things the way they were when it was only the two of us. Before long, nothing here will be the same."

"It's not meant to be the same," Red said. "It's meant to be something new. That's the whole point of me inviting Margaret to live here, and why she and I keep searching for more help. We need fresh ideas and a new approach. If we don't try something soon, none of us will be able to live here much longer."

A step creaked on the wooden staircase leading up to the deck. Hannah swiveled in her chair and peered over her shoulder.

Travis, as tall, brawny, and broad-shouldered as she remembered, stood on the top step a few feet away, his big hand curled loosely around the rail and his dark eyes seeking hers, then lowering. He'd shaved. His handsome features were clearly defined in the sharp sunlight: dark eyebrows, long lashes, high cheekbones, strong jaw, and sensual lips.

Despite the chill in the air, he hadn't worn a jacket. Instead, he wore a long-sleeved shirt and jeans (which had seen better days), and even though his muscular frame still seemed intimidating, in this light, in this setting, he looked less dangerous and more . . . inviting.

Hannah's skin heated beneath her shirt and denim jacket. She gripped the edges of her chair and straightened.

Eyes moving to her grip on the chair, Travis eased back a step and smiled slightly. "I don't mean to interrupt. I walked the grounds for a while but got here faster than I thought I would. Is it okay that I'm early?"

Hannah nodded and lifted a hand to smooth her ponytail, wishing, for the briefest of moments, that she'd taken Margaret's advice and showered. Wished that she was fifteen years younger—twenty, bright-eyed, and trusting. That her flesh had never felt the bruising force of a male fist, and that she'd never learned to fear someone she'd loved.

But she had.

Hand dropping back to her lap, she touched her fingertips to the inside of her elbow where, below thin layers of denim and cotton, a ragged scar marred her skin. It was a tangible reminder of one of Bryan's violent rages involving a knife similar in size to the kind Travis had carried this morning.

"No worries, Travis," Red called out. "You're more than welcome, whatever time you arrive." He jerked his chin toward the table. "Take a load off."

Travis thanked Red, ascended the last step to the deck, and approached the table. He hesitated by a chair opposite Hannah, seemed to change his mind, and moved to another place setting.

The door to the lodge opened and Margaret walked out, carrying a pitcher of sweet tea with sliced lemon floating among the ice. "Oh, how wonderful." She smiled. "You're already here and I can see you freshened up. Please make yourself at home."

Well. Looked like Margaret had expanded the definition of home to more than just family; seemed every stranger off the street was part of it, too. Hannah bit her tongue and remained silent.

"Thank you, ma'am." Travis dipped his head slightly and his gaze settled just to the left of a swan napkin. "I appreciate the supplies and fresh bedding you left at the cabin. Red told me you set things up and I can't tell you how great a shower and good night's sleep will feel."

Margaret beamed. "I'm glad you're happy with the accommodations, although I do wish I'd had time to do a thorough cleaning. That cabin's been empty for too long. But I have to say, even with the bare essentials, you've cleaned up quite well. A shower and shave, and you look every inch the handsome gentleman I suspected you were underneath that beard." She rubbed her chin with one hand. "But, if you were so inclined, I'd be happy to trim your—"

"Easy, Margaret." Smiling, Hannah stood and crossed the deck to the fireplace, carefully leaving a wide berth around Travis. "The man didn't say one word about wanting a haircut." She grabbed a dry log from a stack of firewood, tossed it into the small, stone fireplace in the corner of the deck, and stoked the low blaze. "She's been trying to get her hands on mine for a year."

Margaret made a small sound of irritation but kept her smile in place. "She exaggerates. But the offer remains all the same."

Margaret moved to set the pitcher of sweet tea on the table and Travis intervened, lifting the pitcher from her hands and gesturing toward the table.

"Where would you like it?" he asked.

Margaret pointed to the center of the table. "There, please. Thank you."

"Travis, can I get you a beer?" Red asked as he turned off the fryer. "One's chillin' in the fridge with your name on it."

Hannah returned to her seat and glanced at Travis. Light pink bloomed along his cheekbones. Imagine that. A big, strong man like that actually . . . blushing?

"No, thanks," Travis said. "I don't drink."

Red cocked his head to the side. "Never?"

"No. Never."

"Well, ain't that a first." Red grinned and looked at Margaret. "He doesn't drive anymore either. Never met a man who doesn't do at least one of those. Anything else you don't do that I should be aware of?"

Travis's cheeks turned even redder as he stared at the empty beer bottles on the table.

"Not all men need alcohol to relax," Margaret said quietly. "I think it's an admirable trait."

Hannah squirmed in her chair, wondering if Red realized his misstep. He hadn't meant it that way—of course he hadn't. But Margaret, having lost her daughter, Niki, in a car accident to a drunk driver, would interpret his comments less flippantly.

Red's grin slowly faded. "I'm sorry. I didn't mean—"

"To keep us all waiting," Hannah finished for him. Gracious, the last thing any of them needed were more awkward moments, and as she'd been the cause of most of them today, she was eager to avoid another. "I'm starving." She reached out, took Margaret's hand in hers, and squeezed gently. "What about you, Margaret? We haven't had a decent trout dinner in ages. I bet I can put away at least two times the number of fillets you do."

After a moment, Margaret squeezed her hand back and smiled at Red. "Yes. Get a move on, Red. You have three very hungry people who demand to be fed. You're in for a treat, Travis. Red's fried fish and hush puppies are the finest in east Tennessee."

Relaxing, Red laughed softly. "Only if they're coupled with your potato salad."

"Then Travis is in luck." Margaret released Hannah's hand and headed toward the lodge. "I made a fresh batch and will have it on the table in a jiff."

Travis, Hannah noted, remained silent, his attention following Red's movements as he collected the empty beer bottles and tossed them in a nearby trash can.

A jiff and ten minutes later, all four of them were seated at the table, had said the blessing and dug into a belly-warming spread of fried trout fillets, hush puppies, potato salad, apple pie, and multiple refills of sweet tea. The flaming logs popped and crackled in the fireplace, ice clinked in glasses, and the sun slowly descended behind the mountain peaks in the distance, prompting the strings of solar lights that Margaret had hung around the deck railings to glow softly around them.

The temperature dipped and the chill in the night air turned brisk as they finished their meal. Red discussed his fishing techniques with Travis, a hint of pride in his voice, and Margaret slipped in a few personal questions that Travis responded to with vague generalizations or sidestepped altogether.

Hannah sneaked glances at him every now and then. He hadn't said much or looked up from his plate more than three times during the entire meal. His strong hands moved slowly as he reached for his glass of tea and adjusted his napkin in his lap, and twice, he'd met her eyes briefly before refocusing on his plate.

Soon, Margaret served everyone a cup of hot coffee and Red threw another log on the fire. On the way back to his chair, Red paused to lift Margaret's cardigan from the back of her chair and tucked it around her shoulders. She thanked him quietly as she stirred cream in her coffee.

Hannah smiled. Something about Margaret always brought out the gentleman in Red. He was a good man. The only man Hannah trusted. And despite the presence of a quiet stranger at the table, tonight was one of those increasingly rare but relaxed evenings at Paradise Peak Ranch when a hard day of work had been followed with an abundance of good food, pleasant company, and momentary relief from financial worries. Even the smoke still rising from the distant mountain was easy to ignore when its scent was masked by the smoke from the small, cozy fireplace on the deck.

Sated, with a belly stuffed full to bursting, Hannah eased back in her chair, stretched her weary limbs, and closed her eyes. "Oh, Margaret, I'll wash every fancy dish in the cabinets and mop every floor in the lodge if you and Red serve up another meal like this next week."

Margaret lifted her coffee mug to her lips and smiled. "I take it you enjoyed it?"

"It was delicious."

"And the swan napkins?" Margaret asked. "Did you like those, too?"

Hannah cracked one eye open, shared a look with Red, who covered his smile by rubbing his mustache, then grinned. "I loved the swan napkins. The meal wouldn't have been the same without them."

"Wonderful!" Margaret sipped her coffee, then returned her cup to its saucer. "When business picks up, I'm going to make them every night for dinner in the banquet hall. Swan napkins and fresh flower arrangements on every table. They'll become a permanent fixture of Paradise Peak Ranch." She made a sweeping motion with her hands. " 'Elegant dining in a majestic setting' could be our slogan."

Hannah stifled a groan.

"Everything was delicious. Thank you for inviting me."

The gentle rumble of Travis's voice drifted across the table, sending a delicious tingle over her skin. She kept her eyes closed and sagged further back in her chair. She refused to give in to the aggravating impulse to admire his handsome profile again.

"You're invited to breakfast, too, Travis," Margaret said. China clinked as she lowered her cup again. "I try my best to have it on the table by seven every morning."

A soft palm patted the back of Hannah's wrist.

"Hannah works so hard," Margaret continued. "So does Red. It's the least I can do."

"We all do our fair share, you included," Red said. "And speaking of work—I got a call from Carl Lennox earlier this afternoon."

Hannah opened her eyes and sat up. Carl managed the stables at Misty Ridge Stables—the best riding outfit in Paradise Peak—and he had a knack for picking out horses with the most potential. "Has he spotted a horse for us?"

Red nodded. "A mare. Young, fearful. Was hurt pretty badly wherever she came from. Carl said when he saw her, the first person he thought of was you."

Hannah stood. "Where is she? When can I pick her up?"

Red threw up his hand. "Now, hold up. We'll get to that. First, we need to fix that stable roof. There's rain in the forecast for Tuesday afternoon and, as glad as I am to have this drought broken, that means we got to get a move on fixin' those leaks. You can't be banging on that rickety roof with a terrified animal housed under it."

"Not a problem." Hannah headed for the stairs leading to the field. "I'll get Ruby and Juno settled, turn in for the night, and start on it at first light. That way, it'll be finished tomorrow, and I can go pick up the horse Tuesday morning."

"Whoa." Red waved her back over. "Like I said, you ain't getting up on that roof by yourself, and I promised Margaret I'd help her paint a room in the lodge tomorrow. So . . ." He glanced at Travis. "I'm hoping I can entice Travis into one more arrangement."

"Red, I don't need—"

"That's how it's gonna be, Hannah," Red said, his tone hardening. "You're not getting on that roof without help by your side, and I ain't able to do it tomorrow. Accept the extra hand or it's no-go on the new horse."

Hannah held her breath for a moment, half hoping Travis would refuse and move on like the other nomad Red had brought home two weeks ago. But the other half of her hoped this stranger—a handsome man whose rough exterior had been softened by the gentle glow of Margaret's festive lights—would accept Red's offer, stay a while, and stir the small whirl of attraction deep inside her a bit more.

Travis eased his hands to his lap and narrowed his eyes at Red. "This meal and a night's stay are more than payment enough for the scrap of work I did today. I owe you."

"Enough to fix that stable roof with Hannah?" Red asked.

Travis's dark eyes moved to Hannah as he nodded. "That and more, if you were to ask." He looked down and leaned forward, placing his hands on the table. His fingers toyed with the napkin he'd folded by his plate. "But I need to—"

"There are no buts, hidden expectations, or tricky conditions to this deal." Margaret reached out and covered Travis's hand with hers. "There's work to be had here, and if you're down on your luck, it could be a way to get back on your feet. Red is inviting you to stay and work for as long as you'd like."

A muscle in Travis's forearm flexed. He raised his head and studied Margaret. "Do you want me to stay?"

Margaret smiled. "I'd like that very much."

An odd mix of emotion moved through Travis's expression as he stared down at Margaret's hand covering his. "Then, yes. I'll stay."

Hannah blew out a heavy breath. Looked like the aggravating half of her that was curious about Travis would get its way. "If I'm going to scale rotten planks twelve feet above the ground with someone, I at least need to know his name." Noticing Red's frown, she shrugged, focused on Travis, and lifted her chin. "His full name."

Travis stood slowly, glanced at Margaret, then said, "Miller. Travis Miller."

His tone was warm and steady, but his dark eyes avoided hers.

Hannah watched and waited, wanting more from him. She wanted to be kind, trusting, and accommodating for Red's and Margaret's sake. But something about Travis didn't sit well with her, and she'd learned long ago that good looks could mask a wealth of bad intentions.

"Be at the stable tomorrow morning, seven-thirty sharp," Hannah said. "And get some rest. I'll accept your help, but I won't go easy on you."

CHAPTER 3

Miller. A fake, a fraud. One day in Paradise Peak and he'd already blown it.

Throat tightening, Travis slowed his steps as he passed Hannah's cabin. The front door was closed, the side deck was empty, and sporadic thuds cut through a cold, low-hanging mist blanketing the pastures that sprawled along both sides of the dirt path in front of him. He glanced at his frayed watch and sighed.

Six minutes past seven, the sun barely peeked above the mountain ridge, and Hannah was already hard at work on the stable roof without him. If the expression on her face last night hadn't made her message clear, her actions this morning did.

She was Red's family. Hardworking and capable. She didn't need him.

Travis shook his head and picked up his pace, taking swift strides up the dirt path and around the side pasture. Ruby and Juno were out. They stood several feet from the fence in the larger field, ears perked, heads cocked, studying his every step. Ruby, the gray mare, poised one front leg as if ready to bolt at the first suspicious movement he made.

He stopped and observed her. Watched as Ruby's wide, black eyes fixed on him, then he took in her smooth coat, his fingers flexing at his sides, wondering if the thick hair would feel as soft as it looked. He wanted to touch his palm to her hide gently and offer comfort and reassurance. The same reassurance Margaret had given him last night when she'd placed her hand on his.

Margaret's gesture had been casual and brief. Fleeting, even. But her touch—the kindness behind it, the sheer human connection—had moistened his eyes and almost broken his composure. He had no right to it; he knew that. But in that moment, he'd believed there was a possibility she might be able to forgive him, only he couldn't bring himself to tell her the truth.

How could he when just the touch of her hand had transformed the space around him? In that moment, the cool night air had felt warmer against his skin, the glow of the decorative lights above his head had felt soothing, and the breath he'd taken had felt invigorating and full of promise. As though he'd been given a clean slate and was freed to feel, think, and speak. As though he were entitled to live and be happy like any other man.

Travis smiled at Ruby, lifted his hand, and stepped forward slowly, wanting to share a little of what Margaret had shown him in that small touch, wanting to soothe the mare's fears.

Something heavy struck the ground at his back, the sound magnified by the stable walls. Ruby and Juno jerked, spun, and galloped off, disappearing into the thick mist cloaking the distant field.

"Are you coming, or are you going to stand there and stare some more?"

Travis turned from the chunk of wood that had hit the ground and looked up. Hannah stood on the stable roof, legs wide, feet planted on exposed wood beams, peering down at him. Mist rose in fingerlike tendrils from the ground, reaching midway up the stable wall, and another thin, almost transparent layer swirled around her slender figure.

She motioned with one hand, pointing a hammer at the field behind him. "You act like you've never seen a horse before."

"I haven't." Travis bit his lip at the naïveté of his tone. "Not in person, that is."

She tilted her head, her auburn ponytail swinging over one shoulder. "Not even once? When you were a kid?"

He shook his head. Rockton Park, a small corner in western Tennessee where he'd spent what technically qualified as his childhood, had no horses. Poverty, drugs, and violence, though, had been in high supply.

"Where'd you grow up?" Hannah asked.

Prison. Travis focused on the faint beams of sunlight fighting their way through the mist behind her as the memory of being locked behind high walls evoked a surge of panic.

He might have been eighteen—the legal definition of an adult—when he'd entered prison, but on the inside, he'd been an angry, confused, and terrified kid who'd hurt people in ways in which he'd been unable to fully conceive. Every day he spent inside that gated hell had hurt worse than the one before. He'd been condemned, forgotten, and alone. And one morning a year down the road, he'd woken up on his cot with sober, horrifying awareness of what he'd done, still breathing but completely dead inside.

He was an addict, had driven drunk, slammed into oncoming traffic, and taken the life of twenty-year-old Niki Owens—a medical student, bright, responsible, and vivacious. He'd stolen Niki's future, and scarred Niki's mother, Margaret, and her family forever.

The boy within him was gone; a convicted felon remained, and he'd blown any chance he might've had of becoming someone of character or value. Someone worthy of love.

"I grew up in Rockton Park," he said. At least about location, he could be truthful. One lie was enough; he refused to tell any more. "It's a small place in the middle of nowhere. West Tennessee. Not much to it."

He wondered where Hannah had grown up. Red had mentioned she'd moved to his ranch five years ago, but where had she lived as a child? In the country, maybe? With idyllic views, healthy horses who roamed at will, and a supportive family?

It couldn't all have been good, though, he thought, recalling the defensive panic in her eyes when they'd first met and Red's comment: "She's got reason to be skittish."

What had Hannah seen and felt to put that wounded, angry look in her eyes? And who had inflicted that pain upon her?

His hands flexed at his sides, wanting to cradle her smaller frame, to soothe and support—similar to the urge he'd had to comfort Ruby. The need to protect something—or someone—good and innocent. To replace some of the violence and pain he'd thrown into the world with something well-intentioned and whole.

The questions hovered on his tongue, but he held them back and kept his hands still by his sides. Guessing from first impressions that Hannah was a private person and knowing he had no right to pry.

Hannah studied him, those beautiful blue eyes roving over his chest, abs, and hands, before she motioned toward a twelve-foot ladder that was propped against the side of the roof. "There's a pair of gloves on the bottom rung for you. They might be tight, but they're the biggest size we have."

Travis walked over to the ladder, retrieved the work

gloves, and tugged them on. He flexed his hands twice, loosening the leather.

"Too tight?" Hannah asked.

"No." He smiled up at her. "Thanks."

Her attention lowered to his mouth and lingered, then her chest lifted on a swift breath as she turned away and stepped carefully to another exposed beam. "Then get up here. You're burning my daylight."

He smiled wider, watched her silky ponytail swish across her back as she knelt on two beams. He studied her confident movements as she hooked the claw of the hammer around a nail and tugged.

Hannah didn't want him here—she'd made that obvious—but she liked looking at him. And he had to admit, he enjoyed looking at her. Those soulful eyes, that cute nose, that stubborn chin, and those pink, kissable lips would pull any man in. Her fresh-faced, no frills appearance somehow made her more appealing and feminine than any woman he'd ever seen dressed to the nines.

She seemed sincere, honest, and good. All things he wished he could be.

"Oh, sh—" The hammer slipped, smacked against a beam and, judging by the expletive Hannah failed to silence, hit her finger, too. She brought her finger to her mouth, then lowered it and glanced over her shoulder at him, her cheeks flushing. "Sorry."

"Are you all right?"

"Yeah. Just smacked the stew out of my finger." She shrugged. "Should've kept the profanity to myself though."

He stifled a laugh and climbed the ladder. "It's okay. I've heard"—*and said*, he ruefully admitted—"worse." After easing his weight onto the two beams nearest him, he eyed her waist and asked, "You don't tether?"

"No." She repositioned her hammer and tugged at the

nail again. "I haven't gotten around to picking up a harness. It costs money I'd rather not spend at the moment."

"Do you have ropes? I could rig something up for y—"

"I said I don't tether." She pounded the nail harder. "I've used ropes before, and all they do is get in the way and slow me down."

They'd also keep you from falling. Travis kept his mouth shut, thinking it'd be better to keep that thought to himself, considering her stubborn mood.

"I'll grab you ropes, though, if you'd like to use them?" she asked.

"No, thanks." If she was going without them, he would, too.

She stopped tugging at the nail and frowned at him. "You think I'm going to fall, don't you?"

"I didn't say tha—"

"You didn't have to." She refocused on the nail and yanked at it harder. "I know what I'm doing. I've done this kind of work before on two of our cabins and I'll have to do it again on a third cabin roof before summer. I could do it in my sleep. Besides"—she ripped the nail free from the board, blew a breath to lift her bangs off her sweaty forehead, and narrowed her eyes at him—"isn't that why Red arranged for you to be here? To fetch help for me in case I fall?"

His smile slipped, the lighthearted feeling vanishing. "Yeah. I guess that's the gist of it." He spotted a drill on a tray attached to the top of the ladder. "What's the detail?"

A confused expression crossed Hannah's face. "The what?"

Travis stilled, recalling the frequent assignments of labor he'd been given in prison, when a dark, depressing day inside his cell was exchanged for a few hours spent outside beneath the sun on work detail, each step of which was outlined explicitly. Hannah would be familiar with none of this, and his stint in prison was the last thing he wanted to explain today.

He cleared his throat. "I mean, the details of the job. What would you like me to do first?"

She pointed to several wood beams in front of her. "A few of those boards need to come out. Some are rotten and a couple are cracked. I'll remove the nails, pass the boards to you, and you'll toss them over the edge. Once we finish that, I'll need you to pass me the new boards—they're stacked on the ground by the stable—and I'll nail those in. Then, we'll drill some sheet metal. Sound doable?"

"Yeah." He eased closer to her side and began lifting the beam she'd just loosened. "I'd be happy to take over if you get tired at some point."

She set her hammer aside and lifted the beam with him. "I don't tire easily."

He glanced at her arms as she lifted the hefty beam with ease, noted the sturdy stance of her legs and the stubborn light in her eyes. "I don't imagine you do."

Travis hefted the beam out of her hands, lifted it over his shoulder, and tossed it on the ground by the stable. Hannah's gaze drifted over his upper body once more; then she returned to the beam in front of her, fixed the hammer claw over another nail, and tugged.

And so it went. Over the next two hours, they hit a steady rhythm. Hannah picked out the rotten beams, yanked out the nails, and Travis tossed them into the steadily growing pile. The nails squeaked as they were pried from the weak wood, the beams creaked when Travis shifted his weight to a new position, and loud thuds sounded each time he tossed a board.

When they hit the worst section of the roof, Travis straddled two beams a foot below Hannah, watched her movements closely, and made sure he never positioned his feet on the same boards she did. The wood was weak; it could hold her, but not him, too.

The mist gradually lifted as they scaled the roof, the sun rose higher above the mountain ridge, and soon, the familiar scent of smoke descended on the ranch.

Travis glanced up as Hannah tugged at another nail and eyed the gray streak of smoke above a mountain in the distance. The same one he'd noticed yesterday morning when he'd arrived at Paradise Peak. "That smoke . . . What's it coming from?"

Hannah stopped yanking at the nail, raised her head, and studied the plume of smoke. "Wildfire." She dragged her forearm across her brow as she stared. "We get them from time to time. It's been warmer than usual the last two winters. We've had a drought, and a storm came through four days ago—no rain, but plenty of lightning, which started the fire. That doesn't usually happen till spring."

"Are they trying to put it out?"

"In a way." She returned her attention to the nail and tugged it free. "The fire's weak and in an isolated part of the park. They say it's contained and nothing to worry about."

Her hands shook as she gripped the rotten board and pulled. Travis eyed the pink flush in her cheeks and tight set of her soft mouth. "But you're worried?"

She jerked the board loose and passed it to him. "I'm concerned. After four days, who wouldn't be?"

He took the board and heaved it over his shoulder onto the pile below. Hannah gripped a beam, her boots exploring carefully behind her for a foothold on the next board. Travis moved his feet to lower beams, making way for her as she repositioned herself and attacked the next damaged board.

"How long will they let it burn before they take more aggressive measures?" he asked.

"Not long. There's heavy rain in the forecast for tomorrow afternoon. If they keep it contained until then, it'll be doused." She removed the last nail from the board, slipped it in a small bag at her waist with the others, and lifted the board. "Wildfires aren't all bad; they help healthy growth of the woodland, and some wildlife benefits from them. But despite that"—she passed the board to him—"I still don't like them."

"I don't blame you." He turned, tossed the beam, and watched it hit the pile twelve feet below, scattering a few boards in its wake. "What will they do if it doesn't rai—"

A sharp crack split the air, the board beneath one of Travis's feet gave way, and he caught the flash of an auburn ponytail slipping by in his peripheral vision.

He fell onto the exposed beams, wrapping his right arm around one to secure his position, and his left arm shot out, his gloved hand grasping blindly at the soft material of a shirt, the smooth skin of a forearm, then curled tightly around Hannah's small wrist as she fell through the gap between two beams. Her weight swung to one side, stretching his muscles to the point of pain, but he held on.

She dangled, her legs swaying several feet above the sharp edges of stall walls and twelve feet above the hard ground below. Her free arm flailed, hand outstretched, for a grip on the roof, on the wall, on anything.

Travis looked down, his eyes meeting Hannah's wide, panicked ones. Her mouth opened, her chest lifted and fell on swift breaths, but she didn't make a sound. No scream— not even a plea for help.

Despite the tearing pain in his shoulder and the fear spiking through him at the thought of not being able to pull her back up, he kept his tone calm and said the only words his constricted throat could manage. "Hold on."

Hannah threw her free arm out, straining to reach the wood beams above her head. She slipped a quarter of an inch out of Travis's tight grip, the glove on her hand rolling further up her wrist. His low words barely cut through the pounding echo of her startled heart.

Hold on.

"To what?"

The beams above her were out of reach and the stable wall was too far away to swing over to for a foothold. She searched his eyes, the dark depths blank and unreadable.

Oh, God. This emotionless stranger's grip on her wrist was the only thing preventing her from plummeting to hard earth. She looked down and her legs kicked as silent terror rippled through her at the thought.

"To me."

She stopped kicking and refocused on his face. A muscle ticked along hard-clenched muscles in his jaw, but his mouth curved upward in a tight smile.

"You're gonna have to hold on to me," he said, voice strained. "Seeing as how I decided to catch instead of fetch."

"F-fetch?" Her breath caught. "What're you talking about?"

"I can't fetch help, so I'm gonna pull you up."

A ragged sound—half sob, half laugh—burst from her lips. "Really? You're cracking a joke right now?"

"I'm telling you to grab on to me."

She slipped another quarter of an inch, a gasp escaping her. "I—"

"*Now,*" he rasped. "Please!"

Hannah lunged up, her free hand latching on to Travis's broad forearm. The muscular tendons flexed beneath her hold as his gloved hand tightened around hers and pulled upward.

His wide upper body rose in slow increments and his knee shifted under him, his thick thigh straining against the seam of his jeans as he squatted on the exposed beams and hauled her higher and higher.

Her arm cleared the roof, then her shoulders, chest, and waist. She jerked her right leg up, propped her knee on a beam, and pushed against the wood until her entire body reached the roof and both of her feet were planted on sturdy wood again.

Hannah lay there facedown, her body sprawled across exposed beams, one hand wrapped around a beam and the other still clenched in Travis's grip.

"Are you okay?"

She dragged her attention away from the hard dirt floor of the stable, visible between the exposed beams, and looked at Travis. His lean cheeks were red, his mouth pinched, and his hand holding her wrist shook. The tremors traveled up his arm, making the muscular biceps pressed against her ribs tremble. A sheen of sweat coated his forehead and a soft strand of his black hair had tumbled over his eyebrow.

"I'm fine." She licked her lips and asked, voice catching, "You?"

Emotion flickered in his dark eyes as they met hers. His expression softened despite the pained set of his jaw, and he nodded.

They remained still for a couple moments, their heavy breaths rasping as they stared at the drop below them.

Travis released his grip on her wrist and his gloved hand trailed away across the beams to his side. "Did I hurt you?"

Hannah blinked at the regretful note in his voice. "What?"

"Your wrist." He dipped his head. "Did I hold you too hard?"

She followed the direction of his gaze and studied the sensitive flesh of her wrist, where red blotches the size and shape of his fingers deepened into a purple-tinged shade with each passing second. An intense throb still hummed beneath her skin, but something warm and soothing mingled with the pain.

Bryan had hurt her more often than not during their

ten-year marriage and had broken every promise he'd made to change. The pain he'd inflicted had always been deep, infiltrating every safe space inside her until she'd forgotten how it felt to not be afraid.

But the waves of sensation Travis's tight grip had left behind were different.

It was just a result of the circumstances, she assured herself. A side effect of Travis's pulling her to safety.

Yet, for whatever reason, she yearned to feel his touch again.

"No." Her voice emerged husky and she cleared her throat. "You didn't hold me too hard."

And I want you to hold me again. Her eyes smarted with hot tears at her desire to be protected. To be held, rocked, and assured her life would be right again someday.

It was a silly, stupid whim that would leave her vulnerable to a man's hands.

She squeezed her eyes shut until the moisture in them receded, then tightened her grip on the wood beams and shoved herself to her knees. "I think it's time to take a break."

Hannah eased her way back to the ladder positioned at the edge of the roof. Her legs wobbled as she lowered her feet, one at a time, to the top rung.

"I'm sorry."

Pleasure rippled through her at the deep sound of Travis's voice. She chanced another glance at his handsome face. He'd pushed to his hands and knees, watching her.

"For what?" she asked.

"For not paying attention." He lowered his gaze to her boots. "Some of those boards were too weak for us both. I kept off the ones you stood on, but I wasn't looking when you moved. I didn't transfer my weight to another beam when I should have."

"You were watching out for . . . ?" Hannah looked

away, her chest tightening. "It wasn't your fault." She faced him again. Forced herself to meet his eyes. "Quite the opposite, in fact."

"How's it going up there?"

Hannah started at Red's shout. She glanced to her left to find Red, a water bottle in each of his hands, and Margaret, holding two small paper bags, strolling across the field toward the stable.

"It's after nine." Reaching the stable, Margaret shielded her eyes against the fully risen sun and smiled up at them. "You've been working for over two hours now. Thought we'd bring you breakfast."

A cool breeze swept across the roof, fluttering beneath Hannah's loose shirttails and sweeping over her sweat-slickened belly. She shivered and, face heating at the thought of her close call, glanced at Travis. "Well, I had—"

"To adjust to me getting in the way," Travis interrupted. He pushed carefully to his feet, rubbing his left arm as he looked down at Red and Margaret. "I had trouble keeping up."

Red laughed. "Yep. She's a go-getter, and hardheaded as a mule sometimes. I was hoping she hadn't run you off."

Travis smiled, his brown eyes meeting Hannah's. "No. Not at all."

Cheeks burning even hotter but grateful Travis hadn't mentioned her mishap, Hannah ducked her head and made her way down the ladder until her boots settled on the firm ground below. Travis followed close behind. She studied his scuffed tennis shoes, eyeing the worn heels and loose seams.

"Red," she asked, "you still have that extra pair of hiking boots in your closet?"

"Yep." He handed her a bottled water. "It's hard for a man to chuck his favorite pair of boots, even after he gets new ones."

Hannah looked at Travis. "What size shoe do you wear?"

"Fourteen," Travis said. "But—"

"Perfect." Red laughed. " 'Bout time I met a man with feet as big as mine." He smiled at Hannah. "That's what you were thinking, right?" At her nod, he passed Travis the remaining bottle of water, turned on his heel, and headed back toward the lodge. "Be back in a minute."

"While he's doing that," Margaret said, lifting the paper bags in her hands, "you two might as well eat breakfast. You won't last for much longer up there with growling stomachs. I brought you flapjack sandwiches stuffed with bacon, eggs, and cheese."

Hannah, appreciative of the distraction, took one bag and smiled. "Thanks. That was thoughtful of you."

Travis took the other bag and expressed his thanks as well. "Very thoughtful."

Hannah sat, cross-legged, and opened her bag. The mouth-watering aroma of crispy bacon and maple syrup escaped, and she unwrapped her sandwich and took a bite, humming with pleasure as the delicious flavors of sweet pancake and salty meat hit her tongue.

"Oh, Margaret." Hannah closed her eyes, savoring the hearty bite as a cool breeze swept through her hair, the long strands tickling the back of her neck. "This hits the spot."

Margaret clasped her hands together at her waist and blushed with pleasure.

Travis settled on the ground nearby and dug into his sandwich, too. They sipped water and finished off their breakfast as Margaret walked around the stable, commenting on the large pile of rotten beams they'd removed and remarking on how much the new metal roof would improve the look of the stable. She seemed pleased with the progress Hannah and Travis had made so far and hinted at how relieved she'd be when the walkways were relaid as well. Even went so far as suggesting that different colors of rustic flagstone would really perk things up around the ranch, and wouldn't that be a delightful welcome for new guests?

Despite her impatience with Margaret's extravagant changes, Hannah still managed a smile at that.

Minutes later, Red returned with the boots, handed them to Travis, and waited as he removed his tennis shoes and tried them on.

"How do they feel?" Red asked.

Travis raised his heels a few times, then smiled. "Perfect. Thank you."

"We won't stay and hold y'all up." Red gathered up the empty paper bags and bottles, then waved Margaret over. "We know you've got a lot left to do before the sun goes down. We'll leave you to it."

Margaret called over her shoulder, "I'll be back in a few hours with a late lunch for you."

As they left, Hannah stood, brushed the crumbs off her jeans, and returned to the ladder. "I got to thinking, I might need an extra hand loading up the new horse tomorrow morning. I haven't seen her myself, so I have no idea what condition she's in."

Boots crunched over dry grass and she felt Travis's heavy presence at her back. She pulled in a deep breath and gripped the ladder, ignoring the strange mix of fear and desire clamoring through her.

"You're welcome to go with me and help load up the mare," she continued. "We'll have to drive into town to get her and there's a clothing store on the way. I'm sure Red would throw in a bonus with your pay for new clothes suitable for ranch work if you helped me tomorrow morning." She bit her lip and said ruefully, "That is, if you need them?"

He was quiet for a minute and Hannah tensed, wanting to kick herself for being insensitive.

"I do need them, and I'd like to help with the new horse."

Her shoulders relaxed at his soft words. There was no resentment in his voice, only gratitude and . . . a tinge of eagerness?

Hannah grinned, stepped onto the bottom rung of the ladder, and started climbing. "That's settled then. Now, let's get back to work."

This time, Hannah set aside her pride and worked with more vigilance, stepping carefully, asking for Travis's input and matching her pace to his. She even hauled ropes to the roof and allowed Travis to rig a tether for her, though the contraption was as aggravating this time around as before.

The rotten beams finally removed and replaced with new ones, she and Travis proceeded to install the sheet metal panels. Travis stood on the ladder and passed each panel to Hannah, who slid it in place, measured twice for accuracy, and drilled it into the beams in several places until it was secure.

Soon the sun, which had shone high in the sky for several hours, drifted slowly over their heads and eased west toward the mountain range. Margaret and Red returned with foil-covered plates of fried chicken, mashed potatoes with gravy, and huge slices of chocolate cake, and stood with Hannah and Travis for several minutes, admiring the new stable roof and complimenting their work.

Hannah laughed. "Margaret must be happy with what we've done if she went to the trouble of baking a cake."

Margaret waved her comment aside. "I am pleased with what you've done, but I enjoy baking and couldn't imagine a better occasion for it. You and Travis should be proud of yourselves."

Hannah glanced at Travis. He stood beside Red, one big hand kneading his left shoulder and an exhausted half smile on his face.

Her own smile slipped as she recalled how often he'd massaged his left shoulder and arm while they'd worked. He must have strained his muscles hauling her back up to the roof earlier that morning, and no doubt moving load after load of wood and sheet metal had only worsened his injury. A man who was all bad wouldn't have done something to injure himself to help someone else, would he?

But he had still dodged Margaret's questions at dinner last night and wasn't entirely forthcoming with his past and opinions. Travis definitely fit the strong, silent mold— the kind of man Red had always been—so was it possible she'd misjudged him? That instead of hiding something, Travis was simply private? Or shy?

"I don't know about Travis, but I'm beat," Hannah said, rubbing the back of her neck. "Hope you don't mind if I skip coffee at the lodge tonight, Margaret? It'll be dark soon, so I'm going to settle Ruby and Juno for the night and turn in early."

"I plan to do the same," Travis said.

"Oh." A disappointed expression crossed Margaret's face.

"Travis has agreed to go with me to pick up the new horse tomorrow," Hannah said quickly. "We need to leave early if we're going to be able to load the horse, get back to the ranch and stable her before the rain hits."

Margaret's brows raised, her disappointment vanishing. "You're going with her, Travis? How wonderful!"

Red smiled at Travis. "Glad to hear it. You'll get a chance to see more of Paradise Peak. I'll meet you in front of the stable first thing tomorrow morning and help you hook up the trailer."

"We'll leave you to it then," Margaret said, passing a

plate to each of them and heading back to the lodge with Red. "See you both tomorrow morning."

Hannah set her plate on a fence post and walked toward the pasture, saying over her shoulder to Travis, "If you'll open the first two stalls, I'll bring Ruby and Juno in."

Travis nodded, set his plate on a post beside hers, and walked into the stable. Thirty minutes later, Ruby and Juno were stabled, night had settled in, and Hannah, balancing her plate of food in one hand and holding a camping lantern in the other, walked beside Travis on the dirt path toward her cabin.

An owl's mournful hoot echoed in the woods, and trees rustled in the cool, late-winter wind. The stars were out, winking softly down at them as wispy clouds drifted past. Water splashed against rocks as it moved downstream to their right. Hannah sneaked glances at Travis as they strolled up the dirt path, and she suspected he did the same to her, but neither of them spoke, and before long, Hannah's cabin emerged into view.

Hannah slowed her steps, lifted the lantern higher toward Travis, and said quietly, "I want to thank you for your help today. And for . . ." She looked up at him, admiring the way the soft light of the lantern caressed the strong angles of his handsome face, and blurted, "Holding me."

Oh, wonderful—did she just say that? Out loud? She lowered the lantern to her side and looked away, her mouth opening and closing silently as she searched for a way out of the hole she'd dug.

"Thank you for catching me," she managed to clarify. She stared at the lantern's light spilling over the bottom steps of her cabin's winding staircase. "I might've broken a leg—or my neck—if you hadn't helped me. I want you to know that I do appreciate what you did, and I'm sorry for not being kinder to you when we first met."

Raising her head, she faced him once more, finding him closer than she expected. She caught herself leaning forward to absorb a little more of the heat emanating from his muscular frame.

He lowered his head next to hers, near the lantern's soft light, and his chest vibrated softly with the low words he spoke. "You're welcome."

She caught a brief glimpse of a small smile on his sensual lips before he turned away and walked toward the bridge leading to his cabin on the other side of the stream. His left arm moved stiffly by his side with each step.

"Travis?"

His tall frame stopped, half turned toward her.

"I know you're hurting because you helped me," she whispered. "And what I said—it's not enough. But words never are, are they?" Glancing down, she tightened her grip on the lantern, then walked over and pressed it into his hand instead. "Take this. You'll need it going up the trail, and I know my way in from here."

He stood there silently, the lantern dangling between his blunt fingertips, his dark eyes peering into hers. After a few moments, he moved away and crossed the bridge.

Hannah hugged her arms across her chest and watched as Travis's tall figure blended into the dark night, the glowing lantern bobbing in the dark along the stream's bank, then winding up the mountain trail.

When the lantern's light dimmed to a small speck, barely visible at a high point among the trees, Hannah went inside her cabin, locked the door, and reminded herself of what had happened the last time she'd bared her body— and heart—to a man.

Dear Margaret,
I helped fix the stable roof today. I wish I could tell you that I did it solely for you, at your request. But I

didn't. I wanted to help Hannah, too . . . and I did. Just not in the way I expected.

Hannah thanked me tonight. She looked at me as though I might be someone who mattered, and it was the first time in my life that I came close to feeling happy. Do I deserve that?

Coming to Paradise Peak felt right at the time, but now it doesn't. Hannah doesn't know who I am any more than you do. Neither does Red. I lied to all of you and you've done nothing but welcome me in. It was one thing to imagine being here and asking for your forgiveness; it's another thing altogether to feel the mountain beneath my feet, to look you in the eye and try to find the words.

How can I tell any of you who I am? What can I possibly say that will explain why I felt I had to lie? What can I say to Red and Hannah when they realize how much I've hurt you? When they know I stole Niki's life from her?

Hannah told me tonight that words are never enough. I believe her. There is nothing I could ever say that would right the wrong I've committed. So what do I do now?

I'm so sorry, Margaret—I have no right to ask anything of you, but I don't have the answers.

How is the value of a man measured? With what instrument? And how does a man prove he is worthy of forgiveness?

CHAPTER 4

Travis waved his hand, motioning for Red to continue backing up his truck beside the stable.

"How much further?" Red, seated behind the wheel of the truck, stuck his head out of the open window and hollered over the rumble of the engine. "'Bout a foot?"

"Two," Travis called back.

A swift wind rushed over the foggy grounds of Paradise Peak Ranch, kicking up dust along the gravel driveway and ruffling Travis's hair onto his forehead. Ruby and Juno, standing in the adjacent pasture, jerked their heads and lifted their noses in the air.

Pushing his hair out of his eyes, Travis glanced at the trailer's coupler, then eyed the hitch on the back of Red's truck as it approached. "One more foot and you're there."

When the truck's hitch eased into position beneath the trailer's coupler, Travis held up a fist, signaling for Red to stop the truck. Red turned off the ignition, and the engine ceased its rumble, but a high-pitched whistle took its place, whizzing sharply by Travis's ears.

Travis looked up, taking in the gray, overcast sky and eyeing the darker clouds that rolled with the wind at a lower altitude. From the looks of things, the weatherman's prediction that rain would arrive this afternoon was correct.

"Hannah said y'all planned to stop by Glory Be on the way to pick the horse up." Red had exited the truck and strolled toward Travis. "Might want to make it a quick trip. Way my bones are aching, this storm that's blowing in is gonna be a humdinger, and you don't want to be hauling a nervous horse back in something like that."

"Glory Be?" Travis asked.

Red laughed, bent and cranked the handle on the trailer to lower it. "Gloria Ulman's store. She carries clothes, tools, and plants—bit of everything. Hannah said you two are gonna stop by there so you can pick up a few things."

Travis nodded. "I could use a tougher pair of jeans and a shirt or two. Thanks again for the boots and the bonus."

"Bonus?" Trailer lowered, Red unhooked a pin on the coupler, then secured the coupler to the ball of the hitch.

Travis crouched at Red's side, grabbed both safety chains, crossed them, then attached them to the hitch. "Hannah told me last night that she'd talk to you about throwing in a small bonus with my pay so I could buy work clothes."

Red plugged the electrical cord into the truck's port and straightened. "I'd have been happy to throw in a bonus, but this is the first I'm hearing of it. Hannah told me earlier this morning that you two were gonna shop around and that you'd be back later than you planned, but she didn't mention anything about a bonus. Matter of fact, when I offered her a little extra cash, she turned me down. Said she had plenty for what you needed."

Frowning, Travis stood and glanced toward the stable entrance. After retiring to his cabin last night, he'd taken a shower, had sat at the small wooden desk in front of the window, and had written until his eyes were as heavy as the guilt pressing on his heart. Then he'd crawled into bed and slept like the dead.

The glow of the rising sun spreading slowly over the mountain, brightening the dark interior of the cabin, had awakened him. He'd dressed quickly and walked down the trail and across the bridge to meet Hannah at the stable.

She'd been hard at work mucking the stables and had asked him to go to the lodge and tell Red she was ready for him to bring the truck around to hook up the trailer. Only the top of her auburn head and the flash of her hand were visible as she'd raked and shoveled behind a stall door. Travis had hovered, wanting to offer his help, but she seemed to have a steady rhythm, and instead, he'd done as she'd asked, trekking up to the lodge, riding back in the truck with Red, and helping hook up the trailer for the trip into town.

Since stopping for new clothes was still on the agenda, Travis had assumed Hannah had already talked to Red about the bonus. But clearly, he'd been mistaken.

Hannah emerged from the stable's entrance. She was dressed as she had been yesterday, in jeans and a long-sleeved shirt with her hair pulled back in a ponytail. The long day spent working on the stable roof had given her fair skin a sun-kissed glow and those blue eyes and soft mouth were as pretty in the morning light as they had been last night in the lantern's glow.

Face warming, Travis ducked his head and studied her beneath his lashes as she approached. Every few steps, she glanced up at the sky, her brow creasing.

"The trailer ready?" she asked when she reached the truck.

"What's this about asking me for a bonus?" Red leaned against the truck, one hand propped on the roof's edge as he smiled at Hannah. "Travis must've done pretty good work if you're keen on upping his pay already."

Travis held up a hand. "Hannah did most of the work. I only—"

"Pulled your weight and then some." Hannah's lips curved as she stopped beside Travis and examined the trailer's hitch. "Safety chains on tight?"

"Of course they are." Red nudged Travis with an elbow. "I tell you what—sun's barely up and she's already questioning our competence." He cupped a hand around his mouth and whispered to Travis, "Don't worry, she might act like a tough case, but she just likes to give me a hard time." He lowered his hand and smiled at Hannah. "Go on, give 'em a yank if you're that worried."

Hannah grinned, squatted beside the hitch, and reached for one of the chains. Her shirtsleeve rose with her movements, baring her right wrist. Purple blotches marred her skin in a bruise that wrapped around her entire wrist.

Travis hissed in a breath. "Hannah—"

"What happened to your wrist?" Red shoved off the truck and squatted by Hannah's side. He reached for her wrist, holding it gingerly, and eased the cuff of her shirt up further.

Hannah tugged it back. "It's nothing."

"That's not nothing," Red bit out. He stood, his face paling and mouth trembling. "Those bruises were made by a hand. You think I don't recognize something like that by now? Bryan step foot on this land? 'Cuz I swear, if that bastard even thinks—"

"No." Hannah shoved herself to her feet. Red blotches broke out on her neck and spread to her face. "I told you it's nothing and I'd rather not have this conversation right now."

"Well, we're damn well having it. You don't show up with something like that on you and expect me not to—"

"It was me." Travis stepped forward. "I did it."

Man, the last thing he wanted was to be the cause of an argument between Red and Hannah, though the confession made Travis feel everything but better. Whether he'd saved Hannah from a broken bone or not, he was the cause of those bruises, and the sight of them sent a wave of nausea through him.

Red looked fit to kill.

"I'm sorry." Travis took another step toward Hannah, but the intense glower on Red's face had his feet moving back again. "I didn't m—"

"I fell off the stable roof yesterday," Hannah said, squeezing Red's arm. "Just like you've been hassling me about for the past year. Travis was watching out for me. He caught me and hauled me back up. He has nothing to apologize for because if it hadn't been for him, I'd have broken a bone or two and you would've had to go to the trouble of walking out here and yelling 'you told me so.'" She sighed, frowning as Red continued to stare at Travis. "That's the whole humiliating story—top to bottom. You satisfied now?"

Red's eyes narrowed first on Travis's hands, then his face. "Is that the story? You watched out for her? Hauled her back up?"

Travis stiffened, his body preparing to receive a blow— possibly several. People weren't all that prone to believe him, whether his word was backed by someone else or not, and he'd never raise a hand to Red, no matter the circumstances. "Yeah." Voice weak, he cleared his throat and tried again. "That's how it happened."

Red's scowl dissolved and his expression lit up with a wide grin. "Well, hell. You not only earned that bonus fair and square, I'm indebted to you."

A split second later, Travis's breath left him in a *whoosh* as Red's burly arms wrapped him tight in a bear hug. Red's big hands slapped Travis's back good-naturedly before he released him, and when Red stepped back, his grin had softened to a half smile that trembled. An expression of relief appeared on his face, and moisture gleamed in the crow's feet beside his eyes.

"That story's a damn sight better than the ones she's told me in the past," Red whispered. "Thank you, son."

Travis nodded, his throat tightening to the point that he couldn't speak. The warm pressure of Red's grateful hug still lingered on his back and arms, and an unfamiliar rush of pride filled his chest. The kind Travis guessed a son felt when praised by his father. The sensation was foreign but strong, and he held it tight within him, wanting to preserve and carry it for as long as he could.

"Ah, now, y'all better get while the gettin's good." Red spun away, kissed Hannah's forehead, and walked back toward the lodge, waving over his shoulder. "Rain's coming soon."

Travis watched Red amble away, catching the way his hand rubbed swiftly at his cheeks.

"I'm fine, Red," Hannah called, smiling softly. "There's no need to get sentimental."

Red threw a big hand in the air. "I ain't. These damn gnats are getting in my eyes, is all."

Hannah's smile widened. "It's the last week of February. There are no gnats."

"Go on and pick up that horse, girl. And be back in time for lunch. Margaret's cooking up a big one."

Hannah laughed. "I love you, Red."

"Yeah, yeah." Not looking back, Red quickened his step, mumbling under his breath.

Travis smiled and thought he heard something along the lines of "stubborn women" and "bane of my existence" but the wind whipping across the field fractured most of Red's words.

"Red's got a good heart." Hannah walked to the driver's side of the truck. "I hope he's held on to enough common sense where Margaret's concerned to not let her break it."

Travis glanced at her over the hood of the truck. "Are Red and Margaret a couple?"

Hannah shook her head, her attention still focused on Red in the distance. "No. But not because Red isn't interested. He's been in love with Margaret for as long as I can remember, but never mustered up the courage to tell her. She married Phillip—a banker—about forty years ago. He passed away last year, and when she inherited his stake in the ranch, she sold her house in Gatlinburg and moved in with us." A weak smile appeared as she looked at him. "If you ever wonder what Phillip looked like, just take a stroll inside the main lodge. She's got a picture of him propped on every solid surface in the foyer."

He frowned and looked down at his new boots, fresh guilt assailing him as he thought of all Margaret had lost. First her daughter, Niki, and years later her husband. Had he contributed to that?

During one of the few group therapy sessions Travis had been allowed to attend during his stay in prison, Adam—a thirty-year-old lifer—had asked if bad deeds had a ripple effect. He'd explained that after he'd killed a man in a bar ten years earlier, Adam's wife had committed suicide. His son had visited him in prison to tell Adam he was moving on and didn't want Adam to be a part of his life. Adam had asked if his crime had done that. Had his act of ending one life broken two more? Was there a way he could stop that ripple? Or transform it into something good instead?

Two inmates in attendance had laughed, one had broken down in sobs, and the rest had continued glaring at the concrete wall with dead eyes as the therapist failed to regain control of the conversation.

The session had ended, and Adam never did receive an answer.

The truck door squeaked as Hannah opened it and slid inside the driver's side of the cab.

Travis followed her lead slowly, slid into the passenger seat, buckled up, and shut the door. Hannah cranked the engine and pulled out slowly, easing Red's old truck and trailer up the winding dirt path, then onto the gravel driveway.

Travis glanced at the main lodge as they passed. Red had made it inside, and Margaret stood on the wide front porch, waving good-bye in their direction. Travis lifted a hand in return, and when the driveway ended, Hannah took a right onto a paved road and began the slow, winding descent down the mountain.

The overcast sky had darkened and the wind blew harder. Tall trees lining the road bent and swayed. Leaves hugged their branches and exposed their pale underbellies with each powerful gust.

Hannah's hands moved easily over the steering wheel as she guided the truck around each sharp curve. She'd cracked the window a bit, letting in crisp air tinged with smoke, and a strand of her auburn hair tumbled from her ponytail and danced along the graceful curve of her bare neck.

Travis's hand moved, his finger poised to curl around the silky strand, lift it to his nose, and breathe in Hannah's sweet scent. He yearned to touch her, to revel in her forthright honesty and remind himself that good still existed in this world.

Instead, he pressed his palms flat against his thighs and looked at the steering wheel, glimpsing the purple bruise on her wrist, visible above the cuff of her sleeve as it slid further down her arm when she steered. She hadn't made a sound when he'd caught her as she'd fallen from the roof, and there had been a shadow of resignation in her eyes as though fear and pain had become routine.

Jaw clenching, Travis recalled Red's protective stance and angry comment earlier. Red had made it obvious that someone had hurt Hannah. He'd even named him.

"Who's Bryan?"

Hannah's hands tightened around the steering wheel.

Travis glanced at her and added quietly, "I don't mean to pry. You don't have t—"

"He's my ex-husband."

She didn't offer more. She stared ahead as the paved road unfurled in front of them, looping around the steep mountain.

Travis rubbed his palms over his jeans, knowing it was none of his business and that he shouldn't ask, but the thought of someone deliberately hurting Hannah . . .

"Red said the story behind this bruise was better than the ones you've told him in the past." Travis studied Hannah's delicate profile, watched fiery color bloom in her cheeks and spread down her neck. "What did he mean by that?"

Hannah navigated a sharp turn, then accelerated as they reached a steep incline. "Bryan liked to put his hands on me"—she flashed a tight smile at Travis—"and not in a husbandly way." She shifted gears and the engine rumbled. "No," she said, her voice softening, "that's not true. Bryan never liked hurting me—at least, when he was healthy and sober. When he was high or short on pills, he either didn't know or didn't care."

Travis turned away. The truck had climbed again, and they'd reached a clearing. The tree line receded, the smell of smoke grew heavier, and the dark clouds loomed so low, they enveloped the road ahead, looking as though they'd swallow the truck whole.

He thought of the first time he'd had a drink: whiskey

gulped straight from the bottle as he'd sat on a rocky bank, overlooking the river. He'd been thirteen at the time; his older brother Kyle, sixteen, had smiled as he'd coughed from the burn, told him he could have that bottle (Kyle had his own), and they'd stayed there for hours, drinking, talking, laughing.

The stars had been bright that night, he and Kyle had forgotten all about the empty trailer they'd left behind and the mother who rarely remembered they existed (much less knew when they were gone), and Travis had soaked up the blissful numbness that let him float above it all, have fun with his brother, and not worry about going home. He'd emptied that bottle over the course of a week, then another, and the bigger he grew, the more he drank, until he couldn't remember what life had been like without it.

Travis flinched, shame searing his skin. "Bryan was an addict?"

"Yes." Her tone thickened. "Painkillers. He played football in high school and went pro when he turned twenty-one. Three years into his career he took a bad hit and injured his back and knee." A rueful laugh escaped her. "I guess that's the irony of it all. He didn't get drugs on the street; a doctor wrote a prescription in his office, a pharmacist filled it in a drugstore a block from our house, and Bryan took them with a glass of water in front of me every night at dinner. It was all very professional and routine. Until it became something more."

Travis nodded stiffly. "How long did you stay with him?"

"We married at twenty, had five good years, then five bad ones. I left him five years ago." She slowed the truck as they passed a familiar wooden sign etched with PARADISE PEAK, then took a right onto a wider road. "I tried to stay, but I wasn't a priority for him anymore. And he wasn't the man I married."

"He wasn't a man at all to put his hands on you." Travis

clenched his fists, hating the person Hannah described, and hating the person he used to be. "Couldn't have been if he had no regard for your needs or your life."

The traffic light ahead turned red and Hannah stopped the truck. She faced him then, her eyes peering into his, examining his expression. "He used to be. Bryan was more than a good man; he was one of the best. That's why it was so difficult for me to accept that he'd changed. That he'd never be the same. He had a disease that was stronger than him. After I left, I could see that clearly. I understood."

Several questions hovered on Travis's tongue, but he asked only one. "Did you forgive him?"

Her mouth parted and she looked down, her brow creasing. "I tried," she whispered. "I'm still trying."

A horn honked, startling them both. Hannah glanced at the traffic light—now green—and pressed the pedal, moving the truck and trailer forward.

Travis watched as she turned on the blinker and moved into the left lane. He eyed the way her fingers trembled against the steering wheel, and he wanted to entwine her hands with his own, apologize for the pain she'd endured, and reassure her that she wasn't wrong in being unable to forgive. That forgiveness was a mercy a man like Bryan—or he, himself—might not deserve.

Only the earnestness in Hannah's quiet words, the patient kindness of Red and Margaret, and the sheer beauty of the land that surrounded Travis made him wonder if Paradise Peak might be a place where a man could be forgiven. A place where a man could be embraced for who he was now rather than who he used to be.

"You strong, silent types are good at coaxing confessions out of people," Hannah said, turning into a small parking lot. "Red does it to me all the time." She smiled as she parked the truck and trailer, taking up two parking spaces. "May I ask you a question in return?"

Travis nodded, aching for a chance to forget his past and show Hannah the man he was now. "Anything you want."

"Why do you no longer drive?"

Hannah frowned as Travis's face turned pale. His jaw hardened and his fingers curled tighter around his knees.

Clearly, her question was an uncomfortable one for him and she almost told him he didn't have to answer. But she stopped, pulled the keys from the ignition, held them in her lap, and waited patiently instead.

Heck, she'd opened up a mile wide for him—her cheeks still burned at the thought of the intimate details she'd shared—so it was only fair that Travis reciprocate at least a tad.

For the record, her curiosity had absolutely nothing to do with how protected she felt, having his warm, steady bulk at her side. And it was in no way a result of her wanting to hear the low, steady throb of his voice again and savor the pleasurable thrills his words stirred in her belly— especially when he spoke in her defense.

She glanced at Travis again, watched the slow rise and fall of his wide chest, and acknowledged that maybe this attraction he awakened inside her—one she hadn't felt in years—was why she remained in the truck, waiting for his response, rather than politely ending the conversation along with the tense atmosphere that had descended between them.

He was such a contradiction—this tall, brawny man who possessed such a gentle voice and looked at her with something akin to adoration in the dark depths of his eyes. To be honest, she did want to hear his voice again. Over and over. She wanted his eyes on her, and she wanted to prolong the calming comfort his quiet strength provided.

"I used to drive, but years ago, there was a wreck," Travis said. "I . . ."

He fell silent, and Hannah prompted, "Was it bad?"

He nodded. A strand of black hair slipped over his brow, brushing his thick eyelashes, and an expression of pain crossed his face.

She smothered the urge to smooth her hand over his forehead and cup his stubble-lined jaw. "Were you alone when it happened, or was someone in the car with you?"

"No one was with me." He turned away and looked out the passenger window.

"Were you hurt?"

He nodded.

Hannah studied the way his black hair tapered at the base of his nape, the wavy strands curling around the strong muscles of his tanned neck. "So you chose not to drive anymore?"

A tendon flexed in his neck. "Yes."

She waited for more details, and when they weren't forthcoming, she said, "I understand. Margaret doesn't like to drive much either. She does drive when she needs to, but she says being on the road brings back bad memories." She licked her lips, guilt pricking at her conscience for her recent lack of patience and compassion for Margaret. "Her daughter, Niki, was killed by a drunk driver—some kid who passed out when he hit Niki head-on. He probably didn't feel or remember a thing. The way Margaret described him, he sounded a lot like Bryan. Neil Alden was his name, I think. They put him away, thank God." She stared out the windshield at the heavy smoke and fog hovering above the shopping strip and parking lot. "Margaret said she and Phillip got the call at two in the morning and drove four hours to Nashville to identify Niki. Margaret said she went in alone. Phillip couldn't bring himself to do it."

Travis remained silent.

"Lord, what a downer I am today," Hannah said. "Like you wanted to hear all these sob stories. Bet you'll think twice before you ask a woman questions again, huh?"

An odd sting of jealousy hit her at the thought of Travis by another woman's side, speaking in that low, gentle tone of his, supporting and defending. It was an unexpected emotion that surprised her and left her shaken. When had she dropped her guard? What was it about this big bear of a man that called to her softer, more vulnerable side?

Sighing, she opened her door, and a familiar, acrid stench rushed in. "It's this smoke. Red said it was getting to me, and I'm beginning to believe him." She summoned a smile and scooted to the edge of her seat. "Come on, let's hit up Gloria Ulman for some work clothes, then pick up the horse so we can get back before the rain comes."

Travis's big hand settled on her forearm, stilling her. "I appreciate the offer, Hannah. I do. But you don't have to give me a bonus for clothes."

Hannah stared at his tanned hand as it rested on her arm. The warmth of his palm seeped through her thin sleeve and imprinted itself on her skin. "Yes, I do."

"You don't owe me anything," he insisted. "Neither does Red or Margaret."

"It's not about owing; it's about helping. You helped me, so I'm helping you. That's how it works." She narrowed her eyes, the intense pain and vulnerability in his expression surprising her. "Hasn't anyone helped you before?"

He shook his head. "Red was the first. Then Margaret."

Hannah thought of how warmly Margaret had welcomed Travis the day he'd arrived. How Margaret hadn't hesitated to smile, approach and touch him without a speck of fear, whereas she had been openly defensive and critical.

Bryan had done that; she'd learned fear and distrust from him that she still couldn't shake, even though she'd left him years ago. Yet despite her awful reception of him, Travis hadn't hesitated to help her.

Hesitating, Hannah placed her hand over his and squeezed. Her palm was too small to completely cover his and the firm strength of his big hand lying docile beneath hers sent a wave of warmth through her. "Well, it's my turn to help today—not because I owe you or have to, but because I want to. Will you let me?"

Travis covered her hand with his free one. His thumb smoothed gently over her knuckles. Then he lifted his head and smiled—a small smile tinged with sadness but full of gratitude, revealing a sexy dimple at the left side of his mouth. "Yes."

One little word. That's all he said. But that lone syllable rolling off his tongue melted her on the inside, and every inch of her skin clamored for his palm to move, to slip beneath the cuff of her sleeve and glide up her bare arm. To make her feel the incredible sensations he stirred within her on the outside as well.

Whoa, girl, Hannah chided herself. *Get the clothes, get the horse, and leave the man alone.* All this deep talk and close proximity was making her long for risky things she had no room for in her life.

Hannah removed her hand from his, slid away from his touch, and exited the truck. Immediately, a thick swath of heavy air laced with smoke settled around her. She looked up, straining for a clear view of the burning mountain peak in the distance, but the smoke plume had widened into two parallel columns that obscured the top of the mountain and mingled with masses of gray and black clouds.

"It's spreading."

Travis's deep voice rumbled softly at Hannah's back and she could feel the heat of his muscular frame. She stopped herself from leaning back against the warm support of his chest, shoved her hands in her pockets, and focused on the storm clouds. "Looks that way. But it's a ways off, and the rain should be here soon."

Hannah, heeding Red's advice, put aside her worries and walked toward Gloria's store. Travis followed, his long legs easily catching up with her and matching her pace.

"I'll give you fair warning," Hannah said, motioning toward the bright pink and yellow facade of the little store. The small shopping strip housed three other stores with sedate brown and green trim, and Gloria's shop looked as out of place as a clown behind a preacher's pulpit. "Gloria is the nicest person you'll ever meet, but she's also the nosiest. The best way of handling her is to follow wherever she leads, nod while she rambles, and answer her questions with only one word."

Although, if Travis had the same effect on Gloria that he had on her, one word would be enough to goad her into asking a million more questions just to hear his sexy rumble.

"Okay."

Case in point, Hannah thought as her belly fluttered. One word from this man was enough to turn a woman's head.

She stopped with her hand on the door of Glory Be's entrance and looked up at him. "Just . . . try not to encourage her, okay?"

He frowned but nodded.

Hannah opened the door and they entered, the bell over the door chiming their arrival.

Gloria Ulman, sitting behind a wide desk in front of the entrance, called out, "Welcome to Glor—" Her mouth dropped open and her white eyebrows shot up as she caught sight of them. "Well, Glory be! Look who it is."

She sprang out of her chair and hustled around the counter, her white bun bouncing on top of her head with each of her cheery steps. "Hannah Newsome, I haven't laid eyes on you in forever. Get over here in this old woman's arms."

In the next instant, Hannah was wrapped up in a perfume-laden hug so tight she could barely catch her breath. Wincing, she glanced at Travis, who silently watched the breath being squished out of her, his lips twitching.

"Just last week, I saw Red and told him he'd better tell you to get in here and say hi to me. Vernon," she shouted, her voice ringing in Hannah's ears. "Vernon, you'll never guess who's here! Come say hello!" Gloria squeezed her once more for good measure, then released her and stepped back, frowning over her shoulder. "Oh, gracious. I must not have shouted loud enough. My Vernon's got to where he can't hear much of anything anymore."

Imagine that. Hannah rubbed her ears—still ringing from Gloria's shouts—and her pity for Gloria's husband, Vernon, increased a tad.

Gloria's eyes lit up as they focused on Travis. "And who do we have here?" She cocked her head to the side, excitement shining in her expression as she glanced at Hannah. "A new beau?"

"Oh, no." Hannah shook her head. Good grief, the last thing she needed was for her and Travis's names to be circulated as Paradise Peak gossip. "No. This is Travis Miller—one of Red's new hires—and Travis and I are working

together. We're coworkers and . . ." She smiled apologetically at Travis, searching for the right word as his bright
expression dimmed. "Friends. You could say we're friends."

Of some sort, she guessed. He'd saved her neck yesterday and, Lord knows, she'd shared enough secrets on the
drive into town that she supposed they qualified as something more than strangers.

At her answer, warmth reentered Travis's expression,
but Gloria jostled his slow smile out of him when she
threw her arms around his big frame, too.

"Any friend of Hannah's is a friend of mine," Gloria
said, hugging Travis hard.

Gloria was so short, the top of her gray head only reached
the center of Travis's chest and he hugged her back awkwardly, his cheeks blushing a fiery red as he patted her
back gently and met Hannah's eyes.

Hannah laughed, and when Gloria released him, said,
"Travis plans to stay awhile and help renovate the ranch,
so he needs some work clothes." She glanced around the
interior of the store, eyeing the shelves of jeans lining the
walls and the racks of shirts and jackets. "I'm thinking at
least three pairs of durable jeans, a few long-sleeved shirts,
and maybe a couple T-shirts for layering when it warms up
next month."

Gloria looked Travis over and clapped her hands. "You
came to the right place, my dear. I have plenty of big and
tall apparel for a strapping man like you." She grabbed
Travis's hand and tugged. "Come with me, Travis. I'll set
you right up."

Hannah watched Gloria lead Travis through a maze of
clothing racks toward the shelves of jeans and stifled another laugh. By the time Gloria finished with Travis, the
poor man would be ready to hightail it out of the Smokies
altogether.

CHAPTER 5

"Hope my wife didn't run you off," Vernon Ulman said, patting Travis on the back as he opened the passenger door of Red's truck. "Gloria can talk the hind leg off a donkey. I swear her endless gabbing is what caused me to have to get a hearing aid."

Travis ducked his head to hide his smile. "No. Gloria was very informative."

About everything. His grin widened.

After spending one hour in Glory Be, Travis now knew that Gloria had eight grandchildren, two sons, and one daughter (the latter was currently out of favor for not visiting often enough), and an unhealthy—but amusing—obsession with lantana plants. She'd insisted Travis take the first pair of jeans he'd tried on for a test drive by walking with her through a small greenhouse attached to the back of her store. There, Gloria had formally introduced him to thirty lantana plants—each of which she'd named—and had shoved one potted, yellow lantana into his politely protesting hands, advising him to keep it indoors until the spring planting season arrived.

"This one here's named Joyful Judy. Plant her in full sun after the last frost, and she'll lift your spirits every time she blooms," Gloria had said with a smile. "Consider it a welcome gift to Paradise Peak."

Travis had never felt more welcomed in his life.

"I enjoyed Gloria's company," Travis said, smiling at Vernon and meaning every word.

He could still feel Gloria's wrinkled hands patting his cheeks and see the crow's feet beside her eyes gathering up as she smiled at him. He'd never had a grandmother, and all the time he'd wished for one as a boy, his imaginings had involved someone a lot like Gloria.

"She loaded me down with everything I needed, and then some." Travis lifted the potted lantana he held in one hand, then set it on the floorboard of Red's truck beside two bags of new clothes.

"I was worried she'd hold you up too long," Vernon continued. "Hannah said y'all were on your way to pick up a new horse before the storm hit." He frowned at the gray sky and a strong wind ruffled his white hair over his forehead. "Looks like that could be any minute now." His blue eyes strayed above Travis's shoulder toward the thick blanket of smoke the wind had blown into town. "Not that I wish ill on your trip or anything, but I kinda wish the rain would hurry up."

Yeah, and so did Hannah. Travis glanced at Hannah, who, poised with one leg in the truck and the other outside it, returned Gloria's good-bye hug. She smiled at the older woman and promised to visit again soon, but her eyes, increasingly shadowed, kept returning to the distant wildfire.

Hannah hadn't said much while Gloria had led him around the store. She'd remained by the large windows next to the entrance and stared at the mountain range across the road. Several times, he'd noticed her glancing at her watch and her attention would shift to the dry pavement of the parking lot outside, then the dark clouds hovering overhead, her mouth tightening.

He knew she was worried; he was worried, too. This was only his third day in Paradise Peak and already the fire seemed to have tripled in size. The thin plume of smoke had billowed with each gust of wind, spanning a much wider range than it had when he'd first arrived.

He hadn't had any experience with wildfires—the closest he'd ever been to one had been viewing the resulting devastation on TV in the prison commons—but he knew they were unpredictable at best.

"I hate to rush off, Gloria," Hannah said. "But we really need to get going."

"I know," Gloria said. "Business has been pretty slow today and the weather's turning ugly, so we're gonna close up shop in about an hour, check a few of our rental cabins, and head home to hunker down." She stepped back as Hannah slid into the driver's seat, waited as she closed the door, then leaned in through the open window. "You be careful running these roads with that trailer, and stay safe in the storm."

"Will do." Hannah cranked the engine as Travis slid into the passenger seat, then smiled at Vernon. "If you need anything, let us know."

"Aw, we've seen our fair share of storms and fires." Vernon held his hand out to Travis, who shook it. "Good meeting you, Travis. Safe travels."

Travis shut his door and Hannah pulled off, easing onto Paradise Peak's main street. He looked out the passenger window and eyed the mailboxes, long gravel driveways, and houses as they passed, but the quiet rustle of movement at his side and the prickle up the back of his neck alerted him each time Hannah studied his profile.

Traffic was light but picked up as they drove further

through downtown. There were two more shopping centers, bigger than the one Gloria's shop had been in, one large bank, and an even larger, white-steepled church.

"The farther into town you go, the bigger the banks and churches."

Travis pulled his attention away from the wrought iron cross that crowned the towering steeple and glanced at Hannah.

Eyes on the road, she smiled, then added, "God and money take center stage in Paradise Peak—and not necessarily in that order. Least, that's what my friend Liz Tennyson said after moving here. You'll meet her at the stables. She runs an equine therapy program with Carl."

Travis recalled Red mentioning a man named Carl when he'd spoken about the possibility of a new horse. A Carl Lennox, owner of Misty Ridge Stables. "Is Carl's spread as big as Red's ranch?"

Hannah shook her head. "Not acre-wise, but his stables are top-of-the-line and make our rinky-dink barn look like a shack. He's not lacking for business." She shrugged. "Every now and then, though, he has more animals than he can handle, and he gives us a call. He knows we're struggling, and he does us favors on occasion. He's been a good friend to Red. To all of us, really."

Travis smiled at that, recalling how sweet the word "friend" had sounded from Hannah's lips as she'd introduced him in Gloria's shop. He'd never had a real friend— only acquaintances who liked to get high and party as much as he did. Even his brother, Kyle, hadn't stuck around after Travis had been incarcerated. Drugs and women, it turned out, were more important to Kyle than family.

Travis's smile fell. He couldn't blame Kyle for that. Travis himself had never been much of a brother and he'd learned well from Kyle's example. Drugs and alcohol had always taken center stage in Travis's life. The only thing he'd ever fully shared with the women he'd known had been his body—never his thoughts, dreams, or hopes.

Never his heart . . . or the truth. Those things had begun to swell within him the moment he'd set foot on this mountain, and after meeting Hannah, he'd been moved on the inside by her beauty and steadfast presence. He wanted to ask her to share her secrets, voice his own, and see if she could find something more inside his soul than a liar, murderer, and coward.

He'd had his first shot at being honest with Hannah an hour ago, sitting in this truck, in the same spot, when she'd asked, "Why do you no longer drive?"

And he'd blown it.

But after learning about Bryan, he'd been too afraid. How could a good, honest woman like Hannah take a chance on him after suffering so much pain at the hands of her ex-husband—a selfish addict like the one Travis had been?

With every lie, he dug a deeper hole for himself. He doubted he'd ever climb out of it, much less have a shot at redeeming himself with Margaret, Red, and Hannah.

". . . feeling?"

Travis shook his head, his face heating as he noticed Hannah's eyes on him again. "I'm sorry, what?"

She maneuvered a sharp curve and the road widened—they'd left the center of town and were on the outskirts of Paradise Peak now. Then she glanced at him again. "I said, how are the new duds feeling?"

He glanced down at the long-sleeved Henley shirt, new jeans, and dark belt he'd chosen at Gloria's store. They were the cheapest items Gloria carried but more stylish than he'd expected, and paired with the boots Red had loaned him and the shower and close shave he'd had first thing this morning, Travis had to admit he looked like a new man, even if he didn't feel like one.

"They're comfortable," he said, tugging the soft sleeves up his forearms. The shirt was fitted and warm despite the thin material. "Thank you."

"You're welcome." She glanced at him and flashed a smile before facing the road. "Did Gloria embarrass you? She was hauling you around the store like you were her long-lost son."

He laughed, but the sound was rusty and felt foreign to his chest. "Maybe, but I enjoyed her company. She was very kind."

"I'm sure she was." Hannah laughed, too—the sound feminine, fun and light. Man, even her laugh was gorgeous. "Gloria has always been a sucker for handsome men, and even before you spiffed up, you looked gor—"

Her cheeks reddened and she clamped her mouth shut. She straightened in her seat and her fingers tightened around the steering wheel.

Travis smiled.

"I mean, you . . ." Hannah cleared her throat. "What I meant was, you're easy to look at." She glanced at him, then away and back again as if she couldn't help it, her blush deepening. "I don't mean to stare. Or be rude. I'm sorry."

"Don't be." Chest warming, Travis studied the bloom of color in her cheeks, the soft curves of her pink lips, and the tendril of red hair tucked behind the shell of her small ear. "I appreciate the compliment, and I feel the same about you." He eased back in his seat and softened his voice, hoping not to come on too strong but wanting her to know. "As for being rude"—he shook his head—"anything you do is fine by me, Hannah."

Her lips curved and she ducked her head briefly as if

embarrassed; then she smiled. "So, if I volunteered you to take my place for dinner dishwashing duty the rest of this week, that'd be okay?"

He laughed again—this time, more easily. It felt freeing. "Yeah."

Her smile widened. "And swan napkins? You'd be up for folding those, too?"

"Swan napkins?"

Still smiling, she rolled her eyes. "Margaret. She wants formal dinners to become routine and swan napkins are her go-to for elegant dining. I cringe every time she asks me to help her make them."

Travis nodded as his smile faded. "Can't say I'd be any good at it, but anything you or Margaret asked me to do, I'd do it."

"Just like that?" she asked, one auburn eyebrow raised.

"Like that," he returned quietly. "Every time."

She studied his expression, the teasing light in her blue eyes fading, then refocused on the road. "Guess we'll need to be careful of what we ask, then."

He didn't respond because it didn't matter what Margaret asked of him—he'd do it anyway. He'd decided that before he'd undertaken the long hike up here. What he hadn't been able to foresee or consider was Hannah. He was equally thrilled and dismayed by this attraction he had for every part of her—her tempting figure, strong mind, and honest disposition—and his eagerness to please her.

But it distracted him. Took him off course on his progress with Margaret. And it made him vulnerable, a feeling he'd always detested in the past, but somehow no longer minded when it came to Hannah, her wishes, or this strange urge to protect her.

Hannah remained silent for the rest of the drive, and so did he. The low rumble of the engine and whip of wind against the truck windows filled the cab for the next five miles and, when a gated entrance to a paved driveway appeared, Hannah took a left and eased the truck up to the decorative gate.

She pulled to a stop beside an intercom, lowered the window, and pressed a button.

Moments later, a male voice, brisk and impatient, crackled through the speaker. "Misty Ridge Stables. Name and nature of business, please."

"Carl, it's H—"

"Hannah Newsome." The tone lightened, a slow, pleased drawl taking over. "Come all the way to the other side of the mountain to pick up a mare, I presume?"

Travis glanced at Hannah, who grinned as she listened.

"That's the gist of it," she said into the speaker. "Unless you'd like to rescind your invitation? Sounds like I caught you at a bad time."

"Ain't no such thing when it comes to you." A buzz sounded and the ornate gates swept open. "Come on in, darlin'."

Hannah shifted gears and drove through the opened gates, then down a long, winding driveway flanked by cedar trees. When they reached the end of the driveway, she parked in front of a three-story house positioned in the forefront of sprawling fields. Dark clouds still loomed overhead, seeming to hover inches from the roof of the house, but the haze of smoke that had begun to slowly enter downtown was no longer visible, and the scent of smoke was noticeably lighter.

A man—blond, built, and much younger than the gray-haired good friend of Red whom Travis had envisioned—strode out of one of three massive stables nearby and walked toward the truck.

"Is that Carl?" Travis asked.

"Yep." Hannah opened her door and hopped out, saying before she shut her door, "Come on, I'll introduce you."

Travis eyed Carl through the windshield, noting the other man's confident stride and the slow grin that spread across his face as Hannah met him halfway. Carl held out his hand and Hannah shook it, then Carl leaned closer and smiled as he spoke, causing Hannah to laugh and toss her head, her silky ponytail rippling across her back.

Travis bit his lip and looked away, trying to ignore the jealousy that sparked in his gut. Then, stifling a groan, he climbed out of the truck and walked toward Hannah. He studied Carl as he approached.

The guy looked about forty years old, tall, clean-cut, and, judging from his opulent surroundings, well-off. What was it Hannah had said took center stage in Paradise Peak? Oh, yeah. God and money. It was obvious Carl possessed the latter, whereas he . . .

Travis dragged a hand through his shaggy hair. Well, he'd never had either.

Hannah looked over her shoulder and smiled. "Travis." The welcoming look in her eyes dampened the envious burn that had begun to grow inside him. "I'd like you to meet Carl Lennox, owner of Misty Ridge Stables and good friend of the family."

Travis stopped beside Hannah and held out his hand. He offered a tight smile as Carl reluctantly released Hannah's hand and shook Travis's instead.

"Travis joined the ranks at Paradise Peak Ranch this week," Hannah said. "He's our new hand."

Carl nodded, his green eyes surveying Travis from head to toe, weighing and measuring. "New hand, huh?" His head tilted. "Travis . . . ?"

"Miller," Travis answered. The lie stuck in his throat, but he forced his way through it, feeling more ashamed than ever but unable to voice his real name. The one Hannah had said in the truck, her tone full of contempt. "My name's Travis Miller."

Carl's eyes narrowed on him. "Haven't seen you around Paradise. You're not local, are you?"

"No." Travis grasped at one of the few truths he felt safe in sharing freely. "I'm originally from Rockton Park."

"Rockton Park?" Carl asked. "Never heard of it."

"It's in western Tennessee."

"Travis was passing through town and Red and Margaret offered him a job," Hannah said. "He's been an excellent help so far and he's the reason we made it today. We redid the stable roof yesterday, which means our new horse will have a safe, dry stall to settle in to."

Carl frowned. "Now, I told you and Red both that I'd have been happy to help y'all out with that."

"I know," Hannah said. "And I appreciated the offer, but after Red hired Travis, we managed to get by."

Carl released Travis's hand and half turned away, saying in a low voice Travis had to strain to hear, "You don't have to rely on just getting by. I told you, if you're short on help or cash, I'd be happy to help you out. All you gotta do is ask."

Hannah bristled. "Well, I'm not asking, and neither is Red." Blushing, she glanced at Travis apologetically, then whispered, "Not everything can be solved with money, Carl."

"I'm aware of that, but Red didn't have to go and hire—"

"Well, Red did, and here Travis is." Hannah stepped back from Carl and smiled. "You know as well as I do how hardheaded Red is when he decides on something, and I have to admit"—she glanced at Travis, her eyes warming—"I'm really glad Red stayed stubborn this time.

Like I said, Travis has been a huge help already." She clapped her hands together and rubbed them briskly. "So is this a good time for you to show us the horse? We're anxious to meet her and get back to the ranch before the storm hits."

Without waiting for an answer, Hannah headed for the closest stable, her curvy, jean-clad legs moving quickly and her red ponytail swishing.

Carl blew out a frustrated breath, then chuckled. "And she thinks Red's stubborn?" He faced Travis. "I hope you didn't take offense at what I said. Red sometimes makes a habit of leaping before he looks, you know? And I imagine you've seen for yourself what state that ranch is in. They don't exactly have a lot of money to spare."

Travis nodded. Carl's apparent attraction to Hannah didn't sit well with him, but the sincerity in Carl's voice when he spoke of Red did. "I understand and have every intention of earning my keep."

"I'll take you at your word." Smiling, Carl headed toward the stable Hannah had entered and gestured for Travis to follow. "Lemme show you ar—"

"Giant!"

Travis halted midstep, almost stumbling over the three-foot-tall, brown-haired boy who darted in front of him. Head tilted back, the little boy stood at his feet and stared up at him, openmouthed, a look of wonder in his big, brown eyes. A yellow Labrador pup ran up, nudged the boy's legs, then took to sniffing Travis's boots.

Carl laughed. "That's Zeke and his dog pal, Blondie. Zeke helps in the stables from time to time. Go on, Zeke, tell the man hello."

Zeke's wide gaze roved over Travis's legs, hands, chest, and face. " 'lo, Giant."

Travis moved away, carefully sidestepping the pup, and rubbed the back of his neck. "Hello."

"Travis is here to pick up the new horse." Carl smiled at Zeke, who continued to stare. "You know, the overo you like?" He looked at Travis and shrugged. "Just step around him and he'll follow. The mare's right through here. I'll turn her out into the paddock, give you a chance to get acquainted, then y'all can . . ."

Travis watched Carl's back as he walked further away toward the stable. He glanced down at Zeke, who still stood in his way, studying him. The kid was cute but tiny, and Travis didn't know a thing about toddlers. Something about Zeke's direct stare made Travis's hands clammy.

"You've got a good-looking pup," Travis said, smiling down at the Lab snuffling around his boots.

He leaned down, let the dog get a few sniffs of his hand, and patted it on the head. Blondie yipped, then resumed sniffing his boots, pants leg, and the dirt.

Straightening, Travis shifted from one foot to the other, then cleared his throat. "Excuse me." He stepped carefully around the boy and the pup. "I need to—"

Zeke shot right back in front of him, short legs planted, and big eyes fixed firmly on Travis's face.

"I'm sorry, but I gotta go," Travis said. "I need to help Hannah load up the horse."

No response. The kid kept staring, and the dog stuck her nose right back on his boot.

Travis spread his hands. "Look, I've got to go now."

Zeke didn't budge, and neither did the dog.

Travis glanced at the stable and noticed Hannah and a brunette walk out of the entrance and lean on the fence by a paddock adjacent to the stable, casting glances his way. Nice. Hannah was waiting for his help and here he was, trying to figure out how to reason with a pup and . . . what—a four-year-old?

"How old are you?" Travis asked.

Zeke held up his fingers and smiled.

Travis smiled back. "Three." Okay. He'd guessed pretty close. "That's good. Now I hate to run, but—"

"Walk me." Zeke darted to Travis's side and looked up at him expectantly. The dog followed him, tail wagging.

Travis frowned. "What?"

Zeke stuck out his small hand. "You walk me."

"Oh." Travis looked at the stable. Carl had already made it inside. "All right."

Travis rubbed his left hand over his jeans, then held it out awkwardly, waiting until Zeke clutched it. Gently, Travis closed his hand around the boy's and nodded.

"Off we go," Travis said, taking the first step forward.

His stride was much longer than Zeke's and Blondie's, so he took slow, measured steps and waited after each one as the boy and pup caught up. After a few steps, they achieved a comfortable pace and Travis smiled down at Zeke, who talked to Blondie as they walked.

When they drew close to the stable, a black and white horse darted out from behind the back corner and galloped into the paddock adjacent to the stable. Powerful muscles flexed along the mare's frame as she moved, her black mane rippling behind her.

Zeke squealed and pointed with his free hand. "Oreo!"

"Overo," a male voice corrected.

Travis tore his attention away from the energetic horse and focused on the man exiting the stable and striding toward him. He'd expected Carl. Instead, a man wearing a dark uniform, gold badge, and duty belt packed with a firearm approached.

Travis's blood ran cold.

"See you found my boy," the man said. "Or rather, he found you. Carl said he lost you somewhere along the way." He drew closer, glanced at Zeke's grip on Travis's hand, then said, "I'm Ben Tennyson. You're Travis Miller?"

*   *   *

"Is that him?"

Hannah leaned against the paddock fence beside her friend Liz and watched as Travis, standing several feet away, spoke to Ben. She could see the sensual curves of Travis's mouth move, but she was too far away to hear his voice. "Yeah. That's our new hand."

Liz Tennyson, Ben's wife, craned her neck for a better look at Travis, propped her hands on her hips, and grinned. "Well, isn't he something?"

Hannah narrowed her eyes and smiled. "You better watch that. It's not exactly proper to ogle strange men in front of your husband, is it?"

Liz laughed and held up her hands. "The only man I ogle is my husband. I'm just looking this guy over for a moment or two and have absolutely no intention of touching." She cocked her head to the side. "But you, however—"

"Oh, no." Hannah shook her head. "Nope. We're not going there."

Liz elbowed her good-naturedly. "Why not? You're single and if he is, too . . ." She surveyed Travis again, her lips pursing as he shook Ben's hand. "Besides, Travis doesn't look strange. He looks polite and possibly charming."

"He's definitely polite." Hannah looked at Travis again, a pleasant flutter stirring within her belly as she noticed the way his big hand engulfed Zeke's loosely, then said, "I guess you could say he's charming."

"Like I said, you're single and if he's si—"

"Okay, let's not pull a Margaret." Hannah wrapped her hands tight around the fence and watched Carl approach the mare on the other side of the paddock. The horse bolted for the other end of the fenced-in space. "I don't need a matchmaker and I'm not looking for a man right now."

"I know," Liz said, grinning. "But he's caught your eye,

hasn't he? I know your face, Hannah, and I haven't seen that spark in your eyes in a long time."

Hannah moved to deny it, but faced with the knowing look in Liz's eyes, she remained silent.

Liz knew her too well. Originally from Michigan, Liz had traveled the rodeo circuit for years as an on-site equine vet. Fifteen years ago, Ben, Hannah's friend from high school, had accompanied Hannah and Bryan to a rodeo in Nashville, where they met Liz. Over the following two weeks, Hannah had shared a lot of laughs with Liz and had found a friend. Ben had shared a lot of long, sweet looks and conversation with Liz and had fallen in love. Ben and Liz had married less than a year after they'd met, and Liz had relocated to Paradise Peak.

Hannah had been happy for her—still was—but Liz's marriage was the exact opposite of what Hannah's had been, and though Liz and Ben had helped see her through the worst with Bryan, they'd never fully know what a hell it'd been. Or how many scars Bryan had left her with—on the inside as well as on the outside.

Taking a chance on a man—on anyone, really—was a dangerous gamble. A risk Hannah wasn't sure she'd be able to muster up the courage to take again.

"I hardly know the guy," Hannah whispered.

"So you get to know him."

"His flaws, too, I suppose?"

"Hannah—"

"Not every man is a hero willing to put his life on the line like Ben." Hannah shoved her hands in her jeans pockets and glanced back at Ben and Travis. "I'm happy for you and Ben—I am. But not everyone has the happy-ever-after the two of you do—you have no idea how rare what you have is. Trust me, I know."

"Cop or not, Ben will always be a hero to me," Liz said softly. "But he's still a man underneath that uniform and we have our bad patches like every other couple. All I'm saying is, every man and relationship is different; they're not all like Bryan and what you went through." She sighed. "What's the alternative? Being like Red and never taking a chance?"

Hannah looked at her in surprise.

Liz's brows raised. "Don't look so shocked. Everyone knows Red has been sweet on Margaret for years, and that he hasn't had the courage to tell her." She shook her head. "All I'm saying is, it's okay to take a chance when you think you're ready."

"I know." Hannah grew still as Liz gently squeezed her upper arm.

"Zeke seems to like Travis," Liz said, smiling at her son. "You know what my grandmother used to say about kids?"

Hannah shook her head.

"She said all it takes is one good, long look and they can see straight through to a person's soul."

Hannah laughed, glancing at the brown-haired toddler. "The first time I babysat Zeke, he took one look at me and kicked me in the shin. What's that say about my soul?"

Liz laughed with her. "He'd just turned terrible two, I'd refused to give him a third chocolate chip cookie, and Ben and I were leaving him at home without us for the first time. He would've kicked anyone in the shin to get out the front door and chase us down the driveway."

"I suppose." At the sound of gravel crunching underfoot, Hannah straightened off the fence as Zeke skipped toward her, still clutching Travis's hand, and smiled. "Hi, Zeke. Did you find a new buddy?"

"Giant," Zeke piped, hopping in place and smiling up at Travis, who stood beside him. Zeke's puppy sat beside Travis's boot, his tail scattering bits of gravel as it wagged.

Hannah noted the flush along Travis's angular cheek-bones, met his eyes and grinned. "Giant?"

Travis's lips curved as he shrugged. "He's little, you know? Everyone probably seems big to him."

"Not everyone." Ben walked up, squatted, and called the puppy over, scratching her behind the ear when she snuggled against his knees. "Zeke's hooked on *Tom the Giant* cartoons. The giant guards the castle, protects the king and queen, and always saves the day." He chuckled. "Tom is Zeke's—"

"Hero," Liz finished for him, tugging a belt loop on the back of Hannah's jeans. "The giant is the hero of the show."

Hannah tucked a strand of hair behind her ear, her cheeks burning.

"It's nice to meet you, Travis," Liz said, edging forward. "I'm Liz—Ben's wife—and I manage the stables with Carl."

Travis returned her greeting with a nod and small smile. "Ben's been telling me about the great work you do here, and all the horses you've saved."

Liz beamed. "That was kind of him, though I have a lot of help, and if I ever come across a really difficult horse, I know it's time to hand the reins over to Hannah."

"Has she been very difficult?" Hannah asked. "This new mare you're giving us?"

"Not really." Liz glanced at the black and white horse. The mare was standing still at the other end of the paddock now, eyeing Carl as he approached with a rope. "She prefers a male hand though, for sure. Won't let me get too close to her. I think the original owner was a woman, and she had a rough touch." Her mouth hardened. "Way too rough, considering the state the mare was in when she arrived."

An ache spread through Hannah as the mare lifted her

nose into the air, her nostrils flaring against the push of a swift wind. Her dark mane fluttered against the rich splashes of color along her back. "I've never understood how people can be so cruel."

A low rumble of thunder rolled overhead, and Hannah looked up at the dark clouds drifting above them. "What do you think, Ben? Is the rain going to hit soon?" She pulled in a deep breath and surveyed their surroundings, picking up on the faint scent of smoke. "That fire doesn't seem like it's settling down."

Ben patted the dog once more, then stood and looked over his shoulder toward the mountain range. "It's not, but it's contained. I just left Steep Creek, letting 'em know there's a voluntary evac, but those folks are located in the foothills of Blue Top Mountain, where the fire started. We don't expect it to make it that far before the rain arrives, but with the winds picking up, we thought it best if they considered moving out for the night."

"Should we do the same?" Hannah asked.

Ben hesitated, then said, "The official answer is no—it's not required. Crews are working around the clock on the fire, and honestly, I don't see those flames jumping all the way to Paradise Peak. We've got a river and ten miles between us and that fire, and once the rain gets there, it's done."

"You'll let us know if something changes?" Hannah asked.

Ben nodded. "You've got my word, Hannah. I'm off-duty now, just swung by to check on Liz and Zeke, and we're heading home soon. We got a clear view of that mountain from our side of Paradise Peak, and if we see something different happening, you'll be the first person I call."

Hannah blew out a breath. "Thanks, Ben. You'll be the first person I call, too."

He smiled. "Now having said that, if you're looking to get that horse home before the rain, you better get going."

Hannah shoved off the fence and moved toward the paddock gate. "I'll walk her to the—"

"Oh, no." Liz halted her with a hand on her forearm. "She's calmer around men, and she won't let them get too close either. Let Travis give Carl a hand." She glanced at Travis. "If you don't mind?"

"Not at all. Excuse me, Zeke." Travis slid his hand free from Zeke's hold and maneuvered his way past the frisky puppy and into the paddock.

"Travis," Hannah called.

He glanced back at her.

"Go easy, okay?" she asked. "Follow Carl's lead?"

He smiled. "You got it."

A delicious shiver raced along Hannah's skin as Travis turned away. *Anything*, he'd said. He'd do anything she asked, every time. If there'd been a flirtatious gleam in his eye when he'd said it, she'd have been tempted to brush his comment aside as a bad pickup line. But there hadn't been. The only look in his eyes at the time had been honest sincerity—the kind she'd been unable to find in Bryan's eyes during the last five years of their marriage.

Zeke, excited expression falling at Travis's departure, banged on a fence rung and thrust out both arms. "Up, please."

"Yes, sir." Smiling, Hannah picked Zeke up, sat him on the top rail of the fence, and circled an arm around his waist to help him keep his balance.

"Oreo!" Zeke bounced and pointed at the mare.

"Shh." Liz touched a finger to her lips. "You have to speak quietly around the horse, okay? Otherwise, you'll scare her."

Zeke pressed his finger to his lips and nodded solemnly at his mother.

"Travis seems like a nice guy," Ben said, moving behind Liz and looping his arms around her. "But he doesn't offer up a whole lot about himself, does he?"

"Ben, you're as bad as Hannah." Liz smacked his arm playfully before snuggling back against his chest. "There's no need to pick apart every stranger's character the moment you meet them."

Ben grinned. "Hazard of the job, baby. I just noticed he's standoffish. So did Carl." He glanced at Hannah. "Or are we wrong? Is he more open with you?"

Hannah shook her head. "Sometimes, but only when he's asked directly." She watched Travis walk slowly across the paddock, his muscular frame relaxed and his steps soft. "He said he grew up in Rockton Park, and he'd never been around horses until Red brought him to the ranch two days ago. He doesn't drink and chooses not to drive."

Ben frowned. "Where'd Red run into him?"

"On a trail by the river," Hannah said. "Red said he bumped into him on the way back from fishing. Travis had been hiking and looked tired, so Red offered him a room for the night; then he and Margaret offered Travis a job."

She made a face as Travis reached the mare, who took a startled step back. Carl said something, held out a rope and a small bag of sliced carrots, and Travis took them.

"What do you think of him?" Ben asked.

Hannah hugged Zeke closer as Travis tossed a slice of carrot on the ground and waited off to the side. The mare lowered her head and ate the treat.

"He's been a hard worker so far," she said. "I'd never have finished the stable roof in one day if he hadn't helped me."

Ben leaned on the top fence rail and looked at Hannah, his eyes meeting hers. "But do you trust him?"

"I . . ." She hesitated, watching as Travis took a step

away from the mare, tossed down another piece of carrot; the mare followed. "I don't know."

Ben studied Travis for a few moments, then said quietly, "I can run a background check, if you'd like me to."

Hannah leaned closer to Zeke and rested her temple against his. Zeke leaned into her, his attention rapt on Travis and the mare.

"I'll think about it." Eyes on Travis, Hannah tensed as the skittish mare approached Travis from behind. "Guess we'll see a bit more of what he's made of." She glanced at Liz. "Animals see as much as kids do when it comes to people."

Liz nodded, but didn't answer, and she and Ben continued to watch Travis and the horse. Zeke remained still in Hannah's arms, save for the lift and fall of his small chest on excited breaths as he stared, too.

The mare reached Travis's side, eyed the bag of carrots, then lowered her head and nudged the back of Travis's arm. Travis lifted his arm slowly, presented his upturned palm, and the mare nibbled a carrot from his hand.

"Well, what do you know?" Liz winked at Hannah. "He's a natural."

Zeke, shivering with excitement, smiled up at Hannah and whispered, "Giant."

"A gentle giant," Liz added, leaning over and kissing Zeke's cheek.

Zeke giggled and Hannah hugged him closer.

A gentle giant. Hannah turned the words over in her mind as Travis slid the rope slowly over the mare's head. She wondered if Liz and Zeke were right.

CHAPTER 6

"Who do you see, beautiful?"

Travis watched the black and white mare, her dark eyes wide on him, shift inside her stall in Paradise Peak Ranch's stable. Her gaze stayed steady, just as it had been hours earlier when he'd loaded her into Red's trailer.

Carl had said the mare trusted men more than women, but even he had been amazed at how quickly she'd taken to him. Hell, Travis had been amazed himself. He knew the treats he'd offered the horse must've sweetened the deal, but he still couldn't figure out exactly what drew her to him.

"When you look at me"—Travis propped his hand on the ledge of the open stall window, offering a slice of apple—"do you see a good man?"

The mare eyed his open palm, eased forward, and took the apple. Chewing slowly, she backed away and continued watching him.

"Or do you see a liar?" Travis asked, lowering his hand to his side. "Because that's what I am. I've lied not just to Hannah, Margaret, and Red, but to Hannah's friends now, too."

Ben Tennyson, in particular—a cop whose suspicions

Travis knew he'd raised earlier this morning at Misty Ridge Stables with his short, guarded answers to the man's questions.

He hadn't meant to come across as shifty or untrustworthy, but being approached by a cop—off-duty or not—had placed Travis's spirit, if not his physical being, right back behind bars, where he'd been unable to do anything but lower his head and endure the scrutiny of officers in uniforms, lawyers in suits, and society as a whole, who'd judged, then condemned him.

Judging from first impressions, Ben was a good man. And the punishment Travis had been sentenced to twenty years ago had been deserved. Only, it didn't fit the man he'd been received as in Paradise Peak.

From the moment he'd met Red on the mountaintop, Travis had felt welcomed and encouraged by the older man. When Red had embraced him after learning of how he'd saved Hannah from falling off the stable roof, he'd experienced what it felt like to be approved of for the first time in his life. And when Hannah had smiled up at him last night, had thanked him for helping her, he had known—for the briefest of moments—what happiness felt like.

He wanted all of those things, and he wanted them in Paradise Peak. A place where kindhearted people like Gloria and Vernon greeted an undeserving stranger like him with open arms. A community where a happy kid like Zeke looked up to him—an ex-con with no right to anything good.

Travis flexed his left hand and smiled, recalling Zeke's tight grip, how the boy's small hand had swung his back and forth as they'd walked to the paddock, and the joy in Zeke's voice when he called him "Giant."

In that moment, he'd felt an unfamiliar sense of pride that had made him long to be someone better. Someone like the man whom Hannah had introduced with respect and admiration; Travis Miller, the stranger Paradise Peak had welcomed in.

But he had no right to seek a fresh start in Paradise Peak, or anywhere else, if he didn't tell the truth.

Travis closed his eyes, a wave of guilt and apprehension moving through him. He had to come clean, and he had to do it now. But would Margaret, Red, and Hannah be able to forgive him? Not only for lying, but for the criminal he'd been?

Turning away from the stall, he looked out of the open entrance of the stable to where Hannah, Red, and Margaret stood outside.

Margaret was talking a mile a minute, her hands making wide sweeping motions as she spoke, and her long, gray hair whipped with each sweep of wind across the grounds.

Two hours ago, after leaving Misty Ridge Stables with the mare safely in tow, he and Hannah had returned to the ranch and released the horse into the paddock behind the stable. Travis had provided the mare with fresh feed and water, then had taken up residence beside the paddock fence and watched her eat, drink, and walk slowly about the enclosure as she eyed the view.

Ruby and Juno, whom Hannah had turned out into the neighboring field across the dirt path, stayed close to the fence and watched the new horse from afar. Their ears had flicked meekly as their eyes followed the mare's movements around the paddock, and their noses had lifted as they'd caught her scent in the swift wind.

Hannah had advised that it would be best to keep the animals separate for now and introduce them gradually. The new mare, though docile around Travis, spooked easily, and Hannah hadn't wanted to take a chance on a bad first encounter with the other two horses.

He and Hannah had let the horses stretch their legs, and Margaret and Red had joined them at the paddock for a look at the new mare. While they'd watched the horses roam the enclosures, the dark clouds that had begun gathering earlier that morning had multiplied and glared down at them from overhead, and a thick haze had settled over the ranch, eventually obscuring the stormy sky and bringing with it the heavy scent of smoke.

Increasing winds had ruffled tree branches, scattered leaves, and tossed loose items about outside the stable, but there hadn't been one drop of rain, and the gray columns of smoke in the distance had billowed out and cloaked the landscape.

At Hannah's urging, Travis had led the new mare inside the stable while she'd rounded up Ruby and Juno. He'd fed all three of them apple slices while Hannah had rejoined Red and Margaret outside.

Now, Margaret caught his eye over Red's shoulder, her expression worried. Hannah faced him, too, the same shadows of concern in her eyes, and there, Travis realized, lay the cause of his hesitation.

If he confessed, there was a chance—however, slim—that Margaret might forgive him. But if he confessed, Hannah would no longer look at him with gratitude, appreciation, and the warmth that had begun to grow in her eyes since last night. Instead, when she looked at him, her beautiful blue eyes would be filled with hurt, betrayal, and possibly anger at his deceit. He'd lose her respect, her trust . . . and any deeper emotion he may have been able to earn from her over time.

He wanted to tell Margaret the truth, but would taking ownership of the reckless fool he'd once been cost him a shot at the good man he might be able to become in Paradise Peak . . . and a possible future with Hannah?

"Travis." Margaret waved a hand. "Would you come out here, please?"

Pulling in a deep breath, Travis left the stables and joined Margaret, Hannah, and Red outside. A strong gust of wind spit grit in his eyes, and he dragged his forearm over his face as the thick, smoky haze settled around him.

"I'm not saying we should leave for weeks," Hannah said to Red as she rubbed her temples. "All I'm saying is that we should at least consider loading up the horses and driving into town for a day or two. That way, if things do take a turn for the worse, we'll have a head start on getting off the mountain."

"I think you're jumping the gun," Red said. "Fire breaks are in place—just this morning I heard on the radio that they're adding more—and rain's on the way. I've been watching the news and listening to the radio off and on all day and there have been no warnings or orders for evacuation. Unless you've gotten one on your cell?"

Hannah frowned. "No, but—"

"And you said yourself," Red continued, "that you'd be the first person Ben called if he saw things taking a turn for the worse." He shook his head. "We've been through worse fires than this. We got no reason and no money to spare on needless panicking."

When Hannah moved to speak, Red held up a hand.

"Not that money would matter if the situation were dire," Red added. "I just don't think it is yet. And I ain't abandoning my home on a hunch."

"Normally, I'd be the first to admit that Hannah jumps to conclusions," Margaret said softly, "but I don't think she is, given these circumstances." She lifted a hand toward the sky. "You can't look at that and tell me there's nothing to be worried about."

Travis tilted his head back and followed the direction

of Margaret's hand. The once tranquil mountain range in the distance had darkened into a misshapen mass behind the thick haze that had lowered over the ranch, and above the mountains, the sun, yellow and bright one hour ago, had become a dim, barely visible, bloodred blur amid the smoke.

"It's nothing I haven't seen before," Red insisted. "I've lived on this mountain all my life, and these fires kick up year round. We're sitting up top. There's a lot of wind up here and it blows in more smoke, that's all. It's nothing new."

Hannah sighed. "These fires might not be anything new, but they've continued to get worse every year. I'm telling you, Red, this one just doesn't feel right to me."

"Travis"—Margaret touched his arm—"what do you think?"

What did he think? Travis hesitated, studying Margaret's worried expression, Red's frown, and the shadow of unease in Hannah's eyes. He knew next to nothing about wildfires, but judging from the way their surroundings had changed over the past hour, he'd have to say it warranted concern.

"I can't speak with any authority," he said, "but I think Hannah is right."

Hannah looked at him, her anxious expression easing slightly, and smiled. "Thank you. See, Red? We need to leave."

Groaning, Red dragged a hand over his face and turned away, his narrowed eyes scanning the grounds. "All right, we'll meet in the middle. You and Travis go to your cabins and pack overnight bags. You'll stay at the lodge with me and Margaret tonight, and we'll keep the TV and radio on to catch any warnings. If the rain doesn't make it here by dawn, we'll load up the horses, drive downtown, and find a motel for a night or two until this thing dies down." Lips twisting, he glanced at Hannah. "That suit you?"

"Yes!" Hannah sprang forward and hugged him tight. "Thank you, Red."

He scoffed. "Don't thank me yet. Margaret's still renovating the rooms so you'll have to share a bed with her, and Travis will be sleeping on the living room floor." He smirked at Travis. "See what you let her rope you into? Giving up a perfectly good bed for no reason."

Travis smiled. "I can handle it."

"Yeah, you say that now. Tell me that in the morning when you shove off the hard floor with a crick in your neck and two women gabbing in your ear." Red spun on his heel and headed for the lodge. "Can't do much outside with all this smoke, so we might as well go inside. Get a move on, pack your bags, and join us at the lodge."

"It won't be as bad as he says." Margaret followed Red, grinning as she passed Travis. "I'll blow up an air mattress and find clean sheets for you."

"Later," Red said. "First, we're packing bags."

"No, we're not, and don't boss me around, Red Bartlett. Just because you're in a bad mood doesn't mean you . . ."

Travis chuckled as Margaret walked quickly to Red's side, her long skirt whipping in the wind as she stepped carefully in her high heels and continued to admonish him. Red grunted and walked faster.

"They're a pair, aren't they?" Hannah asked.

Her attention was on his mouth, and the pretty pink blooming in her cheeks made Travis catch his breath. "Yeah," he said. "They are."

Wind gusted against her back and yanked an auburn curl from her ponytail, sweeping it across her soft lips. His eyes traced the curves of her mouth and he leaned forward slightly, wanting to slide his arms around her and brush her lips with his. Wanting to hold her close and ask if she felt the same longing he did—this need to connect, cherish, and belong.

Instead, he reached out, tucked his fingertip beneath the strand of her hair and tugged it off her lips. He smoothed it across her cheek, her skin soft beneath his palm.

She stared up at him, her blue eyes warming, and tucked the strand of hair behind her ear with a shaky hand. "W-we'd better pack."

She studied his mouth once more, then turned away abruptly.

Travis shoved his hands in his pockets and joined her on the dirt path. They walked against the swift kick of the wind, parting ways when Hannah reached her cabin. Travis waited until she made it safely inside, then crossed the bridge and continued along the stone walkway up the steep incline until he reached his cabin.

Once inside, he grabbed his worn bag and tossed in a pair of clean jeans and a T-shirt. Realizing his bag of new clothes was still in Red's truck, he decided to grab it on the way to the lodge.

He scooped up his toothbrush and toothpaste from the bathroom, returned to the small desk in front of the window, and grabbed the lantern Hannah had given him the night before. After dropping the items into his bag, he picked up the unmarked envelopes bound with string, placed them in the bag, then reached for the loose letters scattered on the desk.

Travis stopped, his hand stilling above the name scrawled in ink on the bottom of one letter: *Neil Alden.*

Two simple words against a white backdrop, unspoken, but they resounded through his mind like a sinister hiss inside the silent cabin.

Gut heaving, he covered the words with his fist, then turned his back and exited the cabin, leaving the letters behind.

Outside, the wind had turned fierce. Travis slung his

bag over his shoulder and hustled down the stone walk-way. When he cleared the trees and stepped onto the bank of the river, heading toward the bridge, an odd tint bled into the haze surrounding him.

The smoke-filled air had turned orange. It took on an eerie glow, the haze brightest high above the trees further up the mountain beyond his cabin, and above it, dense clouds of black smoke rose overhead.

An angry wind cut a path down the mountain and through the trees, shoving before it a thick swath of smoke. The black mass loomed low toward Travis like a distorted finger, burning his eyes, clogging his throat, and rushing into his lungs.

"Dear God . . ." Heart pounding against his ribs, he ran across the bridge to Hannah's cabin, climbed the steps, and banged on the door. "Hannah!"

There was no answer.

Coughing to clear the smoke from his throat, he tried the doorknob and, finding it unlocked, thrust it open.

Hannah stopped in midstep two feet from the door, an overnight bag over her shoulder. "Travis, wh—"

"We have to leave." He grabbed her hand, tugged her out onto the deck, and shut the door behind them. "Right now."

She stumbled to a stop on the deck, her head tipping back and mouth parting as she took in the ominous or-ange glow across the stream, above his cabin. A dazed look entered her eyes. "The wind must've shifted."

Something caught Travis's eye; a flutter of gray against an auburn background. "Hannah . . ."

He touched her hair gently, his fingers sifting through the bright strands near her temple, plucked the gray speck out and lowered it in front of her.

"It's ash." She looked at him, then peered above his head, her eyes widening. "It's everywhere."

Large and small bits of gray, black, and white ash began falling like snowflakes from the sky, littering their hair, clothing, the deck and dirt path. The shower of ash started out light, but grew heavier by the second, and the strong gusts of wind barreling down the mountain hurled the flakes in sporadic patterns around them.

"We gotta go," Travis shouted above the roar of the wind.

He grabbed her hand and led the way down the winding staircase of the deck. When their feet hit the dirt path, they bolted, ducking their heads against the wind and sprinting to the stable.

"The horses!" Hannah looked up at him, eyes full of fear. "There's no time to load them, and we'd never make it down the mountain with a trailer in this. We'll have to let them run."

A gust of wind slammed into them, and her free arm shot out, gripping Travis's forearm as her legs shook beneath her. A neigh rang out from the stable and hooves pounded against a stall wall.

Her chin trembled. "But what if they can't outru—"

Her voice broke, but there was no need for her to finish.

What if they can't outrun the fire?

Terror coursed through him at the thought, but Travis leaned close, blocking the wind, and squeezed her upper arms. "They will. I'll let them out and set 'em in the right direction. You go to the lodge and get Margaret and Red. Load up the truck."

She blinked up at him, dislodging ash from her thick lashes, then nodded. "I'll call Ben and Liz and let them know the fire's jumped."

She took off, running across the field toward the lodge.

It took Travis five minutes to unlatch the stalls and urge each horse out, but it felt more like fifteen. Ruby and Juno dashed out of their open stalls without hesitation, darting out of the stable and galloping across the grounds in the opposite direction from the blaze on the mountain.

When he reached the last stall, the new mare, still kicking the walls of her enclosure, tossed her head back, eyes wild.

Travis clutched the latch on the new mare's stall, the metal cutting into his palm, and kept his voice as steady as he could manage. "Don't look back, beautiful." His chest tightened. "You gotta run. Fast as you can."

He swung the stall door open and jumped out of the way as she peeled out of the stable, dirt spraying from beneath her hooves.

Travis grabbed his bag and ran toward the lodge, watching the mare follow the other horses' lead and whispering, "Don't look back."

As he reached Red's truck, parked in front of the lodge, the front door banged open and Red came out, carrying two large bags. Margaret and Hannah followed on his heels down the front steps, each carrying a bag of her own.

"We'll take Margaret's car," Red said, heading toward a car parked on the other side of the lodge. "Hannah, you and Travis take the truck." The wind whipped hard, breaking his next words. "It'll handle better on . . . road and we'll need both in case . . . blow a tire or something worse happens. Follow us."

"I can't," Hannah said, jogging over to the truck. "Cell service is down, and I can't get through to Liz and Ben. I need to make sure they know what's coming their way."

Margaret stopped midstride and shouted against a gust of wind, "No! You follow us."

"I can't." Hannah opened the driver's side door of the truck and threw her bag on the bench seat. "Ben promised me he'd let me know if something changed and I didn't hear a thing from him when the fire changed course and headed our way. He may not know it's crowning, and with the power out, he won't have any more warning than we did." She stabbed a hand at the orange glow in the sky above the mountain, behind Travis's cabin. Small flames licked along a short segment of the tree line. "You see where the wind's carried it. Liz and Ben are below the fire and Ben will be looking in the other direction. It'll rain down on 'em before they see it coming. They might need help getting out."

"It's too dangerous to drive that way." Red dropped the bags, strode over to Hannah, and gripped her shoulders. "As fast as the fire's moving, you won't make it there first."

"But I have to try. Gloria and Vernon are on that side of the mountain. Our other neighbors . . . You'd do the same if Margaret and I weren't here." She shook her head. "I gave him my word. I can't leave without at least trying. We'll take the shortcut, then meet you at the bottom of the mountain. I won't take more chances than I have to."

Red stared down at her, then nodded and hugged her hard. "Travis!"

He met Red's eyes over the hood of the truck.

"You take care of my girl," Red shouted. "Don't leave her side."

Travis nodded, and Red walked back toward the car by the lodge. Margaret stopped Red with a hand on his chest.

"You can't let her go." Fear entered Margaret's eyes as she looked over Red's shoulder at Hannah. "She'll get hurt or—"

Red grabbed Margaret's arms and eased her back, propelling her toward her car. "She knows what's she's doing, and Travis is with her. She'll be okay."

"But she—"

"We gotta go, Margaret." Red hustled her further back.

Travis's chest tightened at the stricken expression on Margaret's face. She'd already lost Niki—he'd done that to her. To lose Hannah, too . . .

Travis pressed his hands on the hood of the truck and leaned forward, calling out to Margaret, "I'll bring her back safe. I promise."

Margaret braced herself against Red, stalling his steps, and locked eyes with Travis. "You swear?"

Travis stared back, his jaw clenching at the vulnerability in Margaret's expression. Terror snaked through him at the thought of failing her. And of failing Hannah.

"I swear."

Hannah hit the gas and a spray of gravel pelted the underside of Red's truck. When she reached the end of the ranch's driveway, she hung a left onto a crude dirt road and floored it. Heavy wind rocked the truck and whirled thick clouds of smoke among the trees, blanketing the sun and intensifying the orange glow around them.

She adjusted the rearview mirror, straining for a glimpse of Margaret's car, then returned her attention to the road. "Are they out?"

Travis shifted on the seat beside her and looked out the back windshield. "Yeah. They just hit the main road, headed toward town."

"How do things look that way?"

" 'Bout the same," he said. "Smoke, orange tint. I can't see them anymore."

Hannah bit her lip, her hands tightening on the steering wheel.

He faced forward again, and she sensed his eyes on her. "You good?"

"Yes. I'm good."

The dirt road narrowed. She moved to the center of it, the truck bouncing wildly over knotted roots and potholes.

"How far is Ben's place?" Travis asked.

"About four miles." Another pothole; their bags bounced off the seat and onto the floorboard. She leaned forward, peering into the thick haze. "But it's mountain road. It'll take longer than normal."

"And Gloria and Vernon?" Travis asked. "How far are they from Ben and Liz?"

"They own guest cabins and live in one of their own a mile further up the mountain."

The dirt road went uphill and Hannah pressed harder on the gas pedal, the engine groaning in response. As the truck ascended higher up the mountain, the orange glow surrounding them deepened and the black smoke grew thicker, turning day into night.

She flipped on the truck's headlights and their bright glow threw tall trees and bare branches into stark relief against the bright orange backdrop. Wind whistled through the thick underbrush lining the road and dead leaves mixed with falling ash and red embers, swirling in the air and tumbling across the windshield.

The air inside the cab warmed and sweat trickled over her temples. "We're getting close to Ben's place."

A loud crash erupted to the left of the road and Hannah flinched, her hands jerking the steering wheel. The truck swerved to the right, tires spinning wildly over rough terrain as she struggled with the wheel, finally managing to drag the truck back onto the dirt road.

Hannah sat up straighter, her spine stiffening.

The truck cleared the top of the incline and sped down the other side. Small flames appeared on the ground, flickered along the sides of the dirt road, blazing thin trails among fallen leaves and thick bushes. More flames licked high in the treetops.

Hannah's foot began to tremble against the gas.

"Slow down."

"What?" Hannah glanced at Travis, his composed expression unnerving her. "Are you crazy?"

He had to be to speak in that low, calm tone of his, completely unfazed when the world was burning down around them.

"I want you to slow down and pull over," he said quietly.

"You are crazy." Her breath caught as she scanned the flames spreading beside the road.

Another crash—this time to the left. Her hands shook so badly, she could barely grip the wheel.

"Stop the truck." Travis's tone was firm. "I'm gonna take over."

A humorless laugh burst from her lips. "You've got to be kidding me." Dear God, he'd lost his mind, and she was beginning to, but at least arguing with him was a welcome distraction from the flames. "We're heading right into the middle of a firestorm."

"I know, and you're rattled. That's why I want you to stop."

"No way. You told me yourself that you don't drive, and you choose now—this moment—to decide to take it up again?" She scoffed and shook her head. "Forget it."

"Hannah—"

"No!" She shot him a glare. "I said, forget i—"

A sharp crack split the air and Hannah caught the flash of something falling toward the road. She slammed on the brakes, heard a screech, the snap of activated seat belts, and felt a broad hand slam into her chest just as the truck jerked to a halt, throwing her forward.

The steering wheel flashed closer into her vision, but the strong palm at her chest propelled her back into her seat, the back of her head thumping against the headrest.

She sat still for a moment, staring at the flaming pine tree that lay across the road in front of them, then down at Travis's strong hand still clamped to the center of her chest. It shook slightly against her.

He slid his hand away as their rapid breaths filled the cab. "Are you okay?"

Heart pounding, she turned her head, met Travis's dark eyes, wide with concern, and nodded. "I'm good. And we're stopped, so you can take over now."

Before he could answer, she unsnapped her seat belt, thrust her door open, and climbed out. Intense heat hit the bare skin of her face and neck, and smoke rushed into her lungs. She doubled over, coughing.

Travis's arms slid around her from behind, lifted her by the waist, and sat her back inside the truck. She slid over to the passenger seat as he followed her in and shut the door.

Reaching over her, he drew the seat belt around her, secured it with a click, then tugged it tight. "Do you want to turn back?"

Hannah dragged the back of her hand across her sweaty face, the pungent smell of smoke wafting up from her clothes, hair, and skin. "I . . ."

Flames flickered along the pines in front of them. Wood crackled and red embers sprayed upward on a gust of wind. They twirled left, right, and left again, then settled gracefully in the top of a cedar tree beside the road as if performing a bizarre dance.

"Hannah. If you want, we can turn back, but we've got to go in one direction or the other, and we gotta go now."

The heat in the cab intensified, and her breaths came quicker now. Oh, Lord, how she wanted to turn around.

Instead, she closed her eyes and thought of Gloria, joyfully prattling on as she had shown Travis around the shop this morning. She thought of Ben, his arms around Liz as they'd stood by the paddock fence at Misty Ridge Stables, both of them smiling and in love. And she thought of Zeke—

"No." Squeezing her eyes shut tighter, she swallowed hard and steadied her voice. "They may need help. We keep going."

"Hannah." A big hand closed around her knee and squeezed. "Look at me."

She opened her eyes and focused on Travis's face. His lean cheeks were flushed, there was a black smudge on his forehead and a tight set to his mouth, but his dark eyes were clear and his gaze steady.

"After we reach Ben and Liz, I'll get you back down this mountain," he rasped. "But you've got to stay focused and tell me which way to go. And you've got to trust my judgment if we run into trouble." He leaned closer, his gaze intense upon her face. "Do you trust me?"

Hannah stared back at him, her chest still humming with the pressure of his protective hand against her. She touched the tender spot with her fingertips, a sense of calm unfurling within her. "Yes."

CHAPTER 7

Travis threw the truck in reverse, hit the gas, and backed up. His fingers glided easily over the wide steering wheel, but the feel of it and the pedal beneath his boot felt forbidden. It'd been over twenty years since he'd sat behind the wheel of a vehicle, and he shouldn't be driving one now.

Memories of metal crunching, shattering glass, and flashes of red and blue lights returned with a vengeance and constricted his chest. He shook his head and blinked hard to regain his focus.

Hannah. He glanced at her seated in the passenger seat, her blue eyes on him, her expression anxious. He'd promised Margaret he'd bring her back safely.

"Brace yourself on the dash." Travis eyed the pine tree lying across the road as flames licked up the long branches. "We're going around it, but this side of the truck's going to run over a limb or two."

"Be careful," Hannah said. "There's a drop off the embankment."

Nodding, he shifted gears again, then eased the truck forward, picking up enough speed as they approached to mount the thinnest limbs.

Wood cracked and flames hissed as the truck crunched over the branches, bounced along the rough embankment, then swerved back onto the dirt road.

"Red was right," Travis said, relief washing over him. "He said this truck had some miles on it, but that it was a tough one."

Hannah removed her hands from the dashboard and relaxed back in her seat. "Yeah. Can't say I've been overly fond of this truck, but I'm grateful for it right now."

Nodding, Travis slowed as they rounded a sharp curve. The flames that had licked along the ground beside the road disappeared in the rearview mirror and the new stretch of road was clear, though orange light still glowed behind distant trees and embers whipped along on the wind.

"How much further to Ben's?" he asked. "Things look better this way."

"We're almost there. Gloria and Vernon's cabin is just ahead, and Ben's place is . . ." As she spoke, they emerged from another sharp curve to find huge flames engulfing a house several feet ahead on the right side of the road. "Oh, no."

Travis had spoken too soon. Cringing, he stared at the burning house.

"Watch out!" Hannah gripped his arm.

Travis hit the brakes just as headlights emerged through the thick smoke covering the road. The truck jerked to a stop in front of a parked sedan. One person stood beside it, outside the open passenger's side door, and another stood several feet away on the right side of the road beside another adult and a child who sat on the ground.

Travis gripped the steering wheel tighter. "Is that Liz and Zeke?"

The passenger door slammed as Hannah ran in front of

the truck toward the figures sitting on the ground, the truck's headlights casting a garish glow over her back.

Travis shoved open his door and ran after her, skidding to a stop by her side. Wind, heat, and ash hit his face and he scrubbed his eyes with the hem of his T-shirt before surveying the figures at his feet.

Liz was sitting on the ground, blank-faced, with Zeke in her arms. The boy pointed to the blaze several feet in front of them, his face red and tears rolling down his cheeks as he sobbed. The fire cast an eerie reddish-orange flicker over the pair.

"I can't get Liz in the car." Vernon stepped forward, covered in soot from head to toe. An anguished expression crossed his face as he looked up at Travis. "Gloria and I have tried, but she won't come." He raised his arm in the direction of the fire, then let it fall limply to his side. "There was nothing—no warning. Just wind and fire. Ben came over and got us out, but . . ."

"Daddy!" Zeke cried, stretching his arms in the direction of the fire.

Vernon's face crumpled and his shoulders shook.

Travis, gut knotting, took a step toward the fire.

A crash erupted from the blaze. The cabin collapsed and the flames shot higher. Waves of heat and hot embers swept across the yard toward them, scattering in all directions on gusts of wind.

"Travis, don't." Hannah halted his steps with a hand on his arm, her eyes panicked and pleading.

He stared at the flames. There was no point in trying to enter the blazing structure; it had already collapsed, and anyone inside it would've been lost long before that.

Throat tightening, Travis grabbed Vernon's elbow and hustled him across the road to where Gloria waited by the car. "Get back in your car and keep the engine running. We'll bring them to you."

Gloria, tears coursing down her face, nodded, then sat in the passenger's seat and closed the door. Vernon followed suit and Travis shut the door behind him.

Zeke's sobs had grown louder by the time Travis returned to the other side of the road.

"Liz, we have to go." Hannah, squatting by Liz, gripped the other woman's shoulders and pulled.

Liz, still dazed, shook her head. "No."

Zeke strained against his mother's hold and cried louder, his arms reaching out in the direction of a downed tree.

Hannah pressed closer. "Liz, you have to—"

"Ben's still in there!" Liz's expression contorted. "I won't leave him."

Zeke, sobbing, pulled at his mother's arms.

"Then at least let us take Zeke," Hannah pleaded, her voice breaking. "Please, Liz!"

"I won't leave him! Ben!" A keening sound escaped Liz's lips and she doubled over, moaning, "Oh, God!"

Chin trembling, Hannah looked up at Travis, her eyes welling, and shook her head. "What do we do?"

Vision blurring, Travis knelt, hooked his arms around Zeke's waist, and pulled him from Liz's arms. "Take him to the car."

He pressed Zeke into Hannah's open arms, then slid his arms under Liz, picked her up, held her tight against his chest, and carried her across the road behind Hannah and Zeke.

When he reached the car, he edged past Hannah and lowered Liz into the backseat with Zeke, who crawled over her lap toward him.

"Blondie!" Zeke cried, pointing out the open door toward the downed tree.

Travis nudged the boy back into Liz's arms, saying softly, "I'll look for her." He smoothed his hand over the boy's soft hair and wiped away a tear from the child's cheek with his thumb. "I promise."

Zeke continued calling for his dog.

Grimacing, Travis shut the door, then rapped his knuckled against Vernon's window.

Vernon lowered it and Travis bent close, saying, "There's a tree down about a mile and a half up the road. Pass it on the left shoulder, then keep going till you clear the smoke—however far that is." He straightened and banged his fist once on the hood. "Go. We'll follow soon."

Vernon nodded, rolled up his window, then pulled off.

Travis spun around and jogged toward the downed tree.

"What are you doing?" Hannah, halfway to the truck, had stopped and looked back at him.

"The dog," Travis said, following along the trunk of the tree and peering at the dark ground. "Zeke pointed over here when he called to her."

Barbed wire snagged Travis's pants leg and he yanked his leg free, stomping further through the dry undergrowth toward the tree's thick branches. He bent low and peered through the smoke for any sign of the pup.

"Travis, the fire's too close. We don't have ti—"

A whimper, then yip, sounded. Yellow fur flashed between a tangle of limbs and a dog's paw kicked in the air.

"Over there!" Travis ran toward the squirming pup and dropped to his knees.

Barbed wire was wrapped around one of the dog's legs and she struggled, trying to kick her way out from under one of the tree's limbs.

Hannah's arm brushed against Travis as she knelt by his side. "Is she okay?"

Travis ran his palm over the pup's belly. It rose on rapid

pants. The pup yipped and licked his hand. "She's all right. Just tangled up." He bent low, looking into the dog's soulful eyes, and spoke softly, "Hang on, girl. We're gonna get you out of this."

A second crash from the direction of the blazing cabin echoed across the landscape. Flames hissed and hot embers spiraled around them on a renewed gust of wind.

Hannah gripped his forearm as she looked up, her mouth parting on a swift breath. "We have to go. Now!"

Fire flickered in the tree directly in front of them, engulfing one thick branch, then another, snaking along dry bark and dead leaves toward the trunk, where high undergrowth waited to ignite.

"Travis, I want to help her as much as you do, but there's no ti—"

"No!" Sweat rolled onto his lashes, clouding his vision. He dragged his forearm over his face and bent closer to the dog. "Not until I've at least tried."

Eyes burning hotter with each gust of smoke, Travis grabbed the limb covering the dog and wrenched at it. Hannah's hands joined his, wrapping around the rough bark and yanking. They jerked and pulled and the limb broke free with a sharp snap.

The pup yipped and flailed in an attempt to roll to her paws.

"Hold her still," Travis said.

Hannah slid her palm over the dog's chest and spoke in low, soothing tones. The dog settled but she still kicked occasionally, and her small belly jerked with heavy pants.

Travis squinted beneath the flickering orange glow and passed his hands gently along each of the pup's legs, searching for the barbed wire wrapped around her paw.

Finding it, he tucked his fingertips under it and tugged.

The dog jerked and whimpered.

"I know," Travis said. "I'm sorry."

He trailed his fingertips along the spiky wire, finding it tangled in a branch above the dog's head. Wrapping it around his hand, he closed his fist and yanked.

Sharp metal cut into his palm and warm blood trickled over his wrist. He gritted his teeth and pulled harder.

"Stop." Hannah leaned closer to him. "Your hand—"

"I don't have a knife on me. Do you?"

She shook her head.

"Then I have to."

Travis yanked again and wood cracked, releasing the wire. He gathered up the slack, then lowered the wire beside the pup and unwound the other end of it from her paw. The dog kicked in Hannah's hold, then scrambled to her belly and crouched low, whimpering.

Fire licked down the tree trunk in front of them and engulfed the brittle undergrowth, which burst into flame.

"Come on!" Hannah shouted.

Travis grabbed Hannah's elbow as she lifted the pup in her arms, and they shot to their feet and ran across the road to the truck. Heat nipped at their heels in waves while smoke and ash swirled in every direction.

Once inside the truck, Travis gunned the engine, executed a U-turn, then sped up the rough dirt road. Fire covered both sides of the road and shot upward, forming scorching walls that swept across the track on violent gusts of wind.

Travis hit the gas pedal harder and the truck barreled through black smoke and bright flames. Fiery embers pelted the windshield and debris banged the underside of the truck. The pup's pants and his and Hannah's heavy breaths rasped inside the hot, smoke-laced air of the cab.

Emerging from the black smoke, the truck groaned as Travis pushed it harder, pressing the gas pedal as far as it would go. Flames danced in every direction, licking at the truck's metal frame. The earth sizzled and hissed as the tires spun past.

Sweat stung Travis's eyes. He squeezed them shut, shook his head, and refocused on the road, his bloody palm slipping on the steering wheel.

"Oh, my God." Hannah, staring at the side of the road ahead, wrapped her hand around his wrist and squeezed tight. "Travis . . ."

To the left, flames on the ground and strong wind converged, twisting into a flaming spiral that stretched high into the red sky. The blazing twister picked up speed, sucking up fiery debris, whirling and spinning in a deadly dance toward the road as if the devil himself had materialized from thin air.

"We can't make it through that." Hannah's hoarse whisper barely rose above the pup's heavy pants as it cowered in her lap. She stared helplessly at him, her face going pale. "It'll burn us alive."

Terror snaked through Travis as he lifted his foot from the gas pedal and slowed the truck. He glanced in the rearview mirror. Everything was aflame, and they couldn't turn back—there was no other way out.

Travis looked at Hannah, the fear on her face increasing his. "Keep holding on to me"—he faced the twisting spiral of fire, then slammed his foot on the gas—"and close your eyes."

They were in hell—there was no other word for it.

Eyes closed, Hannah squeezed Travis's thick wrist with one hand and held the puppy close with the other, cringing as the truck's engine roared.

Tree limbs and sharp underbrush scraped the passenger door and undercarriage of the truck, cracking and snapping as they passed. Heat intensified, stealing Hannah's breath, and a red glow seeped past the black shade of her closed eyelids. Something sizzled and hissed, moving closer with each passing second.

A scream rose from her chest and she opened her mouth, but her throat constricted, trapping the sound.

Clumps of debris pelted the windshield, the sizzling sound nearby morphed into a roar, and something banged against the back end of the truck, sending the vehicle into a fishtailing skid.

Tires squealed and Travis muttered a curse, his wrist jerking beneath Hannah's hold as he grappled with the steering wheel. With each sling of the truck, Hannah cradled the dog closer and pressed back in her seat, her spine stiff.

"Oh, God, please," she choked. "Please get us out."

The slinging motion slowed and the truck righted itself, but the pelting sound against the windshield grew louder.

Hannah froze, then whispered, "Travis?"

His harsh breaths mingled with the heavy pounding on the windshield; then his wrist turned over and his hand slid through her grip to lace his fingers with hers. "Open your eyes."

She closed them tighter, a shaky gasp escaping her as the truck bounced over a pothole.

Travis squeezed her hand. "Look."

Slowly, she lifted her eyelids and focused on the windshield. Small clumps of burned debris clung to the dusty glass, but heavy drops of water pounded the windshield, streaming through the dirt and grime and clearing the view.

A small smile curved her lips. "Rain."

Travis flipped on the windshield wipers.

Cradling the puppy in her lap, she sat up straighter and

glanced around. Fires still roared on both sides of the road and in the tops of trees, and the sky remained a burned orange, but it was raining.

"It finally came!" Relieved laughter burst from her lips, but it turned into a choked sob as Travis rounded a curve, and the truck reached the bottom of the mountain and the outskirts of town.

Cabins, buildings, cars, and trees were on fire in every direction. Power lines littered the streets in snakelike patterns, sparking new fires, and a transformer blew overhead.

Flinching, Hannah twisted in her seat and looked out the back window of the truck. Night had fallen, and orange flames blazed long, glowing trails across the mountain, zigzagging down the rugged landscape. The entire mountain looked as though it was on fire.

"It's burning," she said, her voice catching on a sob. "Everything's burning."

"Don't look back." Travis's deep voice, hoarse, sounded by her side. "We can't look back right now."

A salty tear rolled into the corner of Hannah's mouth. She licked it away, faced forward, and watched as Travis joined a line of cars evacuating the mountain. Blue patrol lights flashed ahead and a police officer waved his arms, directing traffic to a side road that bypassed town.

"Ben." Her throat tightened so much she could hardly speak.

Ben was gone, and Liz would be lost without him.

"What about Red? And Margaret? And Liz and—" She peered up at Travis, her heart pounding so loudly it echoed in her ears. "Do you think they made it out?"

Travis's jaw clenched and he glanced at her, determination flooding his dark eyes. "We'll find all of them. I promise you, once things settle, we'll find them. Right now, we need to get off the road and find a place to stay for the night."

The puppy stirred, raising her head from Hannah's lap, and licked softly at her hand.

"It's okay, Blondie," Hannah whispered, hot tears rolling down her cheeks. "We're going to find Zeke. We're going to find all of them, alive and well."

She said the words but had no idea if they were true.

Travis drove on, following the line of cars in a detour to Crystal Rock, a neighboring town ten miles down the road. Hannah watched Paradise Peak in the side mirror, the blazing mountain growing smaller and smaller with each mile they traveled until another mountain and a heavier downpour of rain hid it from sight. Only the massive black clouds of smoke drifting up to the sky were visible when they reached Crystal Rock.

Headlights flashed by in a continuous stream of traffic, and though several parking lots were full of cars and people milling about, the tall signs standing by each business were dark and all the streetlights were out.

"Looks like the power's down here, too," Travis said, his voice husky. He peered past her, his face lined with exhaustion, and gestured with their clasped hands toward a large building by the road. "Is that a hotel?"

Hannah looked out the passenger window, squinting against the curtain of heavy rain and darkness. "Yeah— Black Bear Lodge. But it's usually full of tourists and it's jammed with cars and people already. There won't be any rooms left by the time we make it inside." She tipped her chin toward the road. "Keep straight and take a left at the next traffic light. There's a small motel on the outskirts of town, kinda tucked away. We'll have a better chance at a room there."

Nodding, he kept driving. When they arrived at the next traffic light, he took a left as she'd directed, and ten minutes later, he pulled into the small, one-story motel's parking lot. The tall, unlit sign above the building was barely readable through the heavy fall of rain: ONE STOP MOTEL. Over a dozen cars were parked in front of room entrances, and a single, dim light shone in the wide window of the office where several people stood, talking and gesturing wildly.

Travis parked in the last empty parking space in front of a room on the end and cut the engine. Rain pounded on the hood of the truck and poured in thick streams from the thin gutters on the motel's roof.

"I'll go to the office and see if this room's available," Travis said. When she moved to open her door, he added, "There's no need for us both to go in. Wait here, okay?"

Hannah grew still, noting his carefully composed expression and the concern in his dark eyes. "You're going to check for information about Red and Margaret while you're in there, aren't you?"

He looked away for a moment, watching the rain bounce off the windshield, then met her eyes and nodded slowly.

She swallowed hard, and his handsome face blurred. "And you don't want to ask about them in front of me because you're worried something has happened to them."

"Hey." He leaned forward, cupping her cheek with one palm and squeezing their clasped hands together on his knee. "I don't know that, and neither do you." He smiled, but his expression was strained. "For all we know, they're tucked safe in one of those plush beds back at that big-ass hotel." His lips lifted. "Red's grumpy because he's trying to sleep and Margaret's still gabbing in his ear."

Laughter burst from her lips, despite the hot tears rolling

down her face. "She'll wake up mad because the power's out and she can't apply her eyeliner properly."

Travis smiled. "And Red'll fuss because he'll wake up with a crick in his neck and Margaret will still be gabbing." He eased closer, studying her grin, and drifted his thumb over her lower lip. "That's better."

His touch, gentle and warm, soothed her on the inside.

Her eyelids drifted shut and she released a heavy breath. "Thank you," she whispered. "For everything."

Gently, he lifted her hand from his knee, and she felt his lips press against the back of her palm. "You're welcome."

Hannah opened her eyes, seeking his handsome smile and comforting expression, but he'd already turned away. The door thudded shut on his exit, and she watched through the window as he jogged through the heavy rain and into the motel office.

Sighing, she rolled her window down an inch to air out the smell of smoke in the cab. Rain sprinkled through the open crack, and she tilted her head back, letting the cool drops mist her overheated forehead and cheeks.

Blondie whimpered and she smoothed her hand across the puppy's fur. "Does your leg hurt, baby?" She touched the injured leg gently, brushing aside blood-coated fur to examine the wound. "It's not too bad. Travis took good care of you, didn't he?"

The puppy snuggled closer to her belly and Hannah leaned down and kissed the top of her head, saying a silent prayer that Red and Margaret were safe in that hotel just as Travis had said. And that Liz, Zeke, Gloria, and Vernon had somehow made it to a safe haven, too.

Ten minutes passed, the smoke in the cab aired out, and cool, late-February air trickled in with the sprinkles of rain. Water sloshed as heavy footsteps approached, and Hannah, shivering, straightened as Travis opened the truck door and stuck his head in out of the rain.

Rain had soaked his hair and shirt, and drops of water rolled down his lean cheeks. "We're in luck," he said, holding up a key. "The room's ours, free of charge, for as long as we need it. The manager's offering rooms to everyone who had to evacuate."

"What about Red and Margaret? Or Liz and—"

"No." Travis shook his head. "They aren't here." He reached over and squeezed her shoulder. "We'll check around again in the morning. Right now, let's go inside, clean up, and get some sleep. Cell service is down and power's out, but the manager said there's running water."

Hannah gathered Blondie close to her chest. "There are first-aid supplies in the tool kit in the truck bed. I'll need it to bandage her leg."

Travis nodded. "I'll open the door for you, then bring that and our bags in."

Hannah took Blondie inside the motel room and stood by the dresser, holding the dog as she waited for Travis. The interior was dark, and out of habit, she tried turning the lamp on, only to sigh with renewed disappointment when it didn't light up. She could make out the shapes of one double bed and a chair in the darkness.

It took Travis two trips to bring in the first-aid kit, all of their bags, and a potted lantana plant. The blooms bounced as he jogged through the rain and shut the door.

"Gloria's gift?" Hannah asked.

A car passed by the window, its headlights flooding the room with light, and she caught a glimpse of his smile before darkness fell between them again.

"Yeah. I didn't have a chance to take it out of the truck." Bags rustled as he set them on the dresser beside her. "My new clothes were still in there, too, and I have something in my other bag"—a zipper rasped open—"that I think will come in handy."

Something clicked, and light glowed in all directions.

Travis lifted the camping lantern and grinned. "Gloria didn't give me this."

Hannah smiled back. "Oh?"

"No. Another woman gave it to me." His grin widened, his sexy dimple denting. "She can be a bit bossy sometimes"—the teasing light in his eyes dimmed, and his voice softened—"but she's the most gorgeous woman I've ever laid eyes on. Inside and out."

His brown eyes darkened even further as his gaze roved over her face.

Face heating, Hannah looked away, noticing their reflection in the mirror on the dresser. "Well, I doubt you feel that way now."

She studied the black streaks of ash and soot on her forehead, cheeks, and nose. Her clothes were soaked from the rain and rumpled from the drive, and water dripped slowly from the hem of her jeans, making a puddle on the carpeted floor.

Travis, she noticed, had fared better. Rain had washed away the ash from his face, neck, and forearms. His black hair, wet, was slicked back from his face, revealing his thick lashes and the strong angles of his handsome features. Dark stubble lined his jaw, and his soggy shirt and jeans clung to his muscular frame, adding to his masculine appeal.

"You're always beautiful, Hannah," he said quietly.

His deep voice sent a delicious shiver through her. She cradled Blondie closer and smiled. "Thank you, but I think I'll feel better after a hot shower."

Travis picked up the camping lantern, eased past her, and entered the bathroom. Something squeaked and then the sound of running water filled the room.

He returned from the bathroom and motioned for her to enter. "Water's warming up." He walked over, holding out his arms. "While you shower, I'll take a look at Blondie's wound."

Hannah passed the puppy to him gently, grabbed her overnight bag, and entered the bathroom. The shower was small, but clean and serviceable, with a thick, opaque shower curtain. She turned around and peered into the dark room where Travis's and Blondie's silhouettes were visible in front of the window. Travis spoke in low, soothing tones to Blondie, who raised her head from his broad chest and nuzzled his chin.

"You won't be able to see well without the lantern," she said. "Once I'm in the shower, I'll let you know so you can come in and get her bandaged up."

Travis turned his head and faced her, his expression unreadable in the dark. "Okay. Thanks."

By the time Hannah had shut the door and peeled off her wet clothes, the water gushing from the tap had warmed up. She turned on the showerhead, placed a towel nearby, and stepped into the tub, drawing the curtain closed.

"You can come in now."

She craned her neck, straining to hear Travis's entrance over the rush of water. When a cool breath of air and Travis's low, gentle voice entered the room, a sense of calm moved through her.

The feeling took her aback. Other than with Red, she hadn't felt that way in a man's presence in years. The sensation was new, comforting, and in a way . . . exciting.

Smiling, she grabbed the shampoo and lathered her hair. The warm, clean water and the shampoo's light, floral scent were heaven and made Hannah feel tons better, but when she grabbed the soap, a flash of reddish brown on her palm caught her eye.

Small amounts of blood had dried on her hand where Travis's palm had pressed against hers in the truck. Chest aching, she recalled the hard set of his jaw and how he'd winced as he'd yanked at the tangled barbed wire earlier. He must've been in a lot of pain, but he'd never said a word. Instead, he'd consoled and protected her without so much as a thought for himself.

She scrubbed her palm hard, then cleaned the rest of her body, moving quickly. After turning off the water, she grabbed her towel and dried off, then wrapped it around her in a sarong and stepped out of the shower.

"Travis?"

Standing by the bathroom vanity, he looked up, his big hands stilling over Blondie's leg as he took in her appearance. He quickly turned away, checked Blondie's bandage once more, then picked her up off the vanity. "I'll step out so you can—"

"Wait," she said, touching his arm. "How's your hand?"

He was silent for a moment, then said, "It's fine."

"May I see?" She slid her hand down his arm, trying not to notice the hard bulge of his biceps and defined forearm through his wet shirt. "Please?"

He hesitated, then nodded and set Blondie on the floor. The puppy left the bathroom, sniffed around, then settled on the floor in front of the bed and closed her eyes.

Travis faced Hannah fully and held out his palm.

She cupped his hand in hers and tugged him closer to the lantern's light to examine his injury. Two deep cuts marred his tanned skin, and dried blood caked the injuries.

"It must hurt," she whispered.

"Not much."

"Will you let me clean it?" She raised her head, her eyes meeting his.

He nodded, and she reached for the first-aid kit by the

sink. She cleaned his wound carefully, then applied antiseptic. Travis had used most of the gauze to cover Blondie's leg wound, but there was just enough left to wrap around his injured palm.

When Hannah finished, she kissed his wrist. "There."

"Thank you." Travis flexed his bandaged hand and looked down at her, his gaze drifting over her mouth and down to her chest where the upper swells of her breasts pressed against the damp towel.

The desire in his eyes warmed her belly.

His cheeks flushed and he ducked his head, his jaw tightening.

"Travis?" Hannah smiled, waiting until he met her eyes again. "It's okay. I know you're a gentleman."

She'd hoped for one of his sexy smiles in return, or at least a relieved shrug. But his cheeks reddened even more as he stared back at her, and his discomfort seemed to grow.

"Am I?" he asked softly, his lips barely moving.

The sadness in his eyes made her heart ache. She reached up and cupped his jaw, smoothing her thumbs over the rough stubble lining his cheeks.

"After what you did for Liz and Zeke? For me? For all of us really." She shook her head. "How could you think otherwise?"

He didn't answer, just held her gaze, a haunted look entering his expression.

She, of all people, knew everyone had events in their past they wished they could forget. She'd already been through hell—in more ways than one. But what had happened to cause Travis to think he was less than the brave, kind man she'd come to know?

And he was just that—a strong, protective man. He could've walked away at any moment today. Could've wished her, Red, and Margaret well, then left to save himself. But he hadn't. He'd chosen to stay, and he'd risked his own life more than once for others.

"Why did you stay for Blondie?" Hannah asked. "The fire was so close and the smoke so thick, we could hardly see. You could've been trapped by that barbed wire just as easily as her, or not made it out in time. Why'd you stay?"

"She was still breathing," he rasped. "She was alive, and worth saving as much as any human." His tone turned adamant. "I don't disregard life. I don't."

"I know." Her throat closed and she swallowed hard past the knot in her throat. "You're the exact opposite of Bryan."

Travis lowered his head as his gaze moved over her, then stopped, his eyes narrowing on her arm. He touched the inner skin of her left elbow and traced his fingertip across the three-inch scar marring her skin.

"Did Bryan do this?"

Hannah nodded, recalling the pain she'd experienced when Bryan, in one of his rages, had used a knife to intimidate and bend her to his will. She recalled all the times she'd allowed Bryan to hurt and control her. The fear she'd carried for years; her refusal to take a chance on anything or anyone. Not really living at all . . . even long after she'd left him.

"You're wrong about something, you know?" She slid her hand down Travis's warm neck and over his sculpted shoulders, then pressed her palm against the center of his wide chest. "Just breathing doesn't mean you're alive."

Travis closed his eyes, a pained expression crossing his face, then refocused on her. "I need to tell you something. Years ago, I—"

"Please don't." Tears burned her eyes and she blinked them back, her fingertips fumbling over his lips. "I don't want to look back right now. I want to do like you said. I want to look forward."

She studied Travis's face, cherishing the warmth in his gentle expression and the desire in his eyes as he looked down at her. Then she pressed closer, aligned her body to him, and savored the way her soft curves filled the hard contours of his, as though, given time, they might be the perfect fit.

Oh, how she wanted that. How she wanted to know his thoughts, his dreams and hopes for the future. Wanted to kiss, laugh, and . . . maybe even love again.

"I haven't lived in a really long time," Hannah whispered, rising on her toes. "And I want to try to again"—she touched her lips to his—"with you."

CHAPTER 8

Travis closed his eyes and parted his lips; the warm press of Hannah's mouth against his and her soft breaths brushing his cheek swept through him on a rush of pleasure, making his legs tremble.

Heaven. He'd never been able to imagine it before—had never been able to conjure it with words or images. But right now, with Hannah kissing him, touching him, approving of him . . . he could feel its pleasurable glow in every dark corner of his heart.

"Hannah . . ."

Her tongue touched his, then retreated, her sweet taste flooding his senses just before she lifted her mouth from his.

Her wide eyes had darkened to a midnight blue and her pink lips trembled. "You don't want me?"

The wounded expression crossing her face turned the pleasure spiraling through his veins into pain. "Yes." He cradled her face and lowered his head, whispering, "I want you."

More than anything. Body hardening, he caressed his thumb over her reddened lips, ran his palms over the delicate skin of her neck and smooth shoulders, then rested his hand over the upper swell of her breast.

Her heart pounded rapidly beneath his touch and he dipped his head, kissing her flushed skin. A sound of pleasure left her lips, making him eager to hear her satisfied sigh again. He trailed more kisses over the upper swells of her breasts, above her collarbone and up her neck, pausing when he reached the sensitive skin behind her ear.

Travis pulled in a strong, steadying breath, the fresh scent of her damp hair filling his lungs, then touched his lips to the soft shell of her ear. "I want you," he whispered. "But we've been through so much today, and when I make love to you, I want it to be because you know me—all of me—and want me for who I am. Not because of something I've done, or as a result of circumstance." He forced himself to release her and step back. "So let me be the gentleman you say I am. Let me not rush this."

Hannah touched her lips with shaky fingertips and stared up at him. Her chest lifted with swift breaths against the towel wrapped around her. "You said you'd do anything I asked."

He had to lean forward to catch her soft words, and they stoked the desire inside him as well as the guilt. "Yes. And I meant it." He flexed his hands by his sides. "If you ask me to, I will."

She studied his face a few moments more, then reached out, her fingers fiddling nervously with a button on his shirt. "Then, will . . ." Tears welled in her eyes and one spilled onto her lashes. "Will you at least hold me?"

Heart aching, Travis wrapped his arms around her and pulled her in, sliding his leg between hers and holding her as tight as he could without hurting her. "All night."

Vibrations and the heavy whir of helicopter blades woke Travis the next morning.

He opened his eyes, and the large window beside the hotel bed caught his attention. The curtains were drawn, but through a small opening in the middle, beneath the dim glow of the rising sun, he could see emergency response vehicles pass along the highway in front of the motel, one after another, in a long line.

Scratching sounds and a high-pitched yip emerged from the foot of the bed near the door.

Travis eased up on one elbow and peered over the bed. Blondie's big, black eyes blinked up at him, her tail wagging furiously across the carpet.

"You need to go out, don't you, girl?" he whispered. "Just a minute, okay?"

A soft, feminine murmur sounded, and Travis looked down, smiling at the auburn curls spilled across his bare chest and abs.

Hannah. He hated to wake her.

After her soul-searing kiss last night, he had showered while she'd dressed in a T-shirt. Then he had donned a pair of jeans and joined her on the bed. She had moved right into his arms, reminding him of his promise and kissing him softly one more time before settling her cheek onto his chest.

He had tucked her head beneath his chin and wrapped his arms around her, gliding his palm in slow circles across her back until she'd fallen asleep. Minutes later, he'd drifted off, too, and they'd stayed that way all night.

Travis's smile fell. Yesterday had been the first day in years that he hadn't sat down to pen and paper and written at least one line to Margaret.

He trailed a shaky hand through Hannah's hair, unsure of how he felt about the realization. Guilt was there, lurking deep inside him—as it always did. But something else had joined it, warring for his attention.

Hannah shifted against him, nuzzling closer to his chest, her soft breaths sweeping over his skin.

Just breathing doesn't mean you're alive.

Her words had whispered through his mind all night, tangling with fractured dreams, and reemerging each time he'd stirred to consciousness. Even now, as he savored the comforting sensation of Hannah's soft body draped over his, they returned to haunt him, bringing his own assertion with them.

I don't disregard life. . . .

But he had—and still did. He disregarded his own.

Not only had he stolen Niki's life from her in a selfish, horrifying way, he'd also destroyed his own life long before his broken existence had ever crashed into Niki's thriving one. He'd poisoned his body with liquor and drugs and had focused only on who he had been rather than who, given time and effort, he might have become.

Yesterday, he'd faced death again when flames had engulfed Paradise Peak. The violent heat ripping through homes and buildings, scorching the earth and spiraling across the road, had seemed intent upon stealing his soul.

And yet, even though a good man like Ben had lost his life saving others, Travis—a man merely a fraction of Ben's worth—had escaped it all with no more than a minor injury.

Hell if he knew why he'd been allowed to emerge from his reckless past, busted up but still breathing. Or why he'd survived the wildfire last night with a renewed chance to start over and become someone of value. But he had.

He'd been given a precious gift, whether he deserved it or not, and he'd be a fool to throw it away again.

Travis ran his finger over Hannah's smooth cheek. It had taken all he'd had not to give in to her last night. The sweet taste of her kiss, the soft feel of her beneath his hands, and the way she'd looked up to him . . . The depth of trust and admiration in her eyes . . .

He had wanted her so much—still did—and for the first time in his life, he could envision how good it might feel to put down roots. To have a home, a family, and be cared for. To love and be loved.

She'd asked him to move forward with her—to not look back—and help her live again. He couldn't do that without telling her the truth about his past, but for now, he had to set his shame aside and make room for this new emotion springing to life inside him. This sensation of . . . hope.

Another helicopter whirred overhead, rattling the window, and the pup ran to the door and resumed scratching the wood.

"Hannah." Travis hugged her close. "We've gotta get up."

She stirred, rubbed her cheek against him, then propped her chin on his chest and looked up at him. A small smile curved her lips, but the beating of helicopter blades grew louder outside, and realization dawned in her eyes, drawing her smile down with it.

"Sounds like a war zone out there." She sat up, pushing the long fall of her hair out of her face, and looked toward the window. "Where will we go first?"

"The detour from Paradise Peak led here last night, so Red and Margaret had to have come this way. I noticed a lot of people camping in parking lots last night when we came in. They might have pulled into one of those lots." Travis swung his legs over the side of the bed and stood. "We'll check this motel again and each parking lot on the way into town. If we don't find them there, we'll go back to the Black Bear Lodge up the road and look for them there."

By the time they'd dressed and walked Blondie in the small strip of grass by the motel's parking lot, the sun had fully risen, peeking between large, gloomy clouds and highlighting last night's destruction.

The distant mountain range had darkened to a deep grayish black and smoke rose in slow curls above the charred landscape. Each rocky peak and its curving slope resembled a large chunk of coal—large swaths of ground appeared ravaged and barren.

A keen sense of loss moved through Travis as he surveyed the damage the once majestic mountains had suffered. He shook his head. "How in the hell did we make it out of that?"

Hannah, standing by his side, entwined her hand with his and squeezed. "You were there, looking out for us." She smiled up at him, then looked at the sky, a grateful expression appearing on her face. "And we weren't on those big rocks alone."

Travis tilted his head back, absorbing the sun's warmth on his face before a dark cloud rolled in and obscured its glow. Heavy thunderheads and a gray haze settled over the view, the scent of rain hanging on the cool air.

"I wonder if Ruby, Juno, and the new mare made it out." Hannah's tone weakened. "Or if there'll be anything left when we go back."

A chill crept up Travis's spine at the thought of the horses running through thick smoke and dodging fire. "They're strong horses," he said, consoling himself as much as Hannah. "As for the ranch"—he lifted her hand and kissed her fingertips—"we'll cross that bridge when we get to it."

Hannah didn't speak, but she squeezed his hand harder as she studied the mountains in the distance.

Blondie yipped, and Hannah bent and scooped her up, cradling the pup against her chest. Travis placed his hand at the small of Hannah's back and they walked across the motel parking lot to the office.

The aroma of hot coffee greeted them as they entered the building. Several people stood in the small lobby area, sipping out of small paper cups, chatting, and craning their necks to look earnestly out the window. Others sat on the floor, some with children in their laps or by their sides, and slept upright, leaning against the wall.

Margaret and Red were not among them.

Hannah leaned against Travis with a sound of disappointment. "They're not here."

"It's okay," Travis said. "We'll find them."

"Travis." Dale Henderson, manager of the motel, whom Travis had met the night before, greeted him from behind the reception desk and waved them over. His blond hair stood up in thick tufts as though he'd raked his hands through it for hours. "How'd the room work out? Did you get any sleep?"

"Yeah, thanks." Travis eyed the dark circles under the other man's eyes. "More than you, I'm guessing. Did you work this desk all night?"

Dale nodded. "Didn't want to leave anyone out in the cold. All our rooms are full, and so is Black Bear Lodge, and we still have a revolving door of people coming in, looking for a place to stay. The city's setting up a shelter at the high school, so I figured I'd at least offer a roof for as many people as we can until it opens." He grabbed two paper cups from the counter and held them up. "Can I interest you in some coffee?"

"Please." Travis glanced around at the dim lobby. "Power's still out?"

"Yep. From what I hear, the main line to the power substation was destroyed, and it'll take several days to replace it." Dale grabbed a carafe of hot coffee from a small table nearby and filled both of the paper cups. "I've got one small generator out back and volunteers are bringing in two more later this morning. They help, but I wish we had one of those big diesel ones." He shrugged. "We're a small joint though, and they're a bit too rich for my budget." He handed Travis one of the cups of coffee, then passed the second to Hannah. "You want creamer, Miss . . . ?"

"Hannah." Smiling, she took it. "No, thank you. This is perfect."

Blondie, catching a whiff of the coffee, squirmed in Hannah's arms and strained toward the cup.

"Here, I've got her." Travis slipped his free hand under Blondie and transferred her from Hannah's arms into the crook of his elbow. He took the cup of coffee Dale offered and sipped the black brew as the whir of helicopter blades returned. "I noticed a stream of emergency vehicles rolling in this morning. Have you received any updates about the fires?"

Dale nodded. "From what I've heard, a few are still smoldering, but the rain from last night and the storms they're expecting today are supposed to help tamp 'em down." He pointed out the window, where a helicopter traveled toward the mountain range. "National Guard and firefighters are out, conducting searches for survivors and taking stock of what they can access. Most of the roads are closed—supposed to stay that way till they're sure they got all the fires contained—and volunteers are pouring in to help. Trouble is, with downed cell towers, no landlines, and no power, it's been hard to coordinate. Everyone's just chipping in where they can."

A baby cried, and Travis glanced around the lobby again, noticing a couple huddled together on a small sofa.

The man spoke in soothing tones to the baby cradled in his arms, and the woman beside him held a little girl in her lap, combing her fingers through the child's tangled hair, a stoic expression on her face.

Dale gestured toward the couple, speaking low. "Some families only got out with what was on their backs and don't know if there's anything to go home to." His tone thickened. "Some families didn't make it out at all."

Travis surveyed the group of strangers, wanting to do so much but having next to nothing to offer.

Dale sighed. "We're tough, though, and take care of our own. We're gonna rise up out of this." He tipped his chin toward Hannah. "You find your people yet?"

The tears in Hannah's eyes made Travis's own burn. He set his coffee cup on the counter and slid an arm around her.

"No," she said. "Not yet."

"Could you please check again?" Hannah raised her voice over the noisy chatter filling the lobby of Black Bear Lodge. "The names are Red Bartlett and Margaret Owens."

The young woman behind the check-in desk flipped through a stack of papers on a clipboard. "They're not on our room occupant list and"—she reached toward the keyboard in front of her, then stopped, her hands spreading helplessly in midair—"our systems are down, so I can't check our digital records to confirm check-ins."

"Maybe they came by looking for a room but you were booked, and you might remember having to turn them away?" Hannah placed her hands on the counter and leaned closer. "Red's about six two, gray hair, mustache. And Margaret's about my height. She's got long gray hair and brown eyes, and she wears high heels all the time— even when she's running from a fire so—" Her voice cracked as she tried for a smile, and she licked her trembling lips. "So you might've heard her clacking around the lobby. And you might've heard Red grumping because sometimes she'll boss him around and—"

"I'm sorry, ma'am. I really am." A strand of hair slipped from the young clerk's topknot and fell over her forehead. She puffed it out of her eyes and shook her head. "But I don't recall meeting anyone of their description and their names aren't on the list as being checked into a room. I have no way of finding them with so many people. . . ."

The clerk's words faded beneath a renewed onslaught of voices. Hannah glanced over her shoulder at the crowd of people standing, sitting, and milling about the large hotel's upscale lobby. Voices—nervous, fearful, and excited— echoed against marble floors and vaulted ceilings. Several people, holding their cell phones high at different angles, searched in vain for a wireless signal, and others paced along a wall of windows, peering outside at the crowds milling about the parking lot.

After speaking with Dale, Hannah had driven Red's truck from the motel where they'd spent the night back into the downtown district of Crystal Rock. It had taken forty-five minutes to make the ten-mile drive on account of traffic, new detours, and delays as they'd pulled over to allow long lines of emergency vehicles to pass and make their way toward Paradise Peak. Travis, holding Blondie, had sat in the passenger seat and peered out the window at each parking lot they'd driven through, searching for any sign of Margaret's or Vernon's car.

Despite not finding either of the cars along the drive, Travis had assured her there was still a good chance Margaret and Red had made it out of Paradise Peak safely and had checked into the Black Bear Lodge. But it had become clear, after scouring the crowded parking lot of the hotel and standing in line for over an hour to check with the clerk for a second time, that Margaret and Red were not safely tucked in one of the hotel beds as Travis had suggested . . . or anywhere else they'd looked.

A happy shout rang out across the lobby and a little girl around six or seven years old darted through the throng of people into the open arms of an elderly man who hugged her and kissed her cheeks.

Hannah bit her lip as a fresh onslaught of tears dampened her lashes. *Oh, Red, where are you?*

"Ma'am?"

A hand, light and consoling, touched Hannah's shoulder. Wiping her eyes, she faced the clerk again.

"Ma'am, is Mr. Bartlett your father?"

Hannah shook her head. "He's my uncle, but I lost my father years ago so . . ." *He's the only father I've ever known.* Eyes burning, she blinked hard to keep more tears at bay, then said, "Red is my uncle, and Margaret is a frien—"

No. Friend wasn't accurate. Margaret had lived with them for a year and had fussed over Hannah's happiness more than she'd fussed with her. And right now, Hannah missed everything about Margaret, idiosyncrasies and all.

"Margaret is family, too," Hannah added.

"Well, I've written Mr. Bartlett and Ms. Owens's names down, and if they do happen to check in, I promise you I'll let them know you're looking for them." The clerk grabbed a different clipboard, flipped to a clean sheet of paper, then hesitated, pen in hand. "May I have your name, please, so I can tell them who's searching for them? And I'd also like to add you to my list."

Hannah frowned. "Your room list? But I'm staying at the other—"

"No, ma'am," the clerk said gently. "Not to the room

list. I'd like to add you to my list of survivors. That way, if someone comes by searching for you, I can at least let them know you're okay."

Hannah stared as memories resurfaced. Absentmindedly, she touched the small scar on the inside of her elbow, then nodded. "Hannah Newsome."

The clerk began writing. "Thank you, Ms. New—"

"And Travis Miller." Hannah stayed the clerk's hand with hers, then glanced out the window, peering through the smoky haze and between groups of people until she noticed Travis still standing on the sidewalk outside where she'd left him.

Travis turned to the side, holding Blondie and scanning the crowds for Red and Margaret. He stood among the chaotic movements in the parking lot, his tall, muscular frame a steady rock amid a turbulent stream of strangers. His big hands, strong but gentle, stroked Blondie's back in slow, sure movements.

Something warm and comforting unfurled inside her at the remembered feel of his callused palm drifting over her back in soothing circles, his touch tender and patient.

She'd been so grateful to have him by her side last night, and again this morning.

"Would you please add Travis Miller to the survivor list as well?" Hannah asked.

The clerk nodded, finished writing Hannah's name, then moved to the next line on the paper and wrote Travis's, too.

Hannah studied the names, printed in ink on the list of survivors, and the sight brought her a small measure of comfort. "Thank you."

"I wish I could've helped you more." The clerk smiled, but it was tinged with sadness. "I hope you find them."

Hannah thanked her once more, then left the lobby and joined Travis outside.

His expression brightened when she joined him, a glimmer of hope lighting his eyes. "Any luck this time?"

"They're not here." She petted Blondie and concentrated on the soft fur beneath her fingertips rather than the hollow forming in the pit of her stomach. "It feels like they're not anywhere."

Travis's strong palm glided through her hair and cupped the back of her head gently. She closed her eyes and felt his lips brush her forehead just as thunder rolled softly overhead.

"Is there another town nearby?" he asked.

"Sutter Gap is thirty miles west of here. It's the only town I can think of that the detour hasn't closed access to. All the other roads are blocked off."

Car horns honked on the traffic-jammed streets surrounding them and the wind picked up, carrying a stronger scent of smoke and rain across the hotel's parking lot.

"Another storm's brewing." Travis slid his hand down her arm and threaded his fingers between hers. "Let's go back to the motel until it passes. I'll drop you and Blondie off and find us all something to eat. Then we'll head to Sutter Gap and look for them there."

Hannah nodded and reached for Blondie. On the way back to the motel, she tried to hold on to that small lift of hope still lingering in her chest, but every mile they traveled stretched on endlessly amid heavy traffic and frantic pedestrians searching for loved ones, and by the time they reached the motel's small parking lot, the world looked bleaker than ever.

Hannah stared out the truck's windshield at the closed door of their motel room. Rain sprinkled across the windows of the truck and thunder sounded.

She hugged Blondie closer to her chest. "What would we do without them?"

Travis's hand left the steering wheel and squeezed her knee. "Hey, let's not talk like that right now. For all we know—"

"They're tucked safe in a big-ass hotel bed?" A sound, half laughter and half sob, escaped her lips as she faced him. "You already mentioned that, and they weren't there."

"I'm just trying t—"

"To help," she said. "I know. But we've checked every parking lot, hotel, and business in Crystal Rock and they're nowhere to be found." Her throat tightened. "They're nowhere, Travis."

His brown eyes, solemn, strayed from her face and looked over her right shoulder. The rain grew heavier, slapping against the windows of the truck with each push of the wind, and the parking lot, devoid of streetlights below the dark cover of clouds, seemed desolate.

"I mean, they should be here—somewhere in Crystal Rock," she said, her voice shaking. "I can't imagine them driving all the way into Sutter Gap with the kind of chaos there was last night, so they should be here. Something has happened to them."

Travis, still staring over her right shoulder, narrowed his eyes. "You sure about that?"

"Oh, Lord, I don't know." She dragged a hand over her eyes, then faced him again. "And I'm sorry for taking it out on you. I'm just scared, and have no idea what to—"

Wait a minute. Was he . . . smiling?

"You . . ." Heart skipping, she touched a fingertip to the dimple forming beside his mouth as his smile widened. "Tell me you're looking at them right now."

His dark eyes met hers; then he bent his head and kissed her, his lips warm and gentle as he whispered, "Look in your side mirror."

She did, and there, right above the phrase OBJECTS IN MIRROR ARE CLOSER THAN THEY APPEAR, Red's reflection jogged across the parking lot toward the truck, his gray head ducked against the rain and wind. Margaret trailed close behind him, clutching her high heels in one hand and holding them over the top of her head as she splashed through puddles.

Hannah squealed, then laughed as hot tears poured down her cheeks. "They're okay!"

Blondie jumped, her ears perking up as Hannah scrambled for the door handle.

"I'm sorry, Blondie." Hannah opened the door, then hesitated as rain splashed against the seat. She glanced at Travis. "Could you . . . ?"

"Got her," Travis said, transferring Blondie into the seat as Hannah exited the truck.

Four swift strides across the wet pavement and Hannah was swept into one of Red's bear hugs, his arms banding tightly around her.

"Dear Lord!" Still laughing and gasping for breath in Red's tight embrace, she shouted above the heavy fall of rain, "I thought we'd lost you!"

"Not a chance!" Red hugged Hannah tighter, then released her and stepped to the side so Margaret could embrace her.

"Oh, my dear girl. We've been looking everywhere for you!" Margaret sobbed, her hands gripping Hannah tight. "I'm so glad you're okay."

Hannah hugged her back. "Same here." She laughed and smoothed her hand over Margaret's wet, tangled hair. "But your hair's getting soaked, and your shoes—"

"Oh, forget the shoes." Margaret's arm jerked behind Hannah's back and Hannah heard the high heels thump against the pavement. "We've found you, and that's all that matters. And we're not alone." She gestured over her shoulder toward the other side of the parking lot where her car was parked. Another car was parked beside it with the headlights and inside dome light turned on, and three faces, their features blurred by the rain, looked back at them. "We ran across Gloria and Vernon not long after we made it out of Paradise Peak."

Hope returning full force, Hannah squinted against the rain and strained for a clearer view. "Are Liz and Zeke with them?"

Margaret nodded and her chin trembled. She wiped her wet cheeks with the back of her hand, the rain and her tears mixing together. "Vernon told us about Ben. Liz hasn't said a word since they left Paradise Peak." Her expression contorted on a sob. "It could've so easily been you caught in that fire. Or Red . . . or any of us, really." She hugged Hannah again. "Red and I were so worried, and we're so glad you're okay."

Hannah cried with her, waved at the group sitting in Vernon's car, then said, "I'm going to tell Vernon, Gloria, and Liz to come in out of the rain. We have a room, and you're all staying with us until we can go back to Paradise Peak. I'm not taking my eyes off any of you until then."

The truck door thudded shut and Margaret released Hannah. She looked over Hannah's shoulder, her wet lashes blinking furiously against raindrops, and a shaky smile appeared.

"Travis." Margaret held out her hands, her shoulders jerking on joyful sobs as she approached him. "You brought our girl back to us. You brought her back. . . ."

Hannah, shivering beneath the cold onslaught of rain, smiled as Margaret and Red both embraced Travis. Then she headed for Vernon's car to invite the rest of the group inside. But the expression she'd glimpsed on Travis's face as Margaret embraced him stayed with her, and her brisk steps slowed, water splashing the pants legs of her jeans as she stopped in a puddle. She looked back, peering at Travis's face through the rain, and noticed the same emotion. Instead of the pleased relief she'd expected to see in his warm, brown eyes as Margaret thanked him, all she saw was guilt.

CHAPTER 9

Hannah leaned over the bed in the motel room and smiled.

Zeke, eyes closed and breathing deeply, rolled to his side and draped one arm around Blondie, who blinked heavy eyes, then snuggled closer against the boy's middle.

"Did they finally drift off?"

Hannah nodded and glanced at Vernon, who looked at her expectantly. He sat on a cot beside the window, a book in his hands, and the lantern sitting on the window ledge cast a soft glow of light over his lap.

"Blondie was tuckered out after playing so much this afternoon," Hannah whispered. "And Zeke..." She looked back down at the young boy, her smile slipping as she studied the flush along his tearstained cheeks. "He misses his dad. He's hurting so much."

And so was Liz. Hannah's gaze moved over her friend, who slept in the bed next to Zeke, her back to Hannah and her shoulders moving in rhythmic breaths.

Earlier, after reuniting with Red and Margaret, Hannah had run through the rain to Vernon's car, informed them all the rooms were taken in both the One Stop Motel and the Black Bear Lodge, and had invited them to stay in the room with her and Travis. Accepting the offer, Vernon had thanked her; then he, Gloria, and Hannah had quickly unloaded the few belongings they'd managed to pack before evacuating and hustled inside the motel room to dry off.

Once inside, Vernon and Gloria had shared relieved embraces with Hannah and Travis, and Zeke had been thrilled to reunite with Blondie. The little boy had thrown his arms around the puppy, his pain at having lost his father the night before fading for an hour or two as he'd hugged and stroked his pet. Blondie had perked up at the sight of her owner and, despite her minor injury, had played on the floor with Zeke for quite some time, chasing a small stick Red had found outside and licking Zeke's chin with gusto.

Margaret and Gloria had taken turns in the bathroom, showering, drying their hair, and donning clean clothes, while Red and Travis had driven to a nearby truck-stop diner that had used backup generators to open for a few hours and provide a limited menu of meals. They'd brought back to-go meals for everyone—including Blondie, who enjoyed a tasty feast of wet and dry dog food on account of a generous donation from the diner's owner.

Red and Travis had experienced equal success in the One Stop Motel's office, where Dale had offered them the last two available cots for Gloria and Vernon to use in the room, and a large thermos of coffee, several paper cups, and a small bag filled with individually sized creamers.

By the time everyone had showered, dressed in clean clothes, and eaten, the afternoon thunderstorm had rolled away, and the sun had slowly set, leaving behind a cool breeze that carried wisps of smoke that periodically covered the bright stars in the dark sky.

Full bellies and a comfortable, quiet place to rest had caused everyone's eyes to grow heavy, and Gloria, stretched out on a cot by the far wall, had been the first to fall asleep. Margaret, sharing the spacious double bed with Liz and Zeke, had been next.

But Liz had stared at the ceiling for what seemed like ages, had not responded to any of Hannah's attempts at conversation, and eventually drifted off with tears still seeping from her closed eyes. Zeke, whom Hannah had hummed to softly for over an hour, had finally joined her.

"You should get some sleep, too," Vernon said. He closed his book and scooted to the edge of his cot. "You're welcome to use my cot."

"Oh, no." Hannah raised her hand to still his movements. "Thank you, but I got a good night's sleep last night, and right now, I don't think I could sleep a wink, no matter how hard I try."

Vernon nodded, a small smile of understanding appearing before he settled back into his cot and resumed reading his book.

Hannah eased away from the bed, stretched tired, aching muscles, then cast one last look at Zeke and Liz before leaving the room.

Outside, a cool breeze ruffled her hair, but the night air had warmed a bit. Slow, even breathing whispered to her right where Travis slumped in a soft camping chair beside the door of the motel room, his chin resting on his left shoulder and his broad chest lifting on rhythmic breaths. The jean jacket he'd draped over his upper body an hour ago had fallen to his lap.

Smiling, Hannah slid the jacket back up his muscular frame, tucked it around his waist, and, being careful not to disturb him, brushed her lips across his forehead in a soft kiss.

He didn't stir, just continued breathing deep and even, his thick, dark hair, stubbled jaw, and sensual lips all the more appealing beneath the faint glow of stars that brightened between the passing wisps of smoke overhead.

"Sleeping beauty still knocked out?" Red called softly. His gray mustache lifted with his grin as he looked back at her from his seated position on the lowered tailgate of his truck.

Hannah stifled a laugh and joined him, hopping up onto the edge of the tailgate and finding a comfortable position. "Yep. He's had a rough couple of days."

"Haven't we all." Red's bushy, gray eyebrows lifted. "And what about mine?"

"Your sleeping beauty?"

When Red nodded, Hannah glanced back at the door of the motel room, her chest warming as she thought of Margaret sitting on the floor with Zeke earlier that afternoon, drying his eyes and coaxing him into laughter as they'd played with Blondie. Margaret had sat by Liz's side for over two hours after that, holding her hand and never speaking—offering silent, unconditional comfort with tears rolling down her own cheeks.

Hannah smiled at the memory of Margaret, an hour ago, hogging the bathroom mirror to braid her long hair, fasten it with a pink bow, then apply three different facial moisturizers before easing carefully into the bed, propping a pillow at just the right angle behind her head to avoid what she referred to as neck wrinkles and suggesting Gloria do the same.

Only Margaret. Hannah laughed and shook her head. "She snores."

Red tipped his head back and chuckled, but his laughter slowly died as he stared up at the sky. "Ain't it something?" he asked softly.

Hannah followed his gaze to the thin puffs of gray smoke that drifted on the wind, stretching and swirling in front of winking stars.

"Yesterday, in Paradise, this sky was red and that smoke

so thick, you could choke on it," Red said. "And to see it now . . ." His voice thickened. "I should've seen it then, before it hit us. Before it reached Paradise and burned it all to hell. Before it killed good people like Ben and left spouses and children like Liz and Zeke with nothing. I should've sensed it, should've—"

"Don't do that," Hannah whispered. "Please don't blame yourself. Pain does that. It makes you want to blame any and everyone. Once things settle, there'll be more than enough blame passed around, and no one person will be responsible for all of it. No one could've foreseen how awful this would become."

"You did." His eyes fixed on hers, regret shadowing the once lighthearted blue depths. "You tried to tell me. You knew what was coming."

"Because I was afraid." Hannah pressed a hand to her chest. "In here. All the time." Eyes burning, she blinked hard, then refocused on the smoke and stars above them. "Did I tell you that when we went to Black Bear Lodge, looking for you and Margaret, the clerk I spoke with added my name to her survivor list?" She laughed, humorless and full of pain. "Funny, that. After I left Bryan, that's what people called me, too—a survivor. A word like that should make you feel strong. Powerful, even. And it did. But inside, I still hurt so much. I was still afraid of him. Of strangers, and the world. Of who I was."

She glanced at Red. The confusion in his eyes made her mouth curve into a sad smile. "How could part of me have been strong enough to walk away, and the other part still too afraid to live? I may be a survivor, but sometimes I still feel like a victim, and I could not find a way to reconcile the two. Some people can't understand that there's no time limit on the fear or the pain—it shows up whenever it chooses."

Red grimaced, his eyes glistening beneath the brief glow

of the stars before another swath of smoke rolled in and cast a shadow over his face. "And here I was, telling you to focus on the good. Demanding you move on and forget."

Hannah covered his hand with hers. "No. There's nothing wrong with looking for the good in life—and in people—instead of the bad." She squeezed his hand. "There was good in Bryan. Otherwise, I wouldn't have fallen in love with him. But there was bad, too. There's bad in all of us, I suppose."

Red sighed, his free hand curling around her upper arm as he leaned against her. "I guess you and I should try to be more like each other, then."

"Yes," Hannah whispered. "That's the sweet spot I was thinking of."

"So tell me," he said softly, "what good things should we look for now?"

Hannah tipped her chin in the direction of the mountain range, its rugged ridges and deep valleys still damaged and dark. "When the roads open, we go back to the ranch and look for the good that's left on the mountain. We find the horses, check the lodge and cabins, and survey the land to assess the extent of the damage. Then, if need be, we rebuild."

The breeze picked up and the curtains of smoke above them parted, revealing bright stars and midnight sky.

Hannah smiled. "And we bring our most valuable asset with us."

When she didn't elaborate, Red nudged her with his shoulder. "And that is . . . ?"

"You." She patted the back of his hand, then looked over her shoulder at the closed door of the motel room. "Margaret." Her gaze moved to Travis, a warm flutter stirring in her belly at the sight of his handsome face. "And Travis." She faced Red again and smiled wider. "Our family."

"Family?" A pleased expression crossed Red's face and moisture seeped into the crow's feet beside his eyes. "You mean Margaret and her swan napkins? And a stranger like Travis?"

Hannah laughed. "I'll get over the swan napkins." She lifted her hands in the air. "Who knows? I may learn to love them."

"And Travis?" Red asked quietly, his solemn eyes searching hers. "Are you learning to love him, too?"

Was she? Hannah thought of how tender Travis had been when he'd kissed and held her last night. How secure his touch had felt in the truck, shielding her from danger. And how sincere her words had been when he'd asked her the same question as Ben.

"I trust Travis," Hannah whispered, glancing back at his sleeping form. "He's a good man. Gentle, protective, and kind. A hero, really, after all he did yesterday. I believe in him." She smiled. "And, yes. I think I may be falling in love with him."

Red chuckled softly, happiness lighting his expression. "Can't say I'm not happy to hear that. I admire him as much as you, and considering all that praise, I imagine he's one person you'd be hard pressed to find any bad in."

Hannah's smile slipped as she thought of the guilt that had haunted Travis's eyes earlier that day when Margaret had hugged him. Some dark secret lurked inside him—a hidden pain of some kind, maybe? One she might be able to persuade him to share with her sometime soon? Once he learned to trust her as much as she trusted him?

"I don't know," she said quietly. "But I hope to learn everything about him."

Red sat up straighter, tipped his head back, and blew out a heavy breath. "I've been thinking about Ben a lot today. About how much he'll miss out on with Liz and

Zeke. And how much they'll miss him." He looked down, his hands gripping his knees. "And I've been thinking about Margaret, and how much time I've wasted standing on the sidelines. I figure it's time to tell her how I feel. I mean, what's the worst that could happen?" He shrugged and tried for a smile, but it fell flat. "She turns me down, and I move on, right?"

Hannah's heart broke at the thought of Margaret rejecting Red. "She'd be a fool to turn you down."

Red's tone turned somber and concern filled his expression. "But you wouldn't hold it against her if she did, would you?"

Hannah shook her head, the question alone making her love Red even more—if that was possible. "I love you both. And I want you both to be happy. In whatever form that takes."

Red smiled, hugged her close, and kissed her forehead. "That's my girl." He kept one arm around her, and she settled against him as they looked up at the smoke and stars. Red spotted the brightest star still visible among the drifting smoke and pointed at it. "Make a wish, and maybe the ranch will still be standing when we get back. Maybe everything will turn out good for both of us."

Hannah closed her eyes, hope stirring within her chest, and whispered, "Maybe it will."

Five days later, on the third of March, Travis returned to Paradise Peak in Red's truck, traveling the same road on which he'd first arrived. Only this time, Hannah drove the truck toward the steep mountain instead of Red, and she had formed a bad habit of taking her eyes off the road—and putting them on Travis.

Travis grinned. Not that he was complaining.

". . . and he said he may make a move." Hannah glanced

at him again, her expression serious as her attention focused on his mouth. "What do you think?"

Travis frowned and reached for the steering wheel, straightening the truck's direction. "Who?"

"Sorry." Hannah, cheeks flushing, faced the road again, tightened her grip on the steering wheel, and narrowed her eyes as though to prove she was concentrating.

Travis studied the smooth curve of her cheek and pink lips. "Who exactly is making a move?" Carl, maybe? "And who are they making this move on?"

Hannah, of course. Travis gritted his teeth and rubbed his hands over his jeans. He'd known from the moment he'd met the guy that Carl had a thing for Hannah.

And what guy wouldn't? With her sharp mind, courage, and compassion for those around her, she'd win any man's heart in record time.

"Red," Hannah stressed. "He told me he's thinking of telling Margaret how he feels about her. Haven't you heard a word I've said?"

No. Face heating, Travis rubbed a hand over the back of his neck. He'd been too busy enjoying having her to himself for a change. He'd watched the way the auburn strands of her hair lifted on the wind blowing through the lowered window as she'd driven out of Crystal Rock's city limits toward Paradise Peak, and had wondered for the thousandth time when he'd be able to run his hands through the silky strands again.

The bright afternoon sun pouring through the windshield, flooding the cab, and the warm March air had brought out a rosy bloom above her cheekbones. Her lips had parted and curved up as she'd spoken, making Travis itch to lean over and cover her mouth with his. To gather her taste on his tongue and see if she was as sweet as he remembered.

And it'd been so long since he'd kissed her. . . .

The first night he and Hannah had spent at the One Stop Motel had been full of worry, fear, and sadness over the devastation the wildfire had wrought. But there'd also been so much comfort in holding Hannah throughout the night. The remembered feel of her lips on his, her warm weight draped over his bigger frame, and the steady throb of her heart against his chest as they'd slept had been sheer heaven.

But the five nights that had followed had been completely different—not bad, per se—but different. The small motel room had been comfortable when he and Hannah had been the only occupants, but the limited space had quickly become inconvenient with the addition of five adults, one toddler, and a pup.

Each night Margaret, Liz, Zeke, and Blondie had taken up residence in the double bed. Vernon and Gloria slept in cots on either side of the bed and Hannah had offered to sleep on a stack of thick blankets on the floor.

Travis and Red had volunteered to sleep outside in Red's truck. Only, on the first night, Travis had fallen asleep in a chair outside the motel room. He'd woken up with a crick in his neck and a wicked backache. The second night, he'd moved to the truck's cab, leaned back on the bench seat as far as he could go and tried to stretch his legs out, but that hadn't worked out much better. So by the third night, he'd tossed a blanket in the bed of the truck, stretched out on it, and spent the first hour or so of the evening staring up at the stars and watching the smoke clear.

Just as he had done each night during his hike to Paradise Peak. But instead of thinking of Margaret, his guilty past, and what steps to take to atone for the wrong he'd committed, his thoughts had been filled mostly with Hannah. He'd thought of a thousand different ways he'd like to make her feel safe and happy again. He'd dreamed of holding and kissing her every day from here on out. Imagined her looking up at him with something more than admiration and respect in her eyes. Something more like love.

But he'd also thought of Red and Paradise Peak. He'd wondered how Red's ranch and the horses had fared during the wildfire and hoped there'd be at least something left of it all when they returned. He'd thought of the sad, fearful expressions on strangers' faces as they'd sat in the One Stop Motel lobby and waited to see if they had a home left when they returned to the mountain. He thought of Gloria, Vernon, Liz, and Zeke, and wondered how difficult it would be for them to rebuild their homes and find their feet again.

And in the darkest hours before dawn, Travis's thoughts had returned to Margaret and the pain he'd caused. The guilt had returned, too, and he'd wished and prayed for hours that he could change the past. That he could roll back the clock, erase his selfish actions, and start over. Put his history behind him and begin anew, as Hannah had asked him to.

But he couldn't move forward with Hannah without telling her the truth. And how would she react when he did?

"You were jealous." Hannah darted glances at him again, a pleased expression on her face.

"Jealous?" he asked.

"Of someone," she countered, her eyebrows raising. "When I said he was going to make a move, you thought I was talking about someone making a move on me, didn't you?"

He shifted uncomfortably in his seat. "Maybe."

"Maybe, as in yes." She watched the road for a moment, then asked, "Whom did you think I was talking about?"

Travis was tempted to evade the question, but noticing

the earnest curiosity on her face, he cleared his throat. "Carl."

Hannah's lips twitched.

He sat up in his seat. "Well?"

"Well, what?"

"Aren't you going to"—he spread his hands—"I don't know, say something?"

"About Carl?"

He bit back a growl of frustration. "Yes."

"No. There's nothing to say because I don't think of him." She glanced at Travis, her smile growing, then refocused on the road. "I'm too busy thinking about you."

The conviction in her soft voice drained the tension from his limbs. He lifted his hand and sifted her tousled hair through his fingers, the warmth of her smooth neck making his palm tingle and his body hum.

"That's a coincidence," he said softly, "because I can't get you out of my head either."

Or my heart. Travis pulled in a sharp breath, his fingers pausing in the bright strands of her hair as the realization set in. Somewhere, in the midst of working together, evading the fire, and searching for Red and Margaret, he had fallen in love with Hannah. And if, once he told her the truth, she couldn't forgive him—couldn't find a way to love him despite his past—he had no idea how he'd move on without her.

A gasp, full of dismay, escaped Hannah. "Oh, no."

"What?" Travis followed the direction of her gaze to the right side of the road as the truck climbed a steep incline.

There, a large wooden sign, once bearing the words "Paradise Peak," had been charred to a blackened slab; the top half of it had broken off and dangled at a precarious angle toward the ground. The tree line, once towering and thick, had been decimated by the fire. Flames had blazed through all the leaves, leaving behind black, twig-like branches that looked as though a stiff breeze could knock them to the ground.

"Everything's gone," Hannah whispered in a strangled voice.

Travis leaned forward, braced his hands on the dash, and studied the landscape more closely as the truck ascended the mountain. The mountain range, full of high peaks that had touched a blue, misty sky, had darkened to midnight black, and a thick, gray shroud had been draped over them, imbuing the air with an eerie, graveyard quality.

The truck's engine groaned when they reached the peak of the mountain, and the sun returned full force. Its thick rays sliced through the gray, smoky air and lit up the broken walls and charred remains of buildings and businesses lining the main road through downtown. Even Glory Be, once a welcoming structure, had been reduced to rubble.

Debris littered the land where homes once stood, and the burned wreckage of cars and trucks slumped amid it. A child's bicycle, its color stripped and covered with ash and soot, lay abandoned in a driveway. Metal porch railings had bent and warped into misshapen angles among the crumbling ruins of homes.

Stomach dropping, Travis swiveled in his seat and peered at Margaret's car, which followed close behind them. Red, driving, looked from one side of the road to the other, a mixture of shock and horror visible in his expression. Margaret sat in the passenger seat and stared out her window at the damage, her hands clasped tightly over her mouth.

"We'll think positive." Hannah's voice, a thin whisper, filled the cab. "This could be the worst of it."

Travis turned back around and stared at the road, hoping what she said was true. Hoping she, Red, and Margaret would at least have one habitable structure still standing when they reached the ranch.

Up ahead, by the left side of the road, a policeman stood outside his patrol car, waving his arms and directing them to stop. Hannah braked slowly, then rolled down her window as the officer approached.

"Where you folks headed?" he asked, leaning closer to the cab.

"Paradise Peak Ranch." Hannah motioned toward the road ahead. "Our place is just up the road, down a ways on the other side of the mountain."

The officer nodded. "Road's open that way but drive carefully. Trees still fall on occasion."

"Power came back on in Crystal Rock yesterday," Travis said. "Has it been restored here?"

The officer nodded. "You'll have lights, running water, and phone lines in working order, but the rest . . ." He looked away, his eyes, full of exhaustion, scanning the landscape. He shook his head slightly, faced them again, and tapped the top of the truck. "Good luck to you, and call if you need us."

Hannah thanked him, then drove on. Red and Margaret followed.

The next few miles seemed to stretch on forever and the view from the truck's windows didn't change. Burned, broken trees stabbed high into the air above the blackened ground, their trunks rocking slightly when the breeze picked up speed.

The truck cleared another tight curve, and then a familiar gravel driveway appeared.

Hannah slowed the truck and turned onto the graveled path. "Please let there be something left. Please, please, please . . ."

Smoky, gray mist thinned as they drove further up the driveway, and then—

"Look." Travis pointed at the wooden sign by the driveway, its post still strong and sturdy. Other than singed edges, the wording, PARADISE PEAK RANCH, remained untouched.

Hannah gripped the steering wheel with one hand and latched on to Travis's knee with the other, squeezing tight. "And the cabins . . ."

Along the driveway, all three cabins—save for a bit of roof and porch damage—were in great shape, too.

"Oh, thank God," Hannah whispered, releasing his knee and pointing at the main lodge. "It's still standing." Her pointing finger moved to the right of the lodge and shook in the direction of the stable. "And the stable and paddock fence are still there. Look at the ground, Travis. Not an inch of it is singed."

And it wasn't. The dormant grass, still brown and unmarred by flames, stretched in every direction. The wooden fences stood sturdy with the exception of several burned and broken rungs along the dirt path leading to Hannah's cabin.

"Come on." Hannah parked the truck in front of the lodge, opened her door, and hopped out. "Let's take a look at our cabins."

Travis followed, shutting his door and waiting by the truck. He smiled as the sound of a car door slamming and Red's joyful bellow echoed across the landscape.

"Would ya look at that?" Red shouted, waving an arm toward the undamaged lodge. "You'll still be able to wallpaper to your heart's content, Margaret!"

Standing beside her parked car, Margaret laughed as she took in the view, tears streaming down her face and amazement shining in her eyes. "It's unbelievable. Just unbelievable . . ."

Travis scanned the grounds of the ranch, the once neglected-looking cabins appearing pristine against the backdrop of the singed mountain range, and the shabby walls of the stable a welcoming haven nestled below the charred tree line.

"Unbelievable," Travis echoed, a smile spreading across his face.

"Oh, but the horses." Hannah, jogging ahead, stopped dead in her tracks, then spun around slowly, scanning the empty landscape. She looked over her shoulder at Travis, her blue eyes widening with fear. "What if—"

"Call them," he said softly. He walked over to her and, standing behind her, slid his arms around her waist. "Let them know we're here."

Mouth trembling, Hannah lifted her hand, slipped her thumb and index finger between her lips, and whistled. The high-pitched sound pierced their silent surroundings and echoed against the black mountains in the distance.

There was no movement in the distance. Only silence.

Hannah's shoulders fell as she slumped back against him.

"Again." Jaw clenching, Travis squeezed her waist and touched his lips to the soft shell of her ear. "Call them again."

Her upper body trembled on a heavy inhale, and she whistled a second time.

Travis closed his eyes and listened intently, a silent refrain moving his lips. *Please let them be okay. Send them back to her. Please . . .*

The silence continued, but then a soft rumble echoed across the grounds as hooves struck the earth in rapid succession.

"There!" Hannah bounced with her excited shout, her soft cheek pressing against Travis's.

He opened his eyes and there they were—all three. Ruby, Juno, and the mare emerged from the damaged tree line in the distance and galloped across the field in front of them, their hooves kicking up bits of dry earth as they ran.

Hannah reached out, her palms running gently over Ruby's and Juno's dusty hides, checking their faces, necks, and legs for injuries, murmuring gentle words of praise as she moved from one horse to the next.

The new mare sidestepped the trio and walked slowly to Travis, dipped her head, and nudged his middle.

"Hi, beautiful." Carefully, he smoothed his hand over her neck, consoling and praising the horse.

The mare stood docilely as Hannah eased over and checked her for injuries, too. After a few minutes, Hannah glanced at him and smiled.

"They're all okay," she said, her tone half relieved, half astounded. "They're exhausted, hungry, and could use a bath, but they've had plenty to drink from the stream, and only a couple minor burns as far as I can tell."

Travis stroked the mare's back gently, then looked up at the sky. A sense of peace unfurled inside him and gratitude swelled in his chest as he eyed the sun shining through the gray mist overhead. "Thank you," he whispered.

To God, the powers that be, or the universe at large. To whatever merciful force had descended on Paradise Peak to protect and defend, saving so much for Red, Hannah, and Margaret when others had lost everything.

"Take those champion horses to the stable and get 'em cleaned up," Red said, clapping a firm hand to Travis's back. "Margaret and I'll check the lodge and the deck to make sure everything's sound."

"Wait," Travis said, stopping Red with a hand on his arm. He looked at Hannah, who stood by the horses, stroking their backs and watching him expectantly. "Do you remember how small that motel room felt?"

Her mouth twisted. "Yeah. It was fine for the first few days, but got cramped real quick once everyone else settled in."

Travis motioned toward the fields, the lodge, and the cabins. "Look at how much room we have here."

He hadn't meant to say "we," to include himself in the close bond holding Red, Hannah, and Margaret together. To place himself within their family. But he had. And none of them objected.

Encouraged, Travis smiled at Red. "We have so much to offer right now, when others have so little. We still need help renovating, and a lot of people will need a place to call their own." He glanced at Margaret. "Imagine how excited Gloria and Vernon would be to know they have a place to stay, free of charge, while they rebuild their cabin and business." He returned his attention to Hannah. "And how much room Zeke and Blondie would have to run, play, and recover."

"And Liz," Hannah whispered, tears filling her eyes. "She wouldn't be alone."

"She'd have all of us." Travis rolled his lips together, hesitating, then added, "But it'd mean opening the ranch to more than just them. It would mean welcoming strangers—"

"No," Hannah said firmly.

Travis grew still, his breath catching at the finality of her words.

She smiled. "It would mean welcoming our neighbors into a safe home they could call their own."

Relieved—and falling more in love with her by the second—Travis nodded. "Paradise Peak Ranch would become a haven."

For a moment, the grounds were silent, save for the whisper of the breeze and the soft neigh of the horses.

Then Red stepped forward, gripped Travis's shoulders, and smiled. "And that's exactly what it'll be, son."

Red's low, approving tone went straight to Travis's heart, relieving some of his guilty burden and raising his spirit and hopes for the future.

"The officer who stopped us on the way in said the phone lines are working," Hannah said.

Margaret smiled and clapped her hands together, rubbing them briskly. "Then I have calls to make, invitations to extend, and rooms to tidy." She headed for the lodge, saying over her shoulder, "Come on, Red. You'll have to help me move some furniture."

Red laughed and shook his head. "There she goes—bossing me around already."

But he followed her, even whistled along the way.

Hannah patted Ruby's back. "I'll get these beauties to the stable, washed up, doctored, and fed."

"I'll be right behind you," Travis said.

Hannah skipped to his side and kissed his cheek, the soft press of her lips lingering on his cheek as she led the horses away.

Travis stood still for a few minutes, watching Margaret and Red cross the field, walk up the front steps, and enter the lodge. He studied the horses as Hannah led them to the stable, and his attention lingered on Hannah's smile as she waved back at him before ducking inside.

He studied the open fields sprawling across the ranch, then stared at the mountains in the distance, his heart filling with emotions so strong they spilled over his lashes and tickled his cheeks.

Travis returned to the truck, grabbed his bag, and retrieved a pen and clean sheet of paper. Legs trembling, he walked to the front of the truck, placed the paper on the hood, and held it down with one hand as the breeze lifted the edges. He pressed the pen to the paper and wrote in sure, clean strokes.

Dear Margaret,
When you read this, I will have already told you the truth. . . .

CHAPTER 10

"This is it." Hannah stopped in the middle of the cabin's living room and set the two bags she carried on the floor. "There are two bedrooms with double beds and one bathroom with a large tub I think Zeke will like. A small kitchen, and"—Hannah lifted her arms and gestured toward the space around her—"a large living room."

Outside, boards creaked along the front porch floor, and then Liz stepped slowly across the threshold and entered the cabin. She looked around the room, her brown eyes lifeless, her expression blank.

Hannah bit her lip and glanced at the sparse furniture. The sofa, its tan upholstery faded, was worn but comfortable. There were two side tables, one at each end of the sofa, with a small lamp on both surfaces. A frayed, forest-green rug covered most of the scuffed hardwood floor and a basket of evenly-sized logs sat next to a stone fireplace on the opposite wall.

"Travis stacked a cord of seasoned firewood out back for you," Hannah said. "I know the fireplace looks a bit the worse for wear, but it functions like a charm." When Liz didn't answer, Hannah crossed to the large window in front of the sofa. "I don't think you'll need it during the day though." She unlocked the window, tugged it open, then stepped back as the curtains billowed out on a fresh breeze. "It's almost sixty-five degrees out there today." She smiled. "I think spring will be here soon."

Liz stared out the window, her brown hair limp around her shoulders and her arms hanging by her sides. The long-sleeved shirt and jeans she wore draped heavily about her thin frame, the hems of her jeans pooling around her ankles.

Body trembling, Hannah turned away and looked out the window, too.

The sun, bright and warm, lit up a clear blue sky above the jagged tops of burned trees and the scorched earth marring the horizon. Though the heart of Paradise Peak Ranch had emerged from the wildfire relatively unscathed, the outskirts of the property had been engulfed in flames, the proof of which remained.

Two days ago, after returning to the ranch, Hannah and Travis had tended to the horses while Red and Margaret cleaned rooms in the lodge. The next day, they'd spent the better part of the day washing towels and bed linens, making beds, restocking bathrooms, and cleaning the cabins that were in good enough shape for guests. They'd attended Ben's funeral yesterday afternoon and, afterward, Margaret had invited Gloria and the rest of the group to come settle at the ranch. Gloria, overjoyed, had accepted, and she, Vernon, Liz, Zeke, and Blondie had all arrived this morning.

Hannah stared at the dark mountains in the distance, their once colorful contours now gray and dreary. She hated that this was Liz's view, but it was the best cabin on the ranch and Hannah couldn't bring herself to stuff Liz, Zeke, and Blondie in one room at the lodge. They needed a new, fresh space to call their own, with plenty of room to stretch, to scream . . . to do *anything*, so long as Liz managed to pull herself out of the emotionless daze she'd remained in since Ben's death a week ago. And yesterday hadn't helped—Ben's funeral may have served as closure for others, but for Liz, it had been another painful reminder that she'd never see, touch, or speak to the man she loved again. The man with whom she'd believed she would share the rest of her life.

Hannah ducked her head and wiped her eyes, then glanced over her shoulder at Liz. She hadn't moved an inch, and her pale cheeks looked sunken, which was understandable, considering she hadn't eaten a bite since Ben's death.

"I told Margaret that you and Zeke both liked peanut butter, and she made you this huge peanut butter pie." Hannah issued a strained laugh. "Travis and I ate two slices of the one she made for us last night, and I swear I could've eaten a third if I'd set my mind to it." She motioned toward the kitchen. "You want me to grab you a slice? It won't take me but a sec—"

Liz left the room, her tennis shoes shuffling across the hardwood floor to one of the bedrooms. A moment later, bedsprings squeaked.

Hannah rubbed her forehead, the small ache behind her eyes intensifying.

Heavy footsteps sounded on the porch steps, and lighter ones pattered close behind. The front door creaked open a bit further and Travis walked in, Zeke by his side.

"Any luck?" Travis asked.

Hannah shook her head, then knelt and held out her arms. "Can I have a hug from my favorite boy?"

Zeke smiled—a very small one, but a smile nonetheless—and walked into her arms. Hannah hugged him close and kissed his forehead, breathing in the soft scent of baby shampoo.

"Where Mama?" Zeke asked, fear lacing his young voice.

Hannah sat back on her haunches and cupped his cheeks, her heart aching at the wet warmth that met her palms. "She's resting, baby."

His chin wobbled, and he looked up at her, his brown eyes wide with confusion. "But I want her."

Hannah blinked back tears. "I know," she said softly. "But your mama doesn't feel too well right now, and—"

"But I want her." Zeke's expression crumpled, and a sob burst from his small mouth. "I want Mama."

Hannah choked back a sob of her own and looked up at Travis helplessly.

"Hey, buddy." Travis squatted beside Zeke and held out his hand, palm upward. "I saw Blondie outside. She found a stick she likes, and she's been carrying it around since she got here. I bet she's waiting for someone to come out there and throw it around for her. What do you say we go out and play with her for a while?"

Zeke's sobs slowed and he rose to his tiptoes, straining to look out the window. He lowered himself back to his feet, glanced at Travis's big palm, then stared up at Travis's face. "Giant . . . go me?"

Travis smiled and nudged his hand closer. "Yeah. I'll go with you."

Zeke pushed Travis's hand away, stretched up, and wrapped his arms loosely around Travis's neck, then lifted his leg in an attempt to climb into his arms.

"Well . . ." Travis glanced at Hannah, the nervous expression on his face making her smile, then looked back down at Zeke. "All right."

Travis bent low, allowing Zeke to wrap his arms tighter

around his neck and shoulders, then slowly scooped the boy up and propped him on his left hip. Zeke, clearly comfortable—and tired, laid his head on Travis's shoulder and fiddled with his collar.

They were a sight: Travis, tall and muscular, cradling Zeke, a small, vulnerable boy, protectively against his massive chest.

"You're a natural," Hannah said as she stood.

Travis met her eyes and smiled. He stepped closer, dipped his head, and kissed her cheek. "We'll be right outside."

She watched them leave. Travis stepped carefully down the front steps and walked slowly across the front lawn, keeping a secure hold on Zeke. Blondie sighted them, popped her head out of a clump of dead bushes, and bounded across the dormant grass toward them, a stick clamped tightly between her teeth. She lost her footing halfway there, did a somersault, then regained her balance and ran over to plop down on Travis's boots.

Hannah heard Zeke cackle from her stance by the window and smiled, wondering if Travis would be as good with his own children as he was with Zeke. Her belly warmed at the possibilities.

"A natural," she whispered.

She turned away from the window, went to the kitchen, and removed the peanut butter pie from the fridge. After cutting a hefty slice and arranging it on a plate with two forks, she grabbed a can of soda—Liz's favorite brand—and walked to the open doorway of the bedroom. Liz was there, lying on the bed, facing the opposite wall.

Hannah set the pie and soda down on the nightstand, then sat on the edge of the bed. "Liz?"

Her eyes stayed closed.

Hannah reached out, slipped her finger under a strand of brown hair that had fallen over Liz's cheek, and tucked it behind her ear. "I brought you something to eat."

She didn't respond.

A puff of wind whistled through the open window in the living room and gusted across the bedroom, carrying the faint sound of Zeke's laughter into the room.

Hannah straightened and stiffened her spine. "This isn't optional. You're going to open your eyes, you're going to sit up, and you're going to eat something."

Liz remained still.

"I'm not kidding, Liz." Hannah's throat closed, a tight knot forming, but she forced herself to speak. "You can cry all you want. You can even hit me if you want, but you're going to at least sit up and eat while you do it. I won't let you give up."

She grabbed Liz's shoulders and shook her gently. When her friend refused to respond, Hannah hooked her hands under Liz's armpits and hauled her resisting form upright.

"L-let go of me."

The croaked sound that emerged from Liz's lips was weak, but she'd spoken.

"That's a little progress," Hannah said, dragging her forearm over her wet eyes. "Now"—she popped the top on the can of soda and held it to Liz's lips—"I want you to drink something."

Liz's eyes began to close, and she turned her face away.

"Nope." Hannah moved the can, pressing it back against Liz's lips. "Not having it. I'm not leaving until you get something in you, and I promise you, I can keep at it all night."

Liz shoved her arm away and soda sloshed out of the can and onto the sheets. "Get away from me."

"No."

Eyes narrowing, Liz stared at her. "I said get away from me."

"N—"

Liz knocked the can out of Hannah's hand. It smacked into the wall and hit the floor, soda fizzing across the floor.

"Okay." Hannah stood and headed for the door. "I'll just get another one."

"Why are you doing this?"

Hannah stopped, midstride, at Liz's shout and turned around.

Heavy sobs racked Liz's chest and shoulders. "Why can't you just leave me alone?"

Hannah swallowed hard. "Because you're my best friend, and I love you. And because there's a little boy outside who loves you more than anyone in the world, and he's hurting and desperate for his mama to get out of bed."

Liz fought to catch her breath, her attention moving to the open door, where Zeke's voice as he called Blondie drifted in. "I . . . I can't." She pressed a fist to her chest and looked at Hannah. "I don't know how to go on without Ben."

Shoulders slumping, Hannah returned to the bed and sat beside her. "I know," she said softly.

Liz shook her head. "So what do I do?"

"You keep breathing and moving. You just keep going until it doesn't hurt as much."

Liz closed her eyes, a stoic expression crossing her face. "You were right. There are no happy-ever-afters."

Hannah scoffed and dragged a hand over her face. "I should never have said that." She sighed. "I've been wrong about so many things. You may not have Ben anymore, but you have Zeke. And he needs you."

A fresh stream of tears coursed down Liz's cheeks.

Hannah scooted closer. "I have no idea how hard this will be for you, but I promise you, you're not alone. You've got to get up—for Zeke's sake, and your own."

Liz opened her eyes, fear and pain mingling in their dark depths. "I don't know if I have it in me," she whispered.

Hannah flinched, recalling the day she'd left Bryan and returned to Paradise Peak. She'd cried in Red's arms and said the same thing, feeling empty and devoid of life. But now, she wanted to start over again. With Travis . . .

She squared her shoulders. "You do. And so do I. After I left Bryan, you and Ben wouldn't let me give up, and I won't let you give up now. So we're both going to start over. Right now. And I swear I'll be with you every step of the way."

Liz sat quietly for a few minutes, listening to Zeke's faint chatter and sporadic laughter. Then, the tears dry on her cheeks, she sat up, shoved her long hair behind her shoulders, and shot a hard look at Hannah. "So what exactly do you want me to do?"

Hannah sagged with relief. Anger, at least, was better than apathy.

"In a few minutes, I want you to get up and take a shower, then help me unpack Zeke's things. But for now . . ." She reached over to the nightstand, picked up the plate of pie, and forked up a big bite. "Please just help me eat this damn peanut butter pie Margaret made for you."

Liz glared at her for a few moments more, then took the fork and put the chunk of pie in her mouth. She chewed slowly, staring at Hannah's face all the while; then her throat moved on a hard swallow and she licked her parched lips.

"Well," Liz whispered, "at least the damn pie is good." The corners of her lips curved up—just a bit.

Hannah laughed, picked up the plate and the second fork, then settled beside her. "The company will be even better."

Travis threw a stick and smiled. "Get it, girl."

Blondie, sitting on his boots, jumped up and shot across the lawn in front of Liz's cabin.

Zeke bounced in place and laughed. "Get it, get it, get it!"

Blondie, the stick clamped between her teeth, trotted back and plopped onto Travis's boots again, her tail wagging.

Travis patted her head. "Good job, Blondie."

"Again, Giant," Zeke squealed. "Again."

"As much as you want, buddy." Travis wrestled the stick away from Blondie, who growled playfully, then threw it across the lawn again.

Blondie and Zeke both took off after it, the little boy laughing the entire way.

After he'd left Hannah in the cabin with Liz, Travis had carried Zeke outside and enticed Blondie over to play. The activity had taken Zeke's mind off his grief and he'd perked up, running, squealing, and playing hard for the two hours they'd been outside Liz's cabin.

"Looks like Zeke's having a blast." Gloria walked along the dirt path leading to the cabin, then crossed the lawn and held out her arms to Travis. "Get over here in these arms, young man. I've been itching for a chance to hug Paradise Peak's hero."

Smiling, Travis complied, bending low and allowing Gloria to squeeze him tight. "It's good to have you here, Mrs. Gloria, but I don't know about the hero part."

"The devil, you don't." Gloria smacked his arm playfully, then hugged him harder. "Way you charged in that night, scooping up Zeke and Liz, then driving Hannah and

Blondie to safety? You're a hero in my book. Vernon's, too." She released him, propped her hands on her ample hips, and sighed. "And you've got no idea how good it is to be here. I was grateful for that motel room—don't get me wrong—but having a real bed again is a treat."

"So the cabin we set you up in is working out okay?"

"Okay?" Gloria laughed. "Vernon's already stretched out on the bed, snoozing away." She cupped a hand around her mouth. "Now, let's keep this between you and me, but Margaret kept us up most nights with her snoring. I love the gal, but I'm glad to have some peace and quiet again."

Travis laughed. "Well, if you need anything—"

Gloria held up her hands. "Nope. We're well taken care of. Having a roof over our heads and a stocked fridge is more than enough. We plan to settle in and rest today, and first thing tomorrow Vernon is going to drive to town to get the ball rolling on rebuilding our house and the store and I'm going to help Margaret prepare rooms in the lodge for more guests. Word's gotten out that you've opened up as a shelter and Margaret said people have been calling all morning."

Travis nodded. "Good. There are a ton of rooms in that lodge, and we want to help everyone we can." He watched Zeke grab another stick off the ground and throw it. Blondie chased it. "How's the outlook on your cabins and business? Did you lose everything?"

Gloria grimaced. "Not everything, but close to it. Our home and all our rental cabins are gone, and the store will have to be entirely rebuilt. The good news is that I placed an order for new merchandise two days before the fire and it hadn't been shipped yet, so at least we have some new stock arriving within the month that will already be paid for. And the cabin y'all set us up in has the perfect space out front for a spring garden, so I'll have lots to keep me busy while we wait for our house to be built. You still got that lantana I gave you?" When he nodded, she winked. "The way the air's warming up makes me think this would be a good time for you to plant it."

Zeke squealed as Blondie rolled onto her back and kicked her legs playfully. He sat beside her and rubbed her belly.

Gloria glanced at Zeke and Blondie, then frowned. "How is Liz doing this morning? She had such a hard time at the funeral yesterday, and she didn't say a word during the drive from the motel this morning."

Travis winced. "Well, she—"

"Good morning."

The porch of the cabin creaked as Liz walked outside to greet them with Hannah close behind. Liz paused at the top of the front steps. She'd changed clothes and, judging from her wet hair, had showered. Dark circles still lingered under her eyes and there was a tight set to her mouth, but some color had returned to her cheeks.

"Good morning, Liz," Travis said, smiling gently.

Liz offered a weak smile in return and smoothed a hand over her wet hair. "I'm sorry you had to babysit for so long."

"Please don't apologize." Travis gestured toward Zeke, who sat with his back to them, petting Blondie. "Zeke's a great kid, and I enjoyed every minute of it. I'm happy to watch him anytime you need me to."

Liz looked down at her bare feet and bit her lip, her shoulders shaking. Hannah moved closed to her side, touched her arm, and whispered something.

Liz raised her head, set her shoulders back, and said, "I'll take over for now. Hannah has helped me unpack a few of Zeke's things, but I'd like for Zeke and me to do the rest." She leaned to the side and, glimpsing her son, called out, "Zeke, would you come here, please?"

Zeke looked back, spotted Liz, then jumped to his feet.

"Mama!" He ran across the lawn and up the front porch steps, then hurled himself against her middle.

Liz hugged him close, another smile—a bigger, more sincere one this time—appearing. "Would you like to help me set up your new bedroom?"

Zeke nodded, smiling as Liz picked him up and headed inside.

Gloria wiped her damp eyes and asked, "I've got nothing on my agenda this morning, Liz. Would you two like a hand?"

"Yes, please." Liz paused, one hand on the door as she waited for Gloria to join them, then said, "Travis?"

He met her eyes.

"Thank you for helping us when we lost—" Her voice broke and she kissed the top of Zeke's head before continuing. "Thank you for helping us during the fire."

Travis dipped his head. "You're welcome."

Liz and Gloria went inside the cabin, with Zeke chattering in Liz's arms as Gloria closed the door behind them.

Hannah walked down the front steps and across the lawn to Travis's side. "She ate two slices of peanut butter pie, drank one soda, and showered, so I guess you can say we made progress."

Travis smiled. "Definitely." He tilted his head back and eyed the blue sky and bright sun. "From what Gloria said, warmer weather's on the way and we've made it past the last frost. Thought I'd head back to my cabin and get Joyful Judy in the ground."

Hannah frowned. "Joyful Judy?"

"The lantana plant Gloria gave me. It survived our drive through the fire and almost a week in that little motel room. Figured I'd find a nice, sunny place to plant it and show it off to Gloria when spring rolls around." He held out his hand. "Want to help me scout out a place for her to put down roots?"

Hannah laughed. "I'd love to." She slipped her hand in Travis's and leaned into him, matching her pace to his as they walked along the dirt path.

It felt good to be outside again, to feel the warmth of the sun on his face and fill his lungs with clean, fresh air instead of thick, ash-laden smoke. They walked over a mile, following the dirt path that led from the three cabins by the ranch's entrance to the gravel driveway, and then continued on to the main lodge.

The sound of brisk sweeping and heavy thumping echoed across the grounds, and Travis shielded his eyes as he peered up at the lodge's deck. Red was there, sweeping the floor of the large deck vigorously and stopping occasionally to wipe his brow, while Margaret beat a large rug against the deck railing and waved clouds of dust away.

"I see Red and Margaret are still hard at work," Travis said. "Gloria mentioned that word has gotten out about us opening up the ranch to those who need shelter and that Margaret received a ton of calls this morning."

"A representative from the city called, too. They're collecting donations of food and clothing, and said they'll send a truck with supplies to us around one this afternoon." Hannah glanced over her shoulder at the gravel driveway. "That's not too far away now, so they should be here soon."

Travis checked his wristwatch. "After I plant the lantana, I'll head back up here and help Red clean the deck, then unload the truck when it arrives."

"I'll help you." Hannah faced him and took his other hand in hers. "And listen, I . . . I wanted to ask you if . . ."

Travis waited as she opened and closed her mouth

twice, preparing to speak, then seemed to change her mind and look away. "Hannah? What do you want to ask me?"

"Nothing." She released one of his hands and tugged him forward. "Let's keep going."

Smiling, Travis shook his head and they continued on, strolling across the field and slowing when they reached the paddock where the horses roamed. Juno and Ruby trotted over to the fence, and the new mare followed their lead and eased her head over the top fence rung for attention.

"You haven't given her a name yet," Hannah said.

Travis's hand slowed on the mare's neck as he caught Hannah's eyes on him. "I haven't, have I? Guess things got out of hand so quickly. . . ." He studied the mare, trailing his palm gently over the black and white markings covering her hide, and smiled as he recalled Zeke's mispronunciation of the mare's color pattern. "Besides, I think Zeke's already given her one." He rubbed the mare's neck. "How about it, girl? Oreo suit you? Zeke seemed to like it."

The mare eased closer and ducked her head for more attention.

Hannah laughed. "I think she agrees."

After visiting the horses for a few minutes, they walked beside the calm stream and across the bridge, then climbed the steep trail to Travis's cabin. They circled the structure, checking for damage they might have missed during the first once-over the day they'd arrived.

"Looks like the wind shifted direction right before the fire reached the cabin," Hannah said, trailing her hand along the wooden porch rail as they walked up the front steps. "Other than some downed trees out back, everything here is sound."

"Yeah. We were incredibly lucky." Travis opened the

door and stepped inside. "I'll grab the plant and be back in a sec. I watered it this morning and put it in the sink to drain."

He went to the bathroom and retrieved the potted lantana from the sink. When he came out, Hannah stood with her back to him by the small desk in front of the window.

"There's a beautiful view from up here." She placed her hands on top of the desk and leaned closer, her fingers spreading over scattered sheets of paper.

Heart pounding against his ribs, Travis stopped in the middle of the room and stared, his hands clenching around the potted plant.

In his haste to evacuate during the fire a week ago, he'd forgotten he'd left the letters behind on the desk, and since he'd returned to the ranch, he'd worked such long hours preparing cabins and rooms in the lodge that he'd fallen, exhausted, into bed the past two nights already half asleep. He'd written his last letter to Margaret two days ago, had stowed it in his bag with the bundle of others, and had no plans to write another.

But right there, beneath the tip of Hannah's thumb, were the words *Neil Alden.*

Hannah lowered her head and drummed her fingers against the papers. "You know, I was thinking. . . ."

Travis froze, his pulse pounding in his ears and filling her silence. "Hannah?"

She didn't speak, but her hands balled into fists against the letters.

Throat tightening, Travis set the potted plant on the floor and stepped toward her on shaky legs. "Hannah, I—"

She spun around, her eyes closed, and inhaled deeply before blurting, "I think you should move in with me."

Travis stood motionless, absorbing her words, trying to

make sense of them amid the panic surging through his veins.

Hannah opened her eyes and blew out a slow, steadying breath. "What I mean is, I have a spare bedroom in my cabin, and if I had a choice, I'd rather you move into it than someone I don't know. And if you were to move in with me, this cabin would be available for wildfire refugees. A whole family even—if we were to put an extra cot or two in here."

Travis studied her face, the uncertainty in her blue eyes, and the way she nibbled nervously on her lower lip.

"Please don't say no," she said quietly. "It's taken me two days and the entire morning to dig up enough courage to ask."

"You . . ." He glanced at the letters behind her, then refocused on her earnest expression. "You want me to move into your spare room?"

She nodded, saying quietly, "It'd be nice to have you around more often. To see you first thing in the morning and last thing at night." Her smile, small and self-conscious, trembled. "I don't want to pressure you or make this into a big deal. I just wanted you to know that since the fire, I've been thinking a lot about the future and what I want out of life. I'm ready for a fresh start, and I'd like for us to get to know each other better so that maybe . . . maybe one day soon, we can both begin again. Together." Shrugging, she gestured at the potted plant on the floor and laughed nervously. "I mean, you can even plant your lantana in my garden if you'd like. There's a lot of sunlight there in the spring, and there'll be plenty of room for it to grow. Like I said"— she spread her hands—"no big deal."

Travis was afraid to speak. Afraid to move. "But what you're suggesting—separate rooms or not—it is a big deal."

Her shoulders slumped. She looked down and picked at her nails. "I know. That's why I was afraid to ask."

Travis moved closer, slid his knuckle under her chin, and gently lifted her face until her eyes met his. "Yes."

She blinked, those beautiful blue eyes of hers fixing on his mouth. "Y-you will?"

"Yes." He dipped his head and kissed her, parting her soft lips with his, gathering her sweet taste on his tongue, and wrapping her up so tightly in his arms that he could feel the excited pounding of her heart against his chest.

Having her in his arms again was the closest thing to heaven he could imagine.

She smiled against his mouth, her teeth bumping his bottom lip, and whispered, "Let's move you in."

Smiling so wide his cheeks hurt, Travis released her and laughed as she grabbed the plant from the floor.

"I know the perfect spot for this." She spun around, her gaze straying to the desk. "And we can take the desk if you'd like." Clutching the plant to her chest with one hand, she reached with the other for the papers. "Your papers, t—"

"Wait." He sprang forward, gathered the letters into a pile, and folded them in half. His hands shook so badly, the papers creased unevenly. "I'll take care of these."

Hannah watched his hands, her eyes studying the awkward movements of his fingers as he folded the papers a second, then a third time. "Are those diary entries?"

He stilled, wanting to tell her, but also wanting so much to hold on to the moment. To hold on to Hannah and the joy of being close to her. Because he had no idea how long it would last.

"Of a sort, I suppose," he answered slowly. "They're private thoughts. Things I want to say but haven't been brave enough to voice yet."

She stared at the papers, then looked up at him, a tender smile appearing. "Will you tell me one day?"

Travis ducked his head, the papers blurring in front of him, and swallowed hard. "Yes." After he helped revive Paradise Peak Ranch for Margaret. Because this . . . Margaret's wishes—and Niki's memory—came first. Before him and everyone else. Even Hannah. "One day soon."

CHAPTER 11

Travis knelt beside the garden in front of Hannah's cabin, spread fresh pine straw around the lantana plant, then grabbed a watering can and poured cool water around the plant's base. The lantana's lush green leaves and yellow blooms danced in the warm May breeze, and butterflies, feeding on the small clusters of flowers, dispersed at the disturbance, fluttering in different directions.

He grinned. "You look gorgeous, Joyful Judy. Gloria will be proud of your progress when she gets a look at you."

Travis stood, tilted his head back, and closed his eyes. Sunlight warmed his face and the rustle of leaves mixed with the chirp of birds high in the trees. He inhaled deeply, filling his senses with the earthy scent of pine, lumber, and the sweet scent of wildflowers.

Two months ago, when he'd planted the lantana in Hannah's garden, it'd been small and unimpressive. But after weeks of sunshine, gradually warming air and plenty of water, the plant had thrived, sprouting new blooms and spreading. Spring, it seemed, had sprung into its full glory, and so had Paradise Peak Ranch.

Bursts of children's laughter joined the chorus of birds.

Travis opened his eyes, turned around, and smiled as

three boys between the ages of eight and twelve years old chased each other down the trail from his old cabin on the opposite side of the stream. They ran over to the grassy bank by the water, and after stopping to catch their breath, rolled up the pants legs of their jeans and waded through the shin-deep water. They splashed each other, howling with laughter when the frigid water hit their skin.

A young couple followed at a leisurely pace behind the boys. They spread a blanket on the grass, sat down, and leaned against each other, smiling as they admired each other, then the view.

And it was a spectacular view.

Travis shielded his eyes from the sun's beating rays with one hand and scanned the terrain in front of him. The steep incline leading to the cabin where he used to stay had greened up nicely, and the thick swaths of grass covered every inch of the grounds.

In the distance, the mountain range still bore scars of the brutal wildfire, but the majority of the landscape had rejuvenated itself. Lush green foliage had fought its way through damaged earth, feeding off the nutrients left behind by ash and scorched woodland debris, and the increase in sunlight to the newly bared forest floor had encouraged new, diverse growth that added splashes of color to the landscape and breathed new life into the majestic mountains.

Blue mist had returned, creating an elegant contrast to puffy, white clouds and golden rays of sunlight, and the smoke that had hovered over the mountain for days after the wildfire had long since departed. Pounding hammers, the playful shouts of happy children, and the faint sound of music echoed across the grounds.

Travis smiled. Since the day Gloria, Vernon, Liz, and Zeke had come, groups of wildfire refugees had arrived every day for two weeks. Word had spread quickly that Paradise Peak Ranch was a welcoming haven, and before long, every room in the lodge was occupied and every cabin on the property was full.

Guests had been eager to help turn the once neglected cabins and outdated rooms in the lodge into temporary homes while they waited through long delays in getting financial assistance to rebuild their own homes and businesses. In the lodge, guests had removed aged wallpaper in the room and applied fresh coats of paint to the walls, pitched in to renovate bathrooms and repair old plumbing. They had helped prepare meals from donated supplies each night, full of comfort foods, to help everyone feel more at home.

Families staying in cabins had helped repair roof damage, stained their decks and porches, and had planted vegetables and flowers in gardens that hadn't been touched in years. And every night, families gathered in the newly restored banquet hall to enjoy meals and listen to the occasional guitar music from guests.

Everyone had come together over the last two months to bring out the best in Paradise Peak Ranch and make it into a home.

Travis studied the boisterous boys and their parents relaxing on the other side of the stream again. The couple waved and he raised his hand and called out a greeting in return.

The Carrollton family—Andrew, Kate, and their three boys, Xavier, Jacob, and Drew—had moved into Travis's old cabin two days after he'd moved into a spare room in Hannah's place. The accommodations had been small for such a large family, but the Carrolltons had been relieved to have a place to call their own while they waited for their damaged house on the other side of the mountain to be rebuilt. They'd lost almost everything in the fire, except for each other, but were grateful they'd all escaped unscathed and had remained optimistic in the two months since they'd arrived at the ranch, pitching in to renovate the cabin they occupied as well as two others.

Kate had even volunteered to sing at a spring dance Red had arranged for tomorrow night—the first event of such kind at Paradise Peak Ranch. Red had been in an unusually anxious mood of late, which Travis chalked up to nerves as he prepared to throw his first ever dance at the ranch.

The scent of charcoal burning drifted by on the spring breeze. That'd be Red, firing up the grill in preparation for a late-afternoon dinner on the lodge deck. It had become a tradition every Friday night at the ranch for himself, Margaret, Hannah, and Travis.

Stomach growling, Travis wiped his hands on his jeans and strode up the dirt path toward the stable. The children's laughter faded as he walked away, and he smiled, recalling the way the boys' joyful shouts had traveled across the stream and echoed against Hannah's cabin last night as they'd chased fireflies after dark.

Their happy sounds had enticed Travis and Hannah outside to sit in rocking chairs on her front porch, where they'd watched the boys play for over an hour. He flexed his hand, the warm feel of Hannah's palm against his own still tingling on his skin. She'd held his hand, rested her head against his shoulder, and smiled as the kids had played.

"Can you imagine having that many rambunctious sons under one roof?" she'd asked.

Her voice had been light and teasing, but there had been something else in her tone and the depths of her blue eyes as she'd looked up at him. Happiness, hope, and . . . love?

He had imagined having sons. Many times.

Each night, as he'd lain in the large double bed in the bedroom across the hall from Hannah, he dreamed of falling asleep with her in his arms and waking up to her soft, even breaths whispering across his chest as she slept. He'd fantasized about rousing her with gentle kisses, making love to her to the slow tempo of the sunrise, and undertaking a full day of ranch work with her by his side.

He'd thought of children—his and Hannah's—and he'd wondered if their daughter would inherit Hannah's red curls and feistiness, or his black hair and reserved disposition. He'd wondered if their son would grow as tall as he and envisioned teaching him to become the kind of compassionate man he endeavored to be. And he'd imagined how full his heart would feel holding Hannah and his children close, protecting them, supporting them, and loving them right here on this mountain for years to come.

He hadn't said any of that out loud.

Instead, he'd simply answered, "Yes." And when he'd walked Hannah to her bedroom later that evening and had shared a slow, lingering kiss good night—as they did every night since he'd moved in—it had taken every ounce of restraint he'd had to pull away from her caressing hands and desire-filled expression and return to his bed across the hall.

He loved Hannah. Putting down roots at the ranch and nurturing a family with her would be sheer heaven. But that choice didn't belong to him. His future in Paradise Peak—and any mercy he might receive—resided in Margaret's hands.

"Hi, handsome," a familiar, feminine voice called. "You looking for me?"

Travis smiled, left the dirt path, and walked over to the paddock fence where Hannah waited, leaning over the top rung.

"Always." He cupped her cheek, dipped his head, and covered her mouth with his, savoring her soft moan of pleasure as he kissed her.

When he released her, she eased away slowly, a dazed look of pleasure in her eyes and a pretty pink flush on her cheeks. She gestured over her shoulder. "After a month of lessons, I do believe Zeke has the hang of it."

Across the paddock, Zeke, wearing a helmet and wide smile, sat astride a small pony. Liz, laughing and praising the boy, held Zeke protectively in the saddle with both hands as Margaret led the pony in a slow walk around the paddock. Blondie padded along the grass on the other side of the fence behind them, tail wagging.

Travis waved. "Looking good there, Zeke."

Catching Travis's eye across the paddock, Zeke grinned brightly and shouted, "Giant, I ride!"

Travis laughed. "You most certainly are. You're as talented as your mama."

"I tell you what though," Liz called out, smiling, "I've never worked harder training a child than I have with Zeke. He's been a handful, haven't you, baby?"

Zeke giggled, bounced slightly in his saddle, and said, "Go, Ginny."

Ginny, along with three other horses, had been found by their owner wandering the charred landscape a week after the wildfire. Though the horses had suffered only minor injuries, the owner's stables had been completely destroyed, so Red had offered to board and care for them at Paradise Peak Ranch until the owner was able to rebuild.

During the first month after Ben's death, Liz had spent most of her time caring for the newly acquired horses as well as Juno, Ruby, and Oreo, comforting Zeke, and trying to heal from the grief of losing her husband. Her recovery had been slow at first, but by the first week of April, she'd begun to rise out of her depression and, after introducing Zeke to the horses, she'd begun giving him and other kids who'd sought refuge at the ranch riding lessons.

"I see you've got things well in hand here."

At the sound of the male voice, Travis looked over his shoulder to find Carl walking around the corner of the stable toward him and Hannah.

"Did you doubt it, Carl?" Hannah asked, smiling.

Reaching them, Carl stopped by Travis and leaned onto his elbows on the top fence rung. "Nah, I expected it. I stopped by the lodge on the way in to deliver a portable dance floor to Margaret for the shindig tomorrow night. She filled me in on the progress you've made." He glanced around, nodding toward the adults and children milling about the ranch, and raised his voice above the pound of hammers in the distance. "Told me all your cabins were full, and how much your guests have pitched in on repairs to the cabins, fences, and banquet hall."

"Together, we've made more progress over the past two months than Red and I alone managed over the course of five years." Hannah smiled at Travis. "Travis even installed that new stone walkway Margaret has been hounding us about, along with just about everything else she asked for." She glanced at Carl and cocked her head to the side. "How are things at your place? And downtown?"

"Slow going," Carl said. "We're rebuilding the stable we lost, and I got a crew coming in next week to repair the damage to my house. Nothing too major. A few businesses have opened up again, but downtown still has a long way to go." He frowned. "I heard over eighteen thousand acres burned, and at last count, more than two thousand homes, businesses, and other buildings were destroyed. Not to mention, we lost twelve people." A sad smile appeared as he watched Liz and Zeke. "It's good to hear Liz laughing again. I was worried sick about her there for a while."

Hannah sighed. "Weren't we all? But she's doing well, and I'm determined she and Zeke will continue to get better every day from here on out. Which reminds me, I need to help untack Ginny and feed the horses since Red will have dinner ready soon." She smiled at Carl. "You are coming to the dance tomorrow night, aren't you? Considering all the work you've done helping Red and Margaret put it together, I'd hate for you to miss the final result."

Carl laughed. "Margaret wouldn't let me miss it. She's already roped me into finding a stage for the band she's going to hire."

"Oh, boy." Hannah rolled her eyes and grinned. "She's probably running you as ragged as she has Red over the past week. They've been bickering something awful." She rose to her tiptoes and kissed Travis's cheek. "See you at the lodge soon, handsome. We'll have another front row seat at dinner for the Red and Margaret Friday night fireworks."

Travis smiled, watching as she jogged to join Liz and Margaret, who led Zeke and Ginny toward the stable.

"Seems you two have gotten close," Carl said, leaning more heavily on the fence. "I heard it mentioned around town last month that you'd moved into Hannah's cabin."

Travis tensed, his smile fading. "News travels fast around here."

Carl nodded. "That it does."

They stood silently for a few moments, listening to the pound of hammers and children's laughter in the distance; then Carl said quietly, "Thing is, that alone wouldn't bother me, considering all the good you've done. Matter of fact, after I heard about what you did for Liz and Zeke—hell, what you've done for all these people when you turned this place into a refuge—I suggested to Ben's partner on the police force that we put together some recognition for you." He glanced at Travis, his eyes narrowing. "You know, have a small ceremony in memory of Ben and present an award of some type to Paradise Peak's newest golden boy. Ben's partner made a few calls to Rockton Park, hoping to get ahold of some of your people and discuss putting together a small ceremony here at the ranch. He couldn't track down any of your family, but he got a call yesterday from the sheriff's department."

Travis clenched his hands around the top rung of the fence, his jaw tightening.

"I know you're not Travis Miller," Carl said. "You're Neil Travis Alden, right? The drunk driver who killed Margaret's daughter twenty years ago?"

Travis faced him then, met his piercing gaze. "That's who I used to be." He straightened and pulled in a heavy breath before saying slowly, "But it's not who I am anymore."

Carl returned his stare for a moment, then nodded slowly. "I'm not here to cause trouble for you. You've served your time, and I believe everyone should have a second chance. But I also think you're wrong to hide the truth." He turned away and refocused on Hannah, watching as she untacked the pony by the stable. "Does Hannah know who you really are? Or Margaret and Red?"

Shame surged through Travis, scorching his skin and drawing his shoulders down. "No."

Carl sighed. "I care about Hannah—always have. She deserves the truth, and I don't want her hurt."

Travis stilled as Hannah caught his attention, waving and smiling from the other side of the paddock as she led the pony into the stable.

"I don't want to hurt Hannah," he said quietly, wishing he hadn't committed such an awful act, wishing he'd been a better man in the past. The kind of man Hannah deserved. "I don't want to hurt Margaret or Red either. But there'll be no way around that, once I tell them the truth."

"And when will that be?"

Travis forced himself to speak. "Sunday morning."

After the spring dance. That way, if he was asked to leave Paradise Peak, he'd at least have one more perfect memory of Hannah and the family he'd grown to love to carry in his heart with him.

Red's hamburgers were grilled to perfection, a warm spring breeze blew across the freshly stained deck of the lodge, and the solar lights strung along the deck rails sparkled to life as the sun slowly set, giving way to a starry night sky.

This Friday evening dinner should've been as pleasant and relaxing as all the others, but Hannah couldn't shake the feeling that something was off. Or, more to the point, something was up with the men who sat at the table.

Red, who sat at the head of the table, had toyed with the swan napkin beside his plate for most of the meal, and shot anxious looks at Margaret as she talked a mile a minute. Travis, seated to Margaret's right, had smiled politely and nodded occasionally, giving the impression that he was interested in every word she said, but each time Margaret had paused to catch a breath, he'd stared at the mountain range with a somber expression on his face.

And those guilty shadows in his eyes—the ones she'd

noticed the night Margaret had hugged him at the One Stop Motel—had returned full force.

Hannah reached across the table and squeezed Travis's hand. "Are you feeling all right? You've barely said two words all evening."

He glanced in her direction and smiled—the action forced and his mouth tight—then looked down at the formal dinner plate, still full of food, that Margaret had placed in front of him an hour ago. "I'm fine."

Hardly. Hannah frowned. He'd barely touched his meal and had yet to look her in the eyes since they'd joined Red and Margaret on the deck for dinner. And over the past few days, she'd noticed that the more the ranch had thrived with the new improvements, the quieter and more withdrawn Travis had become.

Just last night, as they'd sat on the front porch and watched the Carrollton boys chase fireflies, she'd asked Travis in the most undemanding way she could manage if he'd thought about having children. She'd held her breath, waiting for his answer and hoping he'd open up to her about his wishes for the future, hoping that maybe, he'd grown to care for her as much as she had for him. And for a moment, he'd looked at her in such a way that she thought he might finally open up.

But he hadn't. Instead, he'd only offered a quiet, one-word reply, kissed her good night as usual a couple hours later, then returned to his room, leaving her to crawl into her bed, frustrated and longing for his touch, for the umpteenth night in a row.

Seemed it would take a much more drastic act to snag his attention.

Shaking her head, she leaned closer and whispered, "Something's wrong. I can see it on your face. Are you going to tell me what's going on?"

Travis hesitated, then moved to speak. "I need t—"

"And do you know what Phillip and Niki did next?" Margaret tapped her hands on the table and raised her eyebrows at Red. "They took the bet and held an impromptu father and daughter pool tournament after the dinner party, won every round, and donated all the proceeds to a children's charity." Smiling, she sighed. "Oh, Phillip always did know how to have a good time, and Niki was always up for anything when it came to her father."

Red shifted in his chair and cleared his throat. "Speaking of a good time, Carl told me earlier this afternoon, before he left, that you'd asked him to bring by a portable dance floor?"

Margaret nodded. "I hope you and Travis won't mind putting it together tomorrow afternoon before the party? Carl said it's one of those snap together deals, so it shouldn't be too much trouble to set up."

Red smiled stiffly. "No problem. Though, I thought we'd agreed to just use the field across from the stable."

"Oh, but a dance floor will keep everyone's nice shoes out of the grass and dirt." Margaret elbowed Hannah good-naturedly and winked. "Our high heels will be safe."

"Hannah doesn't wear high heels," Red pointed out.

Wincing at the angry note in Red's voice, Hannah sneaked a glance at Travis, her cheeks burning. "It might be nice to dress up just this once." She smiled at Margaret. "I told Margaret I would. As a matter of fact, I was planning to swing by and see Gloria tomorrow to pick out a dr—"

"And not too many people are gonna dress to the nines for an outdoor dance anyway," Red interrupted, eyeing Margaret. "I've told guests it's an informal celebration where they can kick back, relax, and enjoy each other's company."

"But I've already told most of the ladies that the dance is to be a formal affair," Margaret countered. "And it's not just for my enjoyment. Gloria received a shipment of new stock for her store last month that she'd ordered before the fire. There are several beautiful dresses and suits in those boxes, and besides a few hardware items, that clothing is the only merchandise Gloria and Vernon have available at the moment. Selling a few items would help boost their income and several women have already bought dresses. It'd be a shame to change the plan now."

Red frowned. "Well, I wouldn't want to hurt Gloria and Vernon's income, so I'll go along with that, but everything else"—he drew a line in the air with both hands—"stays exactly as I originally planned."

Travis shifted uneasily in his seat, and Hannah glanced at Margaret, who nibbled her bottom lip and twisted her hands together.

"Except for maybe one thing," Margaret said in a small voice. "I asked Carl to set up a stage tomorrow afternoon and I've found two bands that are available for performing tomorrow night. I just need to decide which group to go with."

Red's cheeks turned scarlet.

Laughing, Margaret spread her hands. "And of course, we'll need tables and chairs around the dance floor as well as decorations. And a tent for—"

"Now, that's it," Red snapped. "No tents. God didn't go to all the trouble of hanging stars in the sky just for us to cover 'em up. And we don't need fancy decorations. We've got tons of white outdoor lights stored away that we usually use at Christmas. We'll break those out and string 'em on poles outside the banquet hall. And as for a band, we've got two guitar players staying at the ranch right now, and if we ask around, I'm sure we'll find more than one person willing to sing."

"Kate Carrollton sings at weddings on occasion," Hannah said, hoping to ease the tension. She glanced at Margaret. "You know, the young woman with three boys who moved into Travis's old cabin? She's already said she'd be willing to pitch in."

"Perfect." Red nodded. "Sun's been setting around seven, so we'll start up the music around seven-thirty. That work for you, Travis?"

Travis, cheeks flushing, looked at Red, then Margaret, and back to Red. "I suppose."

"But what about dinner?" Margaret asked. "I thought we could serve a formal meal in the banquet hall around six and—"

"Now, I said no more changes and I meant it," Red snapped. "I've already arranged for finger foods and punch to be served outside. We're not making this into a five-star, hoity-toity event. It's going to be a simple, enjoyable evening."

Margaret's mouth fell open.

Travis held up a placating hand. "Red, Margaret was just trying to help."

"Thank you." Margaret lifted her chin. "All I was doing was—"

"Trying to do things the way you used to do them with Phillip," Red said, his voice cracking. "Well, I ain't Phillip."

Silence fell over the table.

Heart aching, Hannah glanced at Travis, who grimaced and looked down.

Margaret's cheeks flushed. "I—I never thought you were."

"Of course you didn't," he continued. "You barely stop talking about him long enough to think about another man."

Hannah reached out, placed her hand on Margaret's where it rested on the table, and squeezed. "Red, I don't think this is the best time for—"

"I'm sorry, I didn't mean to do this now, and I had something a lot more polite planned, but I've wasted enough time waiting." Red's tone softened as he studied Margaret's pained expression. "Now, I know you loved Phillip. And I know you're still trying to get over him. But you got to start living again, too." He glanced at Hannah. "We all do—including me." He stood and faced Margaret. "I love you, Margaret. I've loved you every day that Phillip did, and maybe a few more. And yes, he was rich and I'm broke. He wore suits and ties and held fancy dinner parties, whereas I'd be just as content dancing around in the dirt, so long as I have you in my arms."

Margaret continued staring, openmouthed, at Red.

"What I'm saying is that I'll be at that dance tomorrow night waiting for you and hoping you're ready to open your mind and your heart to taking a chance on me." Red sighed. "If you're not interested, I'll understand, and I'll move on. This will still be your home and things will go on as before. I just need to know one way or the other."

Red tossed his mangled swan napkin on the table and left, his steps heavy as he descended the stairs.

"I'll go check on him," Travis said quietly as he stood. He glanced at Margaret, then Hannah. "See you back at the cabin."

Hannah watched him go, then looked at Margaret, who braced her hands on the table and pushed her chair back with slow movements.

"I'm going to turn in early tonight," Margaret whispered. "Good night, Hannah."

The deck creaked as Margaret walked across the boards and entered the lodge, the door clicking shut behind her.

"Good night," Hannah said softly, though the evening had been everything but good. She stared at the empty table and twinkling solar lights and wondered if tomorrow night's dance would be any better.

CHAPTER 12

Travis climbed to the top of the nine-foot ladder, attached a long strip of white tulle to a thin metal wire strung between two, tall wooden poles, and draped a string of white lights over the material. "This good?"

Red, standing on the ground by the ladder, shielded his eyes against the late-afternoon sun and squinted up at Travis. "That'll do." He reached into a large box near his feet, retrieved another strip of tulle and a string of lights, and lifted them toward Travis. "Once we get all the tulle and lights hung, I'll go around and tie 'em together in a few places to make 'em look more like curtains."

Travis stepped two rungs down the ladder, took the tulle and lights from Red, then climbed back up the ladder and fastened the materials to the wire. "You want me to run a few extension cords from the stable to power the lights?"

"No need," Red said. "Those lights are battery powered and I got remotes that run 'em, so they'll be good to go with just a few button pushes after dark." He frowned as he passed Travis another handful of tulle and lights. "I thought about asking Margaret to do the honors, but I ain't sure she'd be in the mood to humor me after the way

I acted last night. She didn't come down for breakfast this morning and she's been cooped up in that kitchen with Hannah all day, cooking."

Travis winced and glanced across the open field at the lodge. Several guests moved around the deck, filling coolers with bags of ice and packing each cooler with bottles of water, soda, and beer. Others carried two long tables and several tablecloths toward the field where he and Red worked, presumably in preparation for the buffet of finger foods and punch Margaret and Hannah had spent all afternoon creating.

On the other side of Travis, several guests assembled a twenty-four by twenty-four foot portable dance floor in a light maple wood tone while Carl and three other men erected a portable stage. A small band comprised of guests stood near the grassy area Red had squared-off in the field for the dance, chatting and laughing while they tuned up their instruments in preparation for their performance, which would begin in three hours, at seven-thirty sharp.

All preparations for the spring dance were well in hand, but despite the energetic activity occurring in most areas of the ranch, Travis, like Red, had yet to lay eyes on Margaret or Hannah.

After last night's episode at dinner, he'd followed Red for a walk around the grounds and lent a sympathetic ear. It was past eleven by the time he'd returned to Hannah's cabin and, noticing the lack of light under her bedroom door, he'd decided not to disturb her and had gone to bed himself. By the time he'd risen, dressed, and left his room this morning, she'd already departed for the lodge, so he'd joined Red in the field to begin preparing for the dance.

"I didn't mean to lose my temper and spill my secrets for all and sundry last night," Red said, grabbing another bundle of tulle and lights out of the box. "Matter of fact, I had tonight planned out over a month ago." He passed the materials up to Travis. "I was gonna set the stage with a nice, relaxed party, woo Margaret with a romantic dance or two under the stars, then tell her I loved her." Shoulders sagging, he smacked his knee. "Instead, I spilled my guts across the dinner table in front of my niece and a bunch of swan napkins."

Despite the sympathy he felt at Red's embarrassment, Travis stifled a smile. "I wouldn't go counting yourself out yet." He fastened the tulle and lights securely, then climbed down the ladder. "You might have lost your temper a bit, but at least you were honest." A wave of guilt moved through Travis as he said the words. "Margaret knows exactly how you feel, and the ball's in her court now. You never know—things might turn out better than you think."

"That's what I keep trying to tell myself." Red ran a hand through his gray hair. "Guess sometimes you just gotta let the chips fall where they may."

"Yeah." Travis picked up a section of tulle and rubbed his thumb over the soft material, thinking of Hannah and wondering if there'd be any chance of a future for them once she knew the truth. "Guess you do."

"Getting ideas, are you?"

He looked up to find Red watching him, humor in the other man's eyes. It took Travis back to the day he'd first arrived in Paradise Peak. Back to the moment he'd first sat beside Red in his truck, with Hannah's picture beneath his fingertips and breathtaking mountain scenery all around.

Travis had never felt such promise and possibility as he had when he'd set his eyes on Paradise Peak for the first time. And he'd never imagined he'd fall so deeply in love with the rugged land . . . or with Hannah.

But no matter how high or how far he traveled into these beautiful mountains, his past would never alter, and there was a very good chance that he'd lose everything—and everyone—he held dear now because of it. And maybe, despite his hopes for the opposite, that's how it should be.

"Yesterday," Travis said softly, "when Carl was here, he said he thought everyone deserved a second chance." He studied Red's expression, his eyes tracing the familiar lines of the other man's face—a man he'd grown to love as a father. "Do you believe that? Do you think everyone deserves a second chance, no matter what they've done?"

The teasing light faded from Red's eyes, and he stared at Travis, his gaze peering so deep, Travis took a step back.

"What have you done, Travis?"

His throat closed, and he couldn't speak. Instead, Travis dragged a hand over his face and turned away. He looked down and watched the white tulle billow in the breeze, the long ends trailing across the grass. Then he swallowed hard and faced Red again.

"I tell you what," Travis said, motioning toward the box of tulle and lights. "I can handle this on my own. Why don't you take a break and unwind before the dance gets started?"

"Travis, if you need help with something, I—"

"I got it." Knowing full well Red wasn't referring to tulle and lights, Travis forced a smile. The act made his cheeks ache. "Let me take it from here, okay?"

Red studied Travis's face, then nodded slowly and backed away. "All right. I'll use the extra time to pick up a suit from Gloria. Maybe that'll score me bonus points with Margaret. I'll meet you back here in three hours to flip on the lights." He turned around and walked to the dirt path nearby but stopped a few feet away and glanced over his shoulder. "For the record, I'm not opposed to you getting ideas about Hannah." He gestured toward the tulle and smiled. "So long as it includes making an honest man and woman out of both of you."

"I promise you, an honest man is all I plan to be from here on out," Travis said softly.

Red held his gaze a moment more, then left.

Over the next hour, Travis hung tulle and string lights, then tied loose sections of both together with silver ribbons to form a series of festive curtains around the dance floor. Afterward, he watched guests cross the field to and from the lodge, carrying decorations, supplies, and the like. After casting another glance at the lodge, he followed the long dirt trail around to Gloria and Vernon's cabin, climbed the steps, and knocked on the screen door.

"Just a minute, please," Gloria called out.

Travis ran a hand through his sweaty hair and grimaced, wishing he'd swung by Hannah's cabin and showered before visiting Gloria. He'd turned and made it halfway down the front steps when the screen door banged open behind him.

"Hold up there." Gloria stood in the doorway, holding a cookie cutter in the shape of a star in one hand, and wearing an apron around her waist. "Where you off to in such a hurry?"

Travis stopped on the bottom step, wiped his damp palm on his jean-covered thigh, and smiled nervously. "I wanted to conduct a little business, but I just finished working and realized I'm not exactly presentable."

Gloria made a dismissive gesture with the cookie cutter. "Oh, hogwash. We don't stand on formalities here." She propped the screen door open wider with her elbow. "Come on in and tell me what I can do for you."

Travis thanked her and went inside. The sweet aroma of sugar cookies made his mouth water and he issued a sound of pleasure. "You got it smelling delicious in here."

"Thank you, dear. That'd be warm sugar cookies fresh out of the oven—my mama's special recipe. Margaret asked me to cook up a couple batches to take down to the dance this evening." She walked into the kitchen and waved for him to follow. "Come grab you one. I was just about to throw another batch in the oven and decorate the first with silver icing and edible sparkle."

"I appreciate the offer, but I'm actually here about a dress."

Gloria, her brow furrowed, poked her head around the open door of the kitchen. "A dress, you say?"

Face flaming, Travis dragged a hand over the back of his neck and cleared his throat. "Yes, ma'am. Margaret mentioned that you received that order of stock you'd placed a while back, and that some of the ladies had stopped in to buy a dress for tonight. I was wondering if you had one left. I'm thinking something blue. Cool and comfortable." He shrugged awkwardly. "That is, if Hannah hasn't already been by . . ."

An expression of surprised pleasure slowly worked its way over Gloria's face, and she clapped her flour-coated hands together. "Well, Glory be! How romantic. And, no, she hasn't been by yet." She untied her apron and flung it over her shoulder. "I have just the thing—follow me."

Ten minutes and four dresses later, Travis gave the go-ahead on a short, blue dress the color of Hannah's eyes.

"It's made of light fabric with a cinched waist and loose skirt, so she'll stay cool and comfortable," Gloria said with pleasure. "And it's casual enough to pair with sandals so she won't even have to wear pantyhose."

Travis coughed. "That's . . . good. Thank you, Gloria."

A conspiratorial smile crossed her face. She leaned forward and whispered, "Now, if you really want to sweep her off her feet, you'll let me toss it in a gift box and have it delivered."

"But"—he glanced at his wristwatch—"the dance starts in less than two hours, and—"

"Oh, fiddle-faddle. Vernon might be up in years, but he's swift on his feet. Would you like it delivered to her cabin or the lodge?"

"Well, she's at the lodge right now, cooking with—"

"Excellent." Gloria turned her head, cupped a hand around her mouth, and shouted, "Vernon! Come in the house—we have a delivery to make to the lodge." She faced Travis and smiled. "Now, what was that 'and' you mentioned? Did you need something else?"

Travis nodded. "A suit and . . ."

She raised an eyebrow. "And?"

Travis licked his lips, then asked, "Do you know how to dance?"

"Of course." She blinked. "You mean, you don't?"

Travis shook his head. "Not at all. It's been years since . . ." He shoved his hands in his pockets. "The thing is, I want to do everything I can to make tonight as perfect as possible for Hannah." And for himself, since he had no idea if he'd be able to hold Hannah in his arms again after tonight's dance. "I've got about half an hour to spare for a crash course in dancing before I need to shower and get ready." He reached for his wallet. "I'd be happy to pay for a lesson or t—"

"Oh, no. Your money's no good here, young man, and you knocked on the right door." Her eyes widened with excitement as she looped her arm around his. "This lesson is liable to be more fun for me than you. Now, you just come right over here with me. . . ."

*   *   *

Hannah placed a slice of ham and provolone cheese on raw dough, rolled it into the shape of a croissant, and set it on a large pan lined with at least a dozen others.

"There," she said, wiping her hands off with a paper towel and pinning what she hoped was a sincere smile on her face. "Once this batch is baked, I think we'll have plenty."

Margaret, her hair pulled back tight in a ponytail and eyes puffy, walked over to the kitchen island, picked up the pan and, eyeing the ham and cheese croissants, pursed her lips. "Two more sheets' worth, at least." She whisked the full pan away, shoved it into the oven, and set the timer. "When I come back, we'll start on the mini BLTs."

Hannah slumped on the kitchen island and covered her eyes, watching through spread fingers as Margaret left the room.

"Mini BLTs?" Liz asked, slumping next to Hannah. "And two more pans of ham and cheese croissants?" She waved a hand toward the countertops in the lodge's kitchen, every inch of which was covered with platters, bowls, plates, and dishes full of finger foods. "Where on earth will we put it all?"

Groaning, Hannah shook her head. "On the floor, I guess. That's the only place left."

She uncovered her eyes and looked over the island. Zeke sat on the floor in front of the island, his back against the cabinets, a half-eaten slice of ham clutched in his fist.

Hearing movement above him, Zeke tilted his head back and smiled up at Hannah. Mustard was smeared along his left cheek. "Mmm"—he smacked his lips—"ham."

Blondie, sitting next to him, sprang up and licked the mustard on his cheek, her tail wagging vigorously.

"Never mind," Hannah said, slumping back onto the counter. "Floor's already taken."

"Oh, Zeke!" Liz scrambled to the sink, wet a paper towel, and squatted beside Zeke to wipe his face. "Don't let Blondie lick you in the face. It's not sanitary."

Zeke scowled and batted her hands away.

Liz sat back on her heels and blew a strand of hair out of her eyes. "We can't keep cooking much longer—otherwise we'll miss the party."

"I know." Hannah studied the empty doorway leading to the hall. "Margaret's depressed, and when she's depressed, she cooks."

Liz stood, a helpless expression on her face. "For twelve hours? We've been doing this since six this morning and it's"—she glanced at the clock by the stove—"almost six in the afternoon. What's upset her so?"

"Red." Hannah sighed. "He told her he loved her last night during dinner."

"Oh." Liz's hand rose, her fingers touching her gaping mouth. "Oh, wow. Right in the middle of dinner?"

"Yep. He told me a couple months ago that he wanted to tell her, and last night, Margaret was talking about Phillip—like she does during every dinner—and I guess Red had held his peace for so long that his patience finally just ran out."

"What did Margaret say?" Liz asked.

Hannah shrugged. "Not much of anything, really. She looked shocked and embarrassed, of course. Then Red stormed off and she said good night and left, too. Now, here we are with a million pounds of finger foods and a crowd of guests expecting us to kick off a happy spring dance in an hour and a half."

Liz rubbed her forehead and stood. "Well, as much as I'd like to stay and continue this never-ending bake-off,

I've got to take Zeke back to the cabin and get us both ready." She grabbed a small bag of cooking supplies she'd brought with her, hitched it over her shoulder, and held her hand out to Zeke. "Come on, sweetheart."

Zeke frowned. "We go?"

"Yes," Liz said. "We go. Say good-bye to Hannah. You'll see her again at the dance."

Zeke pushed to his feet, opening and closing his raised hand as Blondie yipped by his side. "Bye, Hannah."

Hannah smiled. "Bye, baby."

Liz paused on the threshold and looked back, a grateful smile appearing. "You know I never have thanked you properly."

"For what?"

"For dragging me off the floor, wiping my face, and nudging me back into the world." Her eyes glistened beneath the overhead lights and she blinked rapidly. "I wouldn't have put one foot in front of the other two months ago if you hadn't done what you did. And now, I don't feel quite as guilty when I smile." She tipped her chin toward the hallway where Margaret had exited. "Maybe that's what Margaret needs right now. One of your tough-love nudges."

Hannah stared at the empty doorway for several minutes after Liz, Zeke, and Blondie departed, then slowly straightened. Shoving her hands in her pockets, she left the kitchen and walked down the hall and into the foyer, where Margaret stood by a table, holding a framed picture in her hands.

Phillip and Niki smiled behind the glass, father and daughter hugging on a beach, waves crashing behind them as they laughed into the camera, their blond hair ruffled by the ocean breeze.

"You still miss them something awful, don't you?" Hannah asked softly.

Margaret started and looked up, her knuckles turning white as her grip tightened on the picture frame. "Yes." A tear rolled down her flushed cheek as she traced the contours of Phillip's face with her fingertip. "I took this at our beach house in Florida a little over twenty years ago. Niki was on spring break from college—it was her birthday; she'd just turned twenty—and Phillip had earned a promotion at the bank the week before." A sad smile crossed her lips. "That was the last time all three of us were together. After that, Phillip returned to work, and Niki went back to college. I had no idea that would be the last good memory we'd have there together." Her voice trembled. "Niki was killed two weeks later, and I never saw it coming." She looked at Hannah, her eyes full of pain and regret. "As her mother, shouldn't I have felt it? When I hugged her that last time, shouldn't I have known?"

Hannah shook her head, her own eyes filling with tears.

"Why is it we never know?" Margaret whispered, staring at the photograph. "It isn't fair, is it?"

"No," Hannah said brokenly. "It's not."

Margaret studied the photograph more closely. "I think that's why I've had such a hard time letting them go—especially Niki. The way she was taken from us . . ." Her voice caught. "I never really had the chance to say a proper good-bye to my family."

Hannah wiped her wet cheeks, searching for the right thing to say. Hoping to offer some small bit of comfort. She'd understood Red's frustration last night—Lord knows, she'd experienced the same feeling when it came to Margaret. But she, of all people, knew there was no time limit on pain or grief. Not on Margaret's pain . . . or her own.

How could she have been so selfish?

"Margaret, I—"

"But I have to say good-bye now," Margaret said softly, cradling the framed photograph in her hands. "For Red." She opened a drawer in the foyer table, turned the framed photograph over, and placed it inside. "For you." She shut the drawer, faced Hannah, and smiled. "And for Travis. Because the three of you are my family now."

"Yes," Hannah whispered, smiling. "We are." She pulled in a shaky breath. "But as glad as I am to hear that, and as much as I love you, I don't want you to feel like you have to do this just because Red—"

"I love Red." Margaret nodded, her voice growing firm. "I fell in love with him months ago but couldn't face up to it because it would mean I'd have no choice but to let Phillip and Niki go. It felt too much like a betrayal." She picked at a pleat in her skirt. "Red has always been so patient and understanding, and even if I didn't mean to take advantage, I did exactly that. I just hope I'm not too late to tell him how sorry I am, and that I do truly love him."

Hannah laughed through the tears pouring down her cheeks. "Red loves you too much to let you apologize."

Margaret grabbed Hannah's hands and squeezed. "Let's hope so." She looked around the foyer, nodding toward the dozens of photographs of Phillip and Niki lining the walls and adorning the table. "Will you help me take down the rest, and pack them away? I'd like to have a clean slate when I tell Red how I feel tonight."

"On one condition," Hannah said. At Margaret's somber silence, she added, "No mini BLTs, and please, no more ham and cheese croissants."

Laughing, Margaret hugged her. "No more cooking, period. We'll just pack these away and freshen up for the dance."

In agreement, Hannah removed photos from one wall

while Margaret took them off another and they stacked them carefully on the foyer table, then transferred them to a sturdy storage container. They'd just secured the lid when someone knocked on the front door of the lodge.

"I'll get it," Hannah said, hugging Margaret once more, then jogging to the front door.

Vernon stood on the porch, a white rectangular box tied with a red ribbon in his hands. "Delivery for you, Ms. Hannah."

Frowning in confusion, she took the box and tilted it one way, then the other, searching for a tag. "Thank you, but who's it from?"

"Here's the card." Vernon smiled, a teasing light in his eyes, and placed a small, red envelope on top of the box. "See you at the dance."

As Vernon left, she thanked him again, then shut the door and opened the card.

> *Dear Hannah,*
> *There are so many things I want to tell you . . . (but with Gloria spying over my shoulder as I write, I doubt I'll have the opportunity).*

Hannah laughed.

> *So I'll leave it at this: Wear this dress tonight if you want—but only if you want. You're as beautiful on the inside as you are on the outside, so what you wear won't matter. I still won't be able to take my eyes off you.*
> *Travis*

Hannah opened the box and touched the blue dress inside, her fingers drifting over the silky material. "If I want . . ."

Oh, she wanted. She wanted Travis—loved him more than anything—and she wanted to share her life with him and add to their new family right here in Paradise Peak. It was time she gave *herself* a tough-love nudge and took a leap of faith for the bright future she hoped waited for her and Travis. Tonight would be the perfect time to tell him.

CHAPTER 13

Festive notes from acoustic guitars and Kate Carrollton's soft, melodious voice filled the open field beside the stable. Bright stars and a full moon lit up the night sky, and the strings of lights Travis had arranged around the dance floor cast a gentle glow over the couples swaying to the slow rhythm of the music. Laughter, happy chatter, and the squeals of children playing nearby floated on the warm spring air, and everyone seemed to be enjoying themselves.

Everyone, that was, except Red.

"Whoever invented the necktie deserves a swift kick in the ass." Red, standing on the grass by the dance floor, hooked a finger under the collar of his dress shirt and tugged. "A man can't breathe—or think—properly with the damn thing on."

Travis smiled by his side. "Nervous?"

Red frowned. "Maybe." His mustache twitched. "I mean, where are they? This shindig started over half an hour ago, and I haven't seen hide nor hair of Margaret or Hannah."

Travis slid his hands in his pockets, hiding the tremors running through his fingers. "They're probably just running behind. Bet they're on their way out here now."

Yeah. That was it. He leaned to the side and peered past Red into the dark stretch of field between the lodge and the dance floor, hoping for a glimpse of Hannah or Margaret strolling through the high grass toward them. But he didn't see either one of them, and the gnawing ache in his chest grew.

"What if I pushed Margaret too far, too fast?" Red asked softly. "What if I blew my only chance to—"

"You did the right thing," Travis said. "You were honest about how you felt, and up-front about what you wanted." He looked away, watching a couple on the dance floor press closer together, smile, and whisper to each other. "That's the only way to begin."

Red blew out a heavy breath. "Lord, I hope you're right."

So do I. Travis closed his eyes, a chill clawing up the back of his neck. There'd be no turning back after tonight. Tomorrow morning, he had to tell Margaret, Red . . . and Hannah the truth. And God knows if he'd be able to find the right words, much less be able to say them out loud. Or if Hannah would ever be able to look at him the same way again.

Warm palms pressed against his cool cheeks and a sweet voice whispered against his ear. "If you're going to keep your eyes on me, you have to open them."

Travis grew still as Hannah's soft words and gentle touch warmed him on the inside, chasing the chill from his skin. He opened his eyes.

She stood in front of him, her hands still cupping his face and her big, blue eyes looking up at him. As he focused on her, she trailed her hands away from his cheeks, stepped back, and lowered her arms to her sides.

Moonlight pooled over her long auburn curls and bare shoulders, casting a soft sheen on the blue dress she wore.

The satin material fit perfectly, clinging to the soft curves of her full breasts and hips, and the flirty ruffle lining the hem fluttered against the smooth skin of her toned thighs in the light, evening breeze.

Smiling, she whispered, "You said to wear it if I wanted." Her graceful hands moved, her pretty, unpolished nails picking nervously at the delicate hem of the dress. "Do you like it?"

The tight ache in his chest receded as he met her eyes, and an intense wave of wanting moved through him, tightening his abs and making his tongue slow. "Yes." His voice, when it emerged, was husky and he cleared his throat. "Very much."

She blushed, the light pink coloring her cheeks deepening as her gaze roved over him slowly, skimming his chest, hips, and legs, then returning to his face. "You look"—her chest rose on a slow inhale—"very handsome."

He grinned. "Thank you."

"That'd be the suit," Red said, clapping Travis on the back. "Might make a man feel miserable, but it makes him look like a thousand bucks." Chuckling, he stepped forward and hugged Hannah, saying as he released her, "You look beautiful, sweetheart."

"That'd be Travis's doing," she said, grinning. "He picked out the dress. And the curls were courtesy of Margaret."

"Oh?" Red looked around, his tone flippant, but his expression anxious. "Did she come out with you?"

"I did." Margaret, wearing a green dress and matching heels, emerged from the darkness covering the field behind them and stopped in front of Travis. "Well, look at you," she said softly, taking in his suit and tie. "A handsome gentleman."

Travis, his face heating, ducked his head as she moved closer and kissed his cheek. The friendly press of her hand against his wrist and the trust in her eyes made his shoulders tighten.

Margaret turned to Red, her smile fading. "I'm a bit late." Her mouth trembled as she whispered, "I hope I didn't keep you waiting too long."

Red, a relieved expression appearing on his face, blinked rapidly and shook his head. "No."

"Good," Margaret said. "Because I'd really like it if you danced with me."

"Of course." Red held out his hand and took a step toward the dance floor.

Margaret placed her hand on the bend of his elbow, stopping him. "I was thinking about something a little less formal." She reached down and removed her heels, dropping them one at a time to the grass, then untied Red's tie and tossed it on top of her shoes. "Right here, with just you, would be perfect."

Red grinned, slid an arm around Margaret's waist, and winked at Travis and Hannah over her shoulder. "Excuse us, please."

With a twirl and the whisper of feet on grass, Red and Margaret danced across the field away from the crowd, their swaying forms gradually fading to dark silhouettes beneath the bright moonlight, their faint laughter drifting on the night air.

"There's a big dance floor behind us," Hannah said quietly. "It'd be a shame for us not to test it out."

"Yeah." Travis smiled, slipped his hands out of his pockets, and reached for hers. "It would."

He led the way to the dance floor, brushed aside a curtain of tulle and lights, and stepped back to allow Hannah to precede him. Weaving between several couples, he followed her to an open space on the dance floor, his heart skipping a beat when she stepped into his open arms and pressed her cheek to his chest.

Heart pounding in his ears, he slid his left arm around her waist and took her left hand in his right, just as Gloria had shown him. He took one slow step to the right, studied the swaying movements of the other couples, then took another step, timing his movements to the slow beat of the song and the slight sway of Hannah's hips.

His arm tightened against the small of her back, and he forced his hand to relax, his fingers shaking against the smooth indentation of her waist.

Hannah lifted her head from his chest and studied his face, surprise in her eyes. "Are you nervous?"

He nodded stiffly and lowered his head, saying softly, "It's been a long time since I've . . ."

His attention strayed to the sprinkling of freckles across her cute nose, the pink blush in her cheeks, and the slight parting of her soft lips.

She smiled, making every nerve in his body tingle. "Danced?"

"Yeah," he whispered. *Among other things.* Like the strong tug of tenderness Hannah evoked deep in his middle.

Her smile faded and her eyes darkened. "It's been a long time for me, too." She slid her free hand along his biceps to his shoulder, her palm curving around the back of his neck. "We'll remember together."

She pressed closer and nuzzled her cheek against his chest. Her soft hair brushed his chin, releasing the light, floral scent of her shampoo, and Travis hugged her closer, absorbing her warmth, his legs moving easily now, his body swaying in tandem with hers.

For the next three songs, they stayed on the dance floor, moving to the slow tunes on the warm night air, and everything melted away for Travis except the feel of Hannah in his arms, the rapid pound of her heart against his chest, and the gentle glide of her legs against his as she danced.

"Travis?" Hannah stopped dancing and looked up at him, her hand leaving his neck and trailing down his arm to weave her fingers with his. "Can we go home?"

Home. His breath caught at her soft words, and he cupped her face, smoothed his thumbs over her cheeks, and nodded, promising himself he'd stop at her bedroom door. That he'd kiss her good night and return to his own bed as usual and keep himself from doing anything else until he'd told her the truth.

But after walking up the winding path lit only by stars, climbing the front steps of the cabin and reaching the hallway, Hannah held his hand tight and stepped closer, her blue eyes steady on his.

"Do you remember what you told me? That when we make love, you want it to be because I know all of you, and want you for who you are?"

Travis grew still, every part of him yearning to pull her close, never let go, and refuse to face the consequences of tomorrow. But another part resisted, knowing things would change when she learned the truth. That this emotion she felt for him could so easily turn to hate when she knew who he really was.

"Hannah—"

"I know you," she whispered, easing closer, her thighs brushing his. "I know how protective and kind you are. How brave, considerate, and passionate." She lifted her hand, her palm pressing against his chest, over his heart. "I know you carry regrets—like we all do. And I hope you share them with me someday, because I love you. Every part of you."

He waited, not breathing, not moving—just holding on

to her words. To the accepting tone of her voice and the admiration in her eyes.

"Do you love me?" she asked.

And he couldn't lie. He wouldn't lie to her. Not anymore.

"Yes." He cupped her face, lowered his forehead to hers, and closed his eyes, listening to her soft, rapid breaths, and savoring her warm touch against his chest. "I love you."

A ragged breath left her lips, and he covered her mouth with his. Her lips parted, and he sampled her sweetness. A soft moan of pleasure and need left her mouth and entered his own.

He wrapped his arms around her, pulled her close, and slid his hands over the silky material of her dress until his palms met her warm, bare upper back.

"Travis . . ." She pulled back, took his hand in hers, and tugged him toward her bedroom.

Unable to resist the need surging inside him, he followed.

When they reached the foot of her bed, her hands went to his tie, her fingers fumbling over the knot and buttons underneath, her blue eyes holding his gaze.

Travis helped her remove his tie and shirt, then stood still, his abs quivering slightly, as her hands explored him, smoothing over his shoulders, biceps, and chest. Then her fingers traveled lower, sliding slowly over his midsection, and removed the rest of his clothing.

He reached for her, skimmed his hands over her curves, then removed her dress, sliding it over her head to trail kisses along her neck, breasts, and belly. He lingered there, nuzzling his cheek against the soft curve of her belly, allowing himself to dream for a brief moment of what it'd be like to feel their child growing there, sheltered, protected, and loved. Then he moved lower still, worshipping every inch of her with his hands, mouth, and heart.

A soft cry of pleasure escaped her, and she speared her fingers through his hair and tugged him to his feet again, her lips meeting his, her hands and body nudging him back onto the bed where she followed.

He let her take the lead, his breath leaving him in heavy exhales as she moved over him, her breasts brushing his chest, and her soft heat surrounding him tightly. Waves of emotion rolled through him, intensifying with each of her movements, until he gripped her soft hips, rolled her gently to her back, and took over, only slowing when they were both overcome, her arms and legs wrapping around him and cradling him close as their hearts spilled over.

Afterward, he rolled to his back and took her with him, hugging her close to his chest and tucking her head beneath his chin. Their pounding hearts slowed in time together and her fingers smoothed through the sprinkling of hair on his chest in slow, relaxed movements.

"I love you," she whispered, closing her eyes, her cheek nestled against the base of his throat.

He wanted to say the same, but emotion—strong and overwhelming—surged over him, threatening his composure. Instead, he held her tighter.

Soon, Hannah's breathing grew deep and even and Travis kissed the top of her head, resisting the pull of sleep, trying to make the moment last forever.

Wet warmth seeped between his lashes and rolled down his cheeks. His eyes grew heavy and a silent plea whispered through his mind as he thought of tomorrow. As he thought of a future empty of Hannah, Margaret, and Red—a bleak world away from Paradise Peak.

Please forgive me.

*   *   *

Warm sunlight urged Hannah's eyes open. She smiled and stretched her arm out, her fingers trailing over the bumps in the bedding, seeking the smooth, hard contours of Travis's chest and shoulders.

Cool, empty sheets met her fingertips.

She sat up and pushed her long hair back. Travis's masculine scent was released with each of her movements and a delicious ache moved through her muscles. Smiling, she touched her lips, still tingling from his tender kisses, and savored the faint throb of pleasure that lingered deep inside her from his passionate movements.

A gentle giant—that's what Zeke and Liz had called Travis. And his touch had been gentle last night. Gentle, protective, passionate, and full of love.

A shadow blocked the bright sunlight streaming between the open blinds of the window and she turned her head, her smile widening as her eyes traced the familiar line of Travis's wide shoulders and muscular back.

He stood outside on the deck, his back to the window, facing the slow rise of the sun above the mountain range. Vibrant shades of gold, pink, and lavender spread across the brightening sky above him, casting his muscular frame into a dark outline that stood in sharp relief against the light projecting from above.

Hannah slipped out of bed, padded to her closet, and dressed quickly, a soft laugh escaping her as she tripped over her jeans twice in her haste.

Joy she'd never felt before spiraled inside her and she pressed a hand to her belly, recalling the light rasp of Travis's stubble-lined jaw against her skin, his big hands cupping her breasts and hips, his thick thighs parting hers and his hard body settling warmly between.

"A perfect fit," she whispered, pleasure unfurling within

her as she envisioned the years ahead, full of love, laughter, and life with Travis.

A great man. One she felt as though she'd waited for forever.

Stealing one last glance at his broad back through the window, she left the room and half jogged to the front door and out onto the deck, drawing to a stop a few feet away from him. Desire stirred within her at the sight of his tall frame clad in jeans and a T-shirt, his strong jaw shadowed with stubble and his black hair rumpled from her touch.

He turned his head, his dark eyes meeting hers, the brown depths warm and loving as they roved over her, just as they had last night.

She smiled again, words leaving her lips in a giddy rush. "You love me."

His sensual mouth curved upward, but there was something lacking in his smile, and in his expression. "Yes. I love you." He faced her, his throat moving on a hard swallow as he held out a folded piece of paper. "Which is why I need to give you this."

Smile faltering at his tone, Hannah moved closer and hesitantly took the paper, her fingers brushing his. "What is it?"

Regret moved through his expression as he said quietly, "Something I should've told you a long time ago. I was going to wait until after I told—" Voice breaking, he grimaced and looked away, his gaze returning to the sunrise. "Please read it."

She studied his profile, then the grim set of his mouth, silently urging him to speak. To ease the fear stirring inside her. Instead, he remained silent and continued staring stoically at the sunrise.

Hands trembling, she unfolded the paper.

Dear Margaret,

"You've written to Margaret?" Frowning, she lifted her head, her gaze returning to him as she tried to sort through her confusion.

He didn't answer.

She looked down at the paper in her hands.

I found you today: twenty years, seven months, and three days after we last saw each other. You looked me in the eyes, shook my hand, and smiled. You didn't recognize the reckless boy I once was in the man I've become. But I recognized you.

A chill swept through Hannah, racking her limbs and stealing her breath.

That same look you had in your eyes twenty years ago—the only time during the trial that you faced me—was still there. The look that said the world is cruel, and God is more cruel.

~~*That same look was in Hannah's eyes, too.*~~

Her hands tightened, crushing the edges of the letter between her fingers. "When did you write this?"

His chin trembled. "The day I met you."

I came to Paradise Peak for you, Margaret. To see you. To beg your forgiveness. . . .

The words blurred and the paper shook in her hold.

Instead of hiding these words with the others, I should tell you all of this. I should tell you that my

*life—however miniscule its worth—is yours in what-
ever way you choose to use it. But if you knew who I
really am . . . If you knew I was Neil Travis—*

"Alden," Hannah whispered, her throat raw. "You're
Neil Alden?"

She knew the answer, but she said the name out loud
again, the words widening the chasm forming between
them, changing the angles of Travis's face, morphing his
once familiar features into the form of a stranger's.

Hannah closed her eyes, the warm glow inside her fading to cold emptiness, every lingering trace of Travis's
touch numbing her sk—

No. Neil Alden. The addict who had driven drunk, who
had killed Margaret's daughter. Neil Alden's hands had
been on her, his hard body inside her.

"You lied to me." Choking back a sob, she shook her
head, opened her eyes, and balled the paper in her fists.
"You lied to all of us. All this time. And last night—"

"No." He shoved away from the deck railing and moved,
hand outstretched, toward her. "Nothing about last night
was a lie. I'm so sorry, Hannah. I never meant t—"

"Don't." She stepped back, ripped the paper into pieces,
and flung them. They scattered in different directions,
some plummeting like stones to the deck and others catching on his shirt, then floating to his feet. "You're a liar."

"I never lied about loving you. I swear." Face turning
pale, he looked down at the scraps of paper littering the
deck, then raised his head, a desperate plea in his eyes.
"When I came here, I had no intention of lying, but when
I saw—"

"When you saw Red, you knew you could take advantage." Hannah held his gaze, struggling to keep her voice
even. "You saw his kindness as weakness, and when you

met me, you saw a damaged woman." She stabbed a finger at the papers strewn across the deck. "How did you
say I see the world? As cruel? As a wounded victim? Someone who was weak and—"

"That's not true. I could tell you had been hurt before
because—"

"You hurt people." She nodded. "That's why. You
could see I had been hurt before because you aim to hurt
and you know what a victim looks like. You're no better
than Bryan." Eyes burning, she dragged the back of her
arm over her face and turned away, her gaze settling on
the lodge in the distance. "And Margaret." She scrubbed
her wet cheek, her chest tightening painfully. "Do you
know she said good-bye to her family yesterday? Just yesterday. She put Phillip's and Niki's pictures away, let go of
their memory for the first time in twenty years, because
she wanted to move on and start a new life with her new
family." She faced him again, forced herself to meet his
eyes. "A family that included Travis Miller."

He flinched, but held her gaze, his eyes wounded and
wet. Moisture gathered on his lashes, and she watched a
lone drop seep onto his lean cheek and roll in a haphazard
trail to settle in the corner of his mouth.

Heart aching, Hannah lifted a hand toward him, wanting
to wipe away the tear and his words, wanting to comfort
the man she'd believed she knew. The strong, gentle, honest
man who'd protected and supported her. Who she had believed loved her, and whom—despite what he'd admitted,
despite the deceit and soul-searing pain he'd caused—she
still loved.

Oh, God. She still loved him. Loved the man she'd believed him to have been.

"Travis Miller doesn't exist." She reached for the rail of
the deck, wrapped her hand around the hard wood, and

followed it backward slowly, her feet blindly feeling their way down the steps. "Travis Miller is just a name. A mask for a liar. A murderer. And a coward."

Pain moved across his face, twisting his features. Hannah forced herself to continue backing away. Forced her hand to tighten around the rail. Forced her feet to continue moving until they touched the ground.

"You're going to tell Margaret the truth," she whispered. "And you're going to tell her now."

CHAPTER 14

Travis tightened his hold on the bundle of letters in his hand and forced himself to take slow, measured steps, keeping a comfortable distance between himself and Hannah as he followed her along the dirt path leading to the lodge.

She glanced over her shoulder, her auburn curls, mussed by their lovemaking last night, bouncing against her slim back. Her red-rimmed eyes remained focused on his boots, never lifting to look into his; then she faced forward again, her steps quickening.

He opened his mouth to call to her, to apologize and beg for understanding, but his voice refused to emerge.

After confessing to Hannah, he'd returned to his room inside her cabin, retrieved the stack of letters he'd written Margaret, and tucked the last one he'd written two months ago beneath the string tying them together.

Hannah had been standing outside on the dirt path, waiting for him when he returned, and without a word, she'd spun on her heel and led the way silently up the path toward the lodge.

Her steps faltered twice as they walked past the dance floor, which still stood in the field, the white tulle and lights surrounding the empty space swaying gently in the morning breeze. A quiet sob escaped her, and Travis shoved his free hand into his pocket and deliberately slowed his steps to keep from reaching for her.

However good his intentions, he'd betrayed Hannah's trust. He'd deceived her. And he'd made love to her before telling her the truth.

She wouldn't welcome his touch, and he couldn't blame her.

Faint laughter emerged ahead, ringing out from the lodge's deck, echoing across the empty grounds of the ranch. The sun had fully risen while they'd walked, and vibrant, golden rays splashed across the green field to highlight the staircase leading to the lodge's deck.

Hannah went first, taking the steps two at a time, and Travis ascended behind her, his heart kicking hard against his ribs.

Margaret sat at the table beside Red. They leaned close together, their elbows propped on the table and hands entwined as Red whispered in Margaret's ear. She blushed, another laugh escaping her, and kissed him.

A board creaked under Travis's weight as he stepped onto the deck, and they both looked up, sleepy smiles—full of joy—on both their faces.

"Well, look who's up and about already." Margaret patted Red's arm and stood, her eyes bright as she glanced at Travis and Hannah. "Red and I weren't sure when you two would venture out this morning after last night's fun, so we haven't put breakfast on the stove." Smiling wider, she gestured toward a carafe, full of coffee, which sat on the table beside two mugs. "But there's plenty of hot coffee and cream, and it wouldn't take me but a minute to crack a few eggs over a skillet if you . . ."

Margaret grew silent, her gaze settling on Hannah, who

stood on the other side of the deck. "Hannah? What's wrong?"

Hannah stared back at Margaret, tears rolling down her flushed cheeks. She opened her mouth to speak, then shook her head and turned away, looking blindly out at the field. Her slim back shook slightly.

Eyes burning, Travis ducked his head.

A chair scraped across the floor of the deck as Red stood. "Travis?" The relaxed, teasing tone had left his voice. "What's going on here?"

Travis drew in a deep breath, raised his head, and met Red's solemn gaze. "It's my fault. All of it." On shaking legs he walked to the table and placed the bundle of letters in front of Margaret. "Over two months ago, when I arrived in Paradise Peak, it wasn't by accident. I came here to find you. To give you these."

Frowning, Margaret picked up the bundle, untied the string, and sifted through the letters. "They're addressed to me, but there's no return information." She shook her head. "Who are they from?"

Breath stalling in his lungs, Travis said softly, "Neil Alden."

The warm blush in her cheeks faded. Her face took on an ashen pallor as she dropped the sealed envelopes to the table and spread her hands, shaking, above them. "But I don't understand. Do you . . . You know him?"

Travis swallowed hard past the tight knot in his throat. "I'm Neil Alden."

Margaret stood still, her gaze moving over his face, recognition leaving her eyes, and pain and distrust taking its place. "But you said your name was Travis Miller."

"I lied to you." He ducked his head. "My full name is Neil Travis Alden."

A sound of dismay left Red's lips. "Why? Why didn't you just tell us who you were to begin with?" His cheeks reddened, anger flashing in the blue depths of his eyes. "Or at least me? When we first met, only the two of us stood on top of that mountain, miles away from here. Why didn't you tell me the truth then?"

Travis's face heated, his throat aching as he answered. "We were strangers then. I didn't know how you'd react, or if you'd trust my intentions." He held up a hand. "That's no excuse. I should've told you from the start, but the way you looked at me, the way you welcomed me . . . I wanted to be the man you thought you saw—a good guy just down on his luck, in need of a hand up."

Wincing, Travis turned his head and studied the sunrise. The golden light spilling over the rugged mountains was just as bright and awe-inducing as it had been the day he'd arrived. "And this place . . ." He blinked hard, holding back the tears burning his eyes and the sob rising in his throat. "There's so much peace here—so much beauty. It was like nothing I'd ever seen. I hated who I'd been, and I thought, maybe, there was forgiveness to be found here. That I could try to do right by Niki's memory and help Margaret in whatever way she'd allow me to. That I could start over and become someone different. Someone better."

"Start over?" Margaret asked, a hard note in her voice. "You wanted to start over, when Niki never will."

Guilt stole through him, cutting deep into his soul. "I'm sorry, Margaret. Sorrier than I could ever say for what I stole from Niki. For how much I hurt you and Phillip. I wish I could take it back. I wish I could—"

"But you can't, can you?" A ragged sob burst from Margaret's lips. "You can't replace all the years of living Niki has lost. You can't give her back a chance at the happy future she was working so hard to build." She lifted her hands and pressed her empty palms to the base of her throat. "You can't give her back to me. You can't replace all the years' worth of memories I've lost with my daughter—" Her voice broke, and her shoulders slumped as Red wrapped his arm around her, pulling her close. "Niki will never grow older. She'll never marry, never hold her own children, never have a family of her own. And you come here and expect to start over? To pursue things Niki will never have?"

"Not at first." Travis looked at Hannah, her rigid back to him, standing only feet away, but unreachable. "But I fell in love with Hannah," he whispered. "With all of you. I never really knew what home or family was until I came to Paradise Peak and met the three of you. I wanted to do right by you, but I also wanted a future with Hannah. And I knew if I told the truth, I'd lose her."

Margaret straightened in Red's hold, glaring. "You don't deserve Hannah, or an opportunity to start over."

"No." Travis flinched at the hate in Margaret's eyes. "I don't. But for whatever reason, I'm still alive. Still breathing. And the only thing I can do from here on out is be a better man than I was. To choose—every day—to do what's right, and good, to make up for the harm I've caused."

Margaret pulled away from Red and wiped her face, her shoulders stiffening. "You won't do it here. I want you to leave."

Travis took a step toward her. "Margaret, please—"

"You're to leave." She held up her hand, palm facing him, then turned away. "Now."

Margaret walked across the deck and entered the lodge. Red stayed behind, his mouth opening and closing silently as he stared at Travis. Then he looked at Hannah, watched her head bow and shoulders jerk, and followed Margaret inside.

Travis stood still, praying silently for Hannah to speak. To turn and look at him or show some sign that she still recognized him for the man he'd become. But she didn't.

"Good-bye, Hannah."

Forcing himself to move, he walked down the staircase leading to the field and placed one heavy foot in front of the other until he reached Hannah's cabin.

It didn't take long to pack. There was only enough room in his bag for two of the new outfits Gloria had helped him choose. He packed the sturdiest jeans and well-stitched shirts, hoping they'd wear well over the journey he'd undertake on foot back down the mountain and out of Paradise Peak.

He looked down at the boots Red had given him and briefly considered taking them off, leaving them behind and wearing his worn tennis shoes instead. But he decided to wear them anyway. They were a good—and perhaps the only—reminder he'd have of the man he'd grown to know and love as a father. And somehow, he felt stronger and more whole when he wore them.

The paper and collection of pens he left behind on the small desk he and Hannah had moved from his old cabin. He no longer needed them. Instead, he grabbed his thermos, took one more look around his room, then left the cabin.

He walked to the bank of the stream nearby, knelt, and filled his thermos with fresh water. His hand lingered in the water's cool current as he recalled the first time he'd plunged his hands in the stream to clean them with Red by his side. When the thermos was full, he withdrew it, secured the cap, then studied his clean hands, watching the clear drops of water trickle along his palms and over his wrists, sparkling beneath the sunlight.

"Good as new," he whispered, his heart heavy.

Guests began to stir about the property as he walked slowly along the stream's edge, then returned to the dirt path. Two men chatted as they slowly dismantled the stage and dance floor in the field, then loaded the heavy pieces of the platform in the bed of two trucks. A group of children played nearby, dashing around the men as they worked, shooting water guns and laughing. And to Travis's left, in the paddock behind the stable, Juno, Ruby, and Oreo strolled along the fence, lifting their noses into the sweet spring breeze, their manes rippling along their strong backs.

Liz, standing on the other side of the paddock, smiled and called out a greeting before walking inside the stable.

Travis managed to smile back, a pang shooting through his heart as he approached the paddock fence. Spotting him, Oreo walked over, dipped her head over the fence, and nudged his chest.

"Hi, beautiful." Travis stroked her neck gently, murmuring low words of praise. "I'm gonna miss you. Take good care of Zeke, okay?"

The mare lifted her head, her nose nearing Travis's face as she breathed softly, then turned and strolled away.

"Where will you go?"

Travis looked to his left where Red stood by the back of the stable, studying him. Red's expression was bleak, and his shoulders drooped as though weighed down.

"I don't know." Travis looked up, above the moisture collecting on his lashes, and peered at the mountain range in the distance. "I've grown to love these mountains, so I imagine I'll look for somewhere similar." He shook his head, a wry smile twisting his lips. "Nothing will compare to Paradise Peak—not really. But I'm hoping to find something almost as beautiful." He faced Red again, an ache spreading through him. "Thank you for bringing me here. For teaching me what it is to be a good man." He shook his head. "I wish I had a better story to tell you this morning—a better past—but I don't."

Red nodded, looked as though he were about to speak, then turned and began walking away, his steps heavy.

"Red?" Travis hesitated, the name sticking in his throat. He should leave Red alone, leave all of them and be on his way. But the journey that lay before him was long, and he'd have to travel it alone. No matter how far he traveled, he'd never be able to forget them. "Do you wish you'd never met me? That you never knew me?"

Red stopped.

"Because I'm not the person I used to be. I swear, I'm not." His voice caught. "I'm a different person now."

Red spun around, walked along the paddock fence, his steps swift in Travis's direction.

"I'm not the same boy that—"

"I know you, Travis." Red wrapped his arms around Travis and hugged him hard, his voice a hoarse whisper in Travis's ear. "Don't you know I know you—and have grown to love you—like my own son?" His words broke on a sob. "Like my own flesh and blood."

Travis closed his eyes and hugged him back, holding on to Red's comforting words long after the older man had released him and gone, taking long strides across the field, up the steps of the deck, and into the lodge.

Dragging the back of his arm over his wet face, Travis resumed walking. He left the paddock fence and rounded the stable, his eyes seeking out the gravel drive leading to the highway.

"Giant!"

Travis stopped and looked back. Zeke stood in the open entrance of the stable, smiling as he stared at Travis. Blondie, sitting beside him, shot to her feet and ran over, jumping up and licking Travis's hand.

Travis knelt and rubbed Blondie behind her ear. "Bye, girl."

Zeke's big, brown eyes moved over Travis, taking in the worn bag slung over his shoulder, and a confused expression crossed the boy's face. "You go?"

Travis stroked Blondie once more, stood, and hitched his bag higher on his shoulder. "Yeah, buddy."

Zeke raised his hand, opening and closing it, and smiled. "Bye, Giant."

Travis smiled back. The fondness in Zeke's voice as he spoke the nickname and the admiration in the boy's eyes lifted his heart with a small sense of pride, and the hope that he might one day live up to Zeke's high expectations.

"Good-bye, Zeke," he said softly, before turning and facing the road ahead.

Hannah eased back in her rocking chair and opened her eyes, taking in the shadowy mountain range opposite her front porch. A thick blue shroud hung over the dark, rugged landscape and dawn had yet to break, its slow approach marked only by a thin strip of lavender just above the mountains' rugged peaks.

The Carrollton boys' laughter, which had echoed across the stream toward Hannah's cabin late yesterday afternoon as they'd played, had vanished hours ago when they'd returned home for supper and bed, their small forms running and jumping along the crooked trail leading to Travis's cabin.

Travis.

Hannah closed her eyes again and rubbed her temples, the painful throb in her head—and heart—persisting as it had all day yesterday after Travis had left, and throughout the night, making sleep impossible.

For a few hours yesterday afternoon, she'd cleaned her cabin from top to bottom, sweeping and mopping floors, dusting every nook and cranny, and raising every window she could reach to air out the place. She'd stripped the sheets from her bed and the one Travis had slept in and drowned them with extra detergent in the washing machine, hoping to erase every trace of Travis's scent from her room, from the room he'd slept in, and from her home in general.

But there was a problem.

No matter how much she washed, scrubbed, and mopped, Travis's presence still lingered in every inch of her cabin . . . and in her heart.

She'd seen him standing in her hallway, smiling down at her, and felt his lips on hers as he'd kissed her good night every night over the past two months. She'd rolled over in bed more than once as she'd strained for sleep last night, her hands fumbling over the sheets, seeking his warm chest. And when she'd given up chasing sleep and had walked outside and sat on the porch, she'd heard his voice, broken and full of pain.

Good-bye, Hannah.

And she'd realized it then—why she had been unable to clear Travis from her home and her heart. It wasn't because she couldn't; she had, after all, undertaken the grueling process of leaving Bryan, a man she had once loved.

No. The reason she was thinking, moving and feeling in circles was not because she couldn't say good-bye to Travis—it was because she didn't want to say good-bye.

Despite his confessions, and despite how badly he'd hurt Margaret, she still loved Travis as the good man she'd met a little over two months ago. She still believed in that man. Still trusted him.

A low groan escaped her as she rubbed her temples harder. But how could she? How could she trust a man—a former addict like Bryan—after all he'd done?

"You couldn't sleep either?"

Hannah lowered her hands to find Margaret standing on the top step of the stairs leading to the front porch, a softly lit camping lantern in her hand and a weary expression on her face. Red stood several steps below Margaret, dark circles under his eyes.

"No," Hannah said. A humorless smile curved her lips. "I gave up hours ago and decided to use the sunrise as my excuse for sitting out here like a heartbroken fool. What's your excuse?"

Margaret sighed and set the camping lantern on the porch rail. "I kept Red up half the night pacing the foyer, so we decided to take an early morning walk and ended up here."

"Do you mind if we join you?" Red asked, his voice gruff.

"Not at all." Hannah waved toward two empty chairs next to her. "Have a seat."

They did, Margaret sitting in a chair beside Hannah while Red settled in a rocking chair on the other side of Margaret. It was silent for a few moments, save for the creak of their chairs as they rocked, and they watched thin shafts of color peek over the mountain range as the sun slowly rose.

"Red and I didn't wander over here by accident," Margaret said quietly. "It was selfish of me, but I hoped you might be up." She slipped a hand inside the pocket of her long skirt and withdrew a folded piece of paper. "I spent yesterday afternoon and half of last night reading the letters Trav—" She bit her lip, then continued, "Reading the letters Neil left, and this is the last one he wrote. Since you were mentioned, I thought you might want to read it."

Hannah stared at the paper in Margaret's hand, her own shaking as she reached for the letter, then turned it over between her fingers. "How many were there?"

"More than I cared to count." Margaret faced the mountain range again, dawn casting warm pink and lavender hues of light across her face. "I wasn't going to read them, but once I started, I found I didn't have the heart to put them down."

Hannah grew still, watching Margaret's carefully controlled expression, then stood slowly and crossed to the lantern. She unfolded the paper, smoothing it between her fingers, then began reading.

> *Dear Margaret,*
>
> *When you read this, I will have already told you the truth. I'm sorry for not telling you who I was from the beginning and for the pain I've caused you, Niki, and Phillip in the past. And I'm sorry for the pain I'm causing you, Hannah, and Red now. I'm ashamed of who I once was and what I've done, which is why this will be the last time I write to you.*
>
> *If I've given you this letter, it's because I know I have to leave Paradise Peak. I'm no longer welcome and must move on. I understand why, and I expected it.*
>
> *What Hannah said about words not being enough is true. There is nothing I could ever say that would right the wrong I've committed, and nothing I could*

ever do that will bring Niki back. I don't deserve forgiveness, and I don't deserve mercy.

I asked you once before, in another letter, how the value of a man is measured. How he can prove he is worthy of forgiveness. What I've come to realize is that I can't earn forgiveness or mercy, but I've been given a gift all the same—the gift of life. The gift of a second chance.

The only way for me to honor Niki's memory is to no longer misuse the life I've been given. So I'm choosing to look forward and work at living a better life. A life of helping others and putting as much good into the world as I can manage. Enough to rival the bad I've caused others to endure . . . even if it costs me a life with Hannah.

I'm afraid leaving her will be harder than I can imagine. I'm afraid of a life without her. Hannah is it for me—there is no room in my heart for another woman. But I'll take comfort in knowing that I'm doing the right thing for her happiness, and for yours and for Red's. And, most importantly, for Niki's memory.

Please take care of Hannah, Red, and yourself. Please be happy.

Travis

Hannah raised her head, blinking back tears as dawn's rosy glow intensified. Bright pink, lavender, and gold kissed the mountain peaks in the distance, enveloped the grassy bank beside the stream, and reflected off the water's surface as it rippled around stones. The sun lifted its head over the mountain range, spilling golden light through the trees.

"I know what Neil did was unforgivable," Hannah whispered. "I hate what he did to Niki, and how much he hurt you." Lips trembling, she pressed them together tightly before continuing. "But I never knew him. I only know Travis as he is now." She faced Margaret, her hands tightening around the letter. "I love Travis as he is now."

Margaret nodded, her eyes glistening in the morning light. "I know. So do I." She pulled in a shaky breath. "But I don't know how I can love a man who killed my daughter. I shouldn't be able to, should I? I shouldn't even want to try."

Red leaned forward in his chair and covered Margaret's hands with his. "Whatever choice you make, Niki would want you to be happy." He looked at Hannah. "Neither of you are alone in this. We're a family, and I'll support you both in whatever you decide." Hesitating, he said, "If we forgive him, it won't be a one-day thing. We'll have to make the choice to do so over and over again—even on the days it hurts the worst."

Red leaned over, kissed Margaret's cheek, and stood. He squeezed Hannah's hand as he passed, walked halfway down the front porch steps, then stopped, his head turning slowly as he took in the sun spilling across the sloping grounds of the ranch.

"This place came to life the moment Travis stepped foot on it," Red said. "And not just this ranch, but us, too." He glanced over his shoulder and smiled at Margaret. "After all these years, I got up the gumption to tell the woman I loved how I felt and found out she loves me just as much." He looked at Hannah. "And I heard my niece laugh again for the first time in years. Her beautiful, brave smile returned, and I finally got the family I've always wanted." His smile slipped. "Including a man I've grown to love as my own son."

Red continued slowly down the steps and Hannah returned to her chair. She reached out and took Margaret's hand in hers, squeezing it gently as she watched Red stop and turn back once more.

"Thing is," Red said softly, "who is forgiveness for, if not sinners?"

CHAPTER 15

Travis recognized Paradise Peak the moment he reached the overlook. He left the gravel path he'd traveled for three miles prior to dawn and walked to the mountain's edge, the muscles in his legs tightening from his morning hike, but his body refreshed by the exercise.

Ahead of him, lush green mountain ranges sprawled beneath a thin, sleepy mist, and healthy evergreen trees stood tall and proud. The sun's golden rays reached out over the mountain peaks, warming the air, and glistened over the dewy, purple petals of rhododendrons that covered the sloping ground in front of Travis's boots.

He tipped his head back, savoring the warmth of the sun's rays on his cheeks and bare neck, and inhaled deeply. Fresh, fragrant air filled his lungs and lifted his chest.

A sense of peace washed over him, and he glanced to his left where the majestic mountain he'd known briefly as home rose gracefully toward the sky.

"Paradise," he whispered.

He hadn't known the land long—his stay in Paradise Peak had been brief—but the strength underlying the mountain, the serene landscape, and cool streams were powerful enough to remake the weakest of men. To make him whole again.

Travis looked down at the boots Red had given him and smiled. That's how he felt. Strong and whole. He was leaving Paradise Peak with so much more than he'd had when he'd arrived.

Except he no longer had Hannah.

His smile faded.

Adjusting the strap of his bag on his shoulder, he took one more look at the impressive landscape before him, then moved on. Each step increased the acute feeling of loss within him, but he returned to the gravel path running parallel to the highway and continued walking.

Travis had made it another half a mile when the familiar rumble of a truck's motor overcame the cheerful chorus of birds in the trees. He stopped as Red's truck passed him, traveled several feet further down the mountain, then made a U-turn and parked on the side of the road. The driver's side door opened, and Hannah stepped out.

Heart pounding, he waited, watching as she shielded her eyes from the sun with her hand and peered up at him. She walked toward him, climbing halfway up the sloping stretch of the mountain, then stood still. Sunlight streamed over her, casting a golden glow over her auburn hair and a pink blush along her cheeks.

"May I come up?" she called, her voice soft in the still morning air. "I need to tell you something."

Travis bit his lip, hesitating. Hoping. "What do you need to tell me?"

Hannah took one small step forward. "I need to tell you that I don't know Neil Alden. And I don't trust him." She took another step. "But I know the man you are now, Travis." And another. "I trust you. And I love you." She stopped again, her blue eyes wide and hopeful as she studied his face. "I want to ask you to come home with me. To share your life with me. I have faith in you, and in us."

Her hands picked at the hem of her T-shirt. "And I hope I'm not too late."

Travis smiled, eased his bag off his shoulder, and lowered it to the ground. "No. You're not too late."

A wide grin spread across her face as he opened his arms and she sprinted up the remaining stretch of mountain that separated them and hurled herself into his arms.

Laughing, he swept her up against his chest and trailed kisses over her cheeks, her forehead and nose, then covered her mouth with his, kissing her deeply and holding her close.

She made a soft sound of pleasure and he released her, cupping her cheek with his hand as his laughter trailed away.

"But Margaret," he said, the ache inside him returning. "She—"

"Wants to see you," Hannah finished for him. She stepped back and took his hand in hers, tugging him toward the truck.

He locked his knees, halting their steps. "I don't want to hurt her anymore."

She reached up and her fingers brushed his hair off his forehead, then trailed gently over his furrowed brow. "Margaret knows that," she whispered. "We all do." She tugged him forward again. "Come with me?"

Hannah drove back to the ranch slowly, her hand squeezing Travis's as it rested on her knee. She glanced at him often, her gaze gentle and loving, but the closer they drew to the ranch, the more tense he became.

The gravel driveway emerged as they ascended an incline and Hannah turned left and proceeded at a slow pace toward the lodge. They passed the wooden sign proclaiming PARADISE PEAK RANCH, its wood freshly sanded and stained, and all signs of the fire damage erased.

Guests strolled about the grounds, a few walking with spouses or children as they admired the view, and others knelt on the ground, planting young, healthy seedlings in the gardens surrounding the cabins. In the distance, the horses grazed in the open field, their long tails swishing rhythmically.

Hannah stopped the truck, and Travis looked at the lodge. Margaret and Red walked down the front steps and across the dirt parking lot toward the truck.

"Margaret was hoping you hadn't traveled too far yet." Hannah smiled encouragingly. "Go ahead."

Travis hesitated, then opened the door and exited the truck. He rounded the vehicle slowly, stopping as Margaret and Red reached him.

Red met his eyes, his voice trembling slightly as he said, "You're late for breakfast, and I'm starving." His mustache twitched and he smiled. "Don't keep us waiting again."

Smiling, Travis shook his head. "Not a chance."

His shoulders tightened as Margaret stepped forward. She studied his face, her gaze moving slowly over his features; then a small smile curved her lips as she opened her arms.

Legs shaking, Travis moved into her embrace, his heart squeezing painfully at the knowledge of how much this must cost her. Of how much she had to sacrifice to invite him in. His body sagged against hers and tears spilled onto his cheeks at the gentle reverence in her touch.

Margaret kissed his temple and her wet cheek brushed his as she whispered, "Welcome home."

EPILOGUE

"Are you ready?" Travis smoothed a hand over his bow tie, eased closer to the partially opened bedroom door, and glanced at his wristwatch. "It's five after one."

Inside the room, something clattered across a solid surface, then thudded to the floor.

He straightened, his hand gripping the doorknob. "You okay in there? If you need more time, I can—"

"No, I'm all right." There was a soft rustle of fabric from inside the room, and the door creaked open.

Travis stepped back, carefully sidestepping the slight swish of a long, ivory, chiffon gown and the shiny toes of high-heeled shoes. His gaze skimmed over the delicate material embroidered with beads and sequins and traveled up to the pretty but nervous eyes of the woman staring back at him.

Margaret raised her eyebrows, an anxious expression appearing on her face. "How do I look?"

Travis smiled, taking in her soft, gray curls and fitted wedding gown. "Absolutely beautiful." He held out his arm, his elbow bent. "May I?"

Margaret nodded, slid her arm through the bend of his elbow, and followed his lead as he walked with her up the hallway, through the foyer, and onto the front porch of the lodge.

Her steps slowed as they emerged into the sunlight and a small gasp escaped her as she looked at the open field before them. White chairs adorned with fresh, spring flowers were lined up in perfect rows and squared off on both sides, creating a center aisle made of lush, green grass that led to a high, floral wedding arch. Beyond this, the scenic Smoky Mountain range provided a breathtaking, natural backdrop of green mountain peaks dotted with colorful spring flowers.

"Oh, it's so beautiful," Margaret whispered, her voice thick with tears of joy. "Hannah must've worked on this all night."

"She was happy to do it. We all were."

Travis smiled, recalling the laughs he, Hannah, and Red had shared into the early morning hours as they'd worked under floodlights in the warm spring air, unloading and arranging chairs in the field, folding swan napkins, and decorating outdoor tables for the reception. He'd even managed to sneak off with Hannah for an hour, sharing soft whispers and passionate kisses on the grassy bank of the stream beneath the full moon and bright stars in the night sky.

Last night had been the first evening since Summer's birth six months ago that he and Hannah had managed to steal a few minutes for themselves. Liz, settled comfortably in her renovated cabin with Zeke, had offered to babysit for the weekend, and Travis, eager for time alone with his wife, had accepted. And though he'd enjoyed every second of having Hannah's beautiful smile and flirtatious laughter to himself, he found himself missing his daughter after only one night away from her.

Wife. And daughter. Travis grinned as he thumbed the silver wedding band on his finger, his gaze seeking out

Hannah as she stood beneath the floral arch beside Red, Summer in her arms, smiling and bouncing with excitement when her dark eyes spotted him. She had his eyes, and Hannah's auburn curls, and she was the most gorgeous baby girl in the world.

Man, he was lucky, and couldn't possibly be prouder.

Margaret pointed a manicured nail toward the big blooms of spring flowers creating floral curtains between rustic, wooden posts lining the aisle. "How'd you manage to hang the roses?"

Travis laughed. "Red's fishing line. When it came to you, he was happy to offer up his entire tackle box."

Margaret laughed and some of the nervous tension eased from her expression. She lifted to her toes and kissed Travis's cheek. "Thank you for walking me down the aisle. You won't let me fall, will you?"

Travis tucked her hand tighter within the crook of his elbow and kissed her forehead. "Never."

After his return to Paradise Peak with Hannah one year and six months ago, Travis had asked Hannah to marry him, and she'd happily accepted. Red had been overjoyed, and Margaret had been ecstatic—she'd already begun planning the wedding before Travis had slid the engagement ring on Hannah's finger. He and Hannah had married on the ranch a month later, choosing to wed simply and quickly rather than wait to arrange a lavish ceremony, and the ceremony had been beautiful. A month after returning from their honeymoon, Hannah had surprised him with the happy news of their pregnancy and Margaret had sprung to action, planning a baby shower months in advance.

The months that followed had been a happy whirlwind, and a period over which Red and Margaret had become engaged and carefully planned a simple but elegant ceremony for the following spring. Travis and Margaret had grown even closer after Summer's birth. Margaret had taken up the role of grandmother—though she preferred to be called Gammy—and showered Summer with love every day.

And more surprisingly, Margaret had, over time, grown to regard Travis as a son. Her motherly pecks on the cheek and caring advice had warmed his heart, and the heavy ache he'd carried for years continued to slowly recede. His life had never been more full of laughter and love. For the first time, he knew he was right where he belonged.

"Well," Margaret said, meeting Red's eyes across the field and smiling, "let's not keep the love of my life waiting."

Thirty minutes later, after a sweet ceremony and heart-felt vows, Red, clad in a tux, swept Margaret up in his arms beneath the floral arch and kissed her soundly in front of a cheering crowd of family, friends, and new ranch guests who'd been eager to attend and celebrate the happy event.

"Red," Margaret gasped, gripping his shoulders. "Put me down before you break a hip."

Laughing, Red hefted her higher up on his chest, her long hair spilling over his shoulder. "Darling, if I put you down, it'll break my heart."

Margaret smiled, cradled his face, and kissed him.

Travis crossed the aisle and lifted Summer from Hannah's arms and into his own, kissing her soft auburn curls before hugging Hannah close to his side. He laughed as Red carried Margaret up the aisle, across the field, and onto the front porch of the lodge, pausing to allow his bride to wave once more at the cheering crowd of guests before carrying her inside.

Hannah laughed. "You think we'll see them again any time soon?"

Travis grinned. "I seriously doubt it."

"Then take me home," Hannah whispered, wrapping her arms around his waist and smiling up at him. "Our little girl's eyes are getting heavy, and I'm in the mood to celebrate with my husband. An entire night together, undisturbed, would be heaven."

Travis bent his head and kissed her. The warm press of her soft lips against his, the comforting weight of his daughter in his arms, and the peaceful breeze sweeping across Paradise Peak stirred his soul and lifted his spirits higher than he could have ever imagined. "Yeah," he whispered, thinking of their cabin by the peaceful stream with the best mountain view in Tennessee. A place with more love and happiness than he'd ever hoped to find. "Let's go home."